"That Jodie's a pretty little thing— you noticed?"

"I'd have to be blind not to notice," Tate said.

"Red hair, those eyes... Like you say, hard not to notice. You goin' to ask her out?"

"No!"

"Why not?"

"Because— Well, when would I have time?"

"I always found time for Maureen."

"You'd been married for ten years before you became sheriff. It's not the same thing as—" Tate stopped.

"Courtin'?" Jack teased. "Seems you've been givin' this a bit of thought." Then he laughed. *"Courtin'.* I always did like that word. Sounds so much nicer than what kids call it today."

"Kids today don't court," Tate said.

"How about grown men like you?"

ABOUT THE AUTHOR

Ginger Chambers says that from her earliest days she's always loved cowboys—the way they look, the job they do and the way they feel about the land. In particular, she loves *Texas* cowboys.

That's because her family roots run deep in Texas. Her great-grandfather raised cattle and drove them on the Chisholm Trail!

This is Ginger's third story about the Parker Ranch in West Texas. Watch for upcoming books!

Books by Ginger Chambers

HARLEQUIN SUPERROMANCE
601—TILL SEPTEMBER
647—FATHER TAKES A WIFE
680—A MATCH MADE IN TEXAS
730—WEST TEXAS WEDDINGS

TEXAS LAWMAN
Ginger Chambers

Harlequin Books

TORONTO • NEW YORK • LONDON
AMSTERDAM • PARIS • SYDNEY • HAMBURG
STOCKHOLM • ATHENS • TOKYO • MILAN
MADRID • WARSAW • BUDAPEST • AUCKLAND

For Bella
Good does triumph over evil.
Sometimes it just takes a helluva long time.

ISBN 0-373-70778-9

TEXAS LAWMAN

Copyright © 1998 by Ginger Chambers.

This edition published by arrangement with Harlequin Books S.A.

® and TM are trademarks of the publisher. Trademarks indicated with ® are registered in the United States Patent and Trademark Office, the Canadian Trade Marks Office and in other countries.

Printed in U.S.A.

TEXAS LAWMAN

CHAPTER ONE

THE BUTTERFLIES in Jodie's stomach increased as, mile by mile, she drew closer to the ranch. It didn't seem to matter that she'd been on her own for all these years—five at the university and the last traveling in Europe. The instant she saw her great-aunt all the hard-won poise and confidence she'd acquired over that time would evaporate and she'd turn into the uncertain young girl she used to be.

Her great-aunt had that effect on people. The pure force of the woman's will invariably rode roughshod over independent thought. As the oldest living Parker, Mae was due respect and deference—and she never let anyone forget it!

Jodie's fingers tightened on the steering wheel and her foot pressed harder on the accelerator. What she wanted most at this moment was to get their first meeting over with. Mae hadn't liked it one bit that after graduation she'd turned down the job arranged for her and gone, instead, with friends to Italy. Nor when, after six months in Italy, she'd moved on to explore other areas of the continent, absenting herself from the ranch for an additional six months. It was the longest uninterrupted period Jodie had ever spent away from her birthplace, the Parker Ranch, an almost living entity in the minds and hearts of the people who resided there.

She could just imagine the upcoming scene. Her great-aunt, her father, her cousins and their wives—Rafe and Shannon, LeRoy and Harriet—Aunt Darlene and Uncle Thomas, not to mention the growing menagerie of Parker children. All would gather at Mae's house to welcome her, even though they'd be surprised by her premature arrival. Originally she'd planned to spend the afternoon and night at a friend's house in San Antonio before setting off for Briggs County in West Texas the next morning. But restlessness had taken hold, so she'd rented a car and come ahead.

Jodie didn't want a fuss made. Particularly not while waiting for her great-aunt's inevitable show of displeasure. But seeing everyone again would be nice. She'd missed them in ways she hadn't anticipated.

Suddenly lights filled the night. Bright flashes of blue, white, red...blue, white, red. Their brilliance bounced off her rearview mirrors as a siren emitted an abbreviated wail.

A police car! Jodie immediately lifted her foot from the accelerator and looked for a place to pull over. As both cars rolled to a stop, the lights continued to dance, illuminating the lonely rugged landscape on each side of the road.

She cut the engine and waited. Just what she needed—a citation for speeding. How fast had she been going?

After what seemed an eternity—she was just about to get out to see what was taking so long—an even brighter light switched on from behind, spotlighting the distance between the two cars.

Jodie twisted to look over her shoulder and, narrowing her gaze against the glare, saw an officer step out of the patrol car and approach. He was long and lean and, judging by the style of his hat and uniform, a member of the Briggs County Sheriff's Department.

He didn't stop until he was at her window, then shined his flashlight in her face.

"Don't do that!" Jodie complained.

The light remained on her for another moment, before darting off to illuminate the passenger and rear compartments. At last it was switched off.

"You in a hurry to get someplace?" the officer drawled.

Jodie's heart gave a surprised little leap. Tate Connelly! What were the odds that he of all people would be the first person she'd meet upon returning home? "I was...yes," she managed.

"You could get yourself killed driving that fast out here at night. You had to be outrunnin' your headlights."

"I could see just fine," Jodie claimed. Didn't he recognize her? It hadn't been that long since they'd seen each other. Two years at most, surely. During one of her brief visits home from the university.

"Mind tellin' me what your business is?" Tate inquired, coolly courteous. "I mean, since you were in such a hurry, maybe I can be of assistance."

Jodie began to see the humor in the situation. For once she had him at a disadvantage. She wondered how long she could string him along. "I doubt it!" she replied.

His tone took on a more official edge. "I need to see your license, ma'am, and your rental agreement. This *is* a rental car—I ran the tags. Briggs County is a long way from San Antonio."

"Since when is it against the law to rent a car?" Jodie challenged. She made no move to retrieve any of the requested paperwork.

"Your license, ma'am," he repeated.

"I'd rather not."

He didn't miss a beat. "Then I'll have to ask you to step outside."

"You're arresting me?" Jodie squeaked.

"Out of the car."

Jodie opened the door and stepped onto the gravel roadside.

"Don't do that!" he barked when she instinctively reached back inside to retrieve her purse. "Keep your hands where I can see 'em."

"But I just wanted to get—"

"Step to the side, face the car and put your hands on the roof. *Now!*" he ordered when she hesitated.

Jodie blinked as she did what he said. Her little joke had gone about as far as she should let it. Before she could speak, though, he reached into the car himself.

"This yours?" he asked, straightening. The strap of her black leather shoulder bag hung from his fingertips. "You don't mind if I have a look inside, do you? You carryin' any drugs? Any drug paraphernalia? Any weapons?"

Jodie had had enough. "Tate!" she exclaimed.

His fingers froze on the partially open zipper.

In the radiance of the spotlight she could see most of his handsome face. The cleanly carved line of jaw and cheekbone, the firm set of his mouth, the brown eyes and close-cropped brown hair that peeked out from beneath his flat-brimmed hat. At one time, when she was going into seventh grade and he had just graduated from high school, his features had been as familiar to her as her own. And far more interesting.

"How do you know my name?" he demanded, frowning.

"Don't you recognize me? Some great policeman you are! I'm Jodie—Jodie Parker! Now may I please put my hands down?" She didn't wait for permission.

He examined her through narrowed eyes, before nodding and saying slowly, "I should've known it was you, drivin' like a bat out of hell."

She snatched her purse away. "It's late and I want to get home." She motioned impatiently to the flashing lights on his patrol car. "Do you think you could turn that off? It's giving me a headache."

He ignored her complaint. "Last I heard you were in Paris."

"That was two months ago."

"Then London."

"One month ago."

"Then New York."

"Last week." She cocked her head. "You've certainly kept up with my whereabouts."

"Couldn't help it. Your trip was a prime subject of conversation around here."

"I'm glad I provided such grand entertainment," she said dryly.

He lifted an eyebrow. "What did you do to your hair?"

Jodie smoothed her new sleek style. In the confusion of being pulled over she'd forgotten the radical change. "I had it cut. What do you think?"

"I didn't recognize you."

She eyed him suspiciously. "You didn't answer my question."

"I liked it long and curly better—and the natural color."

"This is called 'midnight black'."

Tate Connelly shook his head. "No wonder I didn't recognize you. Does your aunt Mae know about it?"

Jodie shrugged. "I'm twenty-four now, Tate. Whether my aunt approves or not makes no difference."

For the first time since he'd pulled her over, a smile tugged at his lips. "You say that now…out here."

Jodie pushed past him to get back into her car. "May I go? Now that you know I'm not an escaped felon? Honestly, the way you behaved you'd've thought I had a gun and was about to…" The words died on her lips. Tate's father, a deputy sheriff, had been shot and killed by a pair of escaped felons he'd pulled over because their car had a faulty brake light. "Oh, Tate, I'm sorry. I didn't mean—"

He cut her off. "I'll follow you to the ranch. We don't want you to get lost or anything."

Her cheeks flushed. "I'm already almost there, Tate."

"Just the same," he returned stubbornly, "it's either that or a ticket for speeding."

"Everybody speeds out here!"

"Not in front of me, they don't. Not for long, anyway."

Jodie slammed the door shut. Obstinate, objectionable, opinionated beast! She didn't want to be escorted home like a delinquent runaway! Her aunt was already disgruntled enough.

As Tate returned to his patrol car, Jodie took several deep breaths, forcing herself to calm down. As she'd claimed only moments before—and it was something she needed to remember—she was twenty-four years old! A fully adult woman who had no need to apologize to anyone about anything.

The light bar on top of the patrol car switched off, as did the spotlight. Tate started the engine and waited. For a fleeting second Jodie wondered what he'd do if she refused to budge, then she reached for the key and twisted it. Within seconds both cars were back on the highway.

True to his word Tate trailed her closely. Jodie, highly conscious of his presence, kept to an unwavering fifty-five, under the legal limit for highway travel at night in Texas.

As before, their cars were the only vehicles on the road. It was past ten o'clock on a weekday night and most of the people who worked the surrounding ranches had called it quits for the day. From Jodie's knowledge of the Parker Ranch, though, her relatives would still be up. But not for long.

Her foot itched to press harder on the accelerator;

she restrained the urge. They would get there when they got there, and there wasn't anything she could do to change it.

When they finally arrived at ranch headquarters, Jodie was relieved to see lights still on in four of the five houses rimming the drive. Without thinking she drove past her father's house and pulled to a stop in front of Mae's larger two-story structure—a telltale sign as to who had the most influence in her life. When she realized what she'd done, she ground her teeth, because Tate Connelly wouldn't miss the significance.

Her cousin Rafe—his house was the nearest Mae's on the right—was the first to step outside. As manager of the ranch, he had both the authority and the force of personality to challenge any intruder. Shannon, his wife, waited in the doorway, her robe drawn tightly about her slender frame. Farther back along the drive Jodie saw her father appear on his porch, while directly across the tree-dotted courtyard her cousin LeRoy had left his house and was coming toward them.

Jodie took a deep breath. She was home.

Tate Connelly eased himself from the patrol car in time to receive Rafe's greeting. "What's all this? Somethin' goin' on I should know about?"

"Yeah," LeRoy chimed in. "It's not every day the sheriff pays a visit. Fact is, I don't remember it ever happenin' this late at night before!"

Jodie felt the sweep of Rafe's dark gaze as she exited her car, but she sensed no spark of recognition. He didn't know her, either!

"Just a little delivery I thought I'd help make," Tate said amicably.

Mae's front door opened. "What in tarnation's goin' on here?" she demanded irritably, giving the sash of her robe a sharp tug as she stepped onto the porch. "What couldn't wait until morning? Rafe, what is it?"

"I don't know, Aunt Mae. I was just askin' Tate that."

"Tate Connelly?" She moved closer to the rail and squinted. "Tell him I can't see him. He needs to get into better light."

Tate complied with her direction, and as he passed Jodie, he collected her by the arm and brought her along.

"Look who I ran into, Miss Parker," he drawled.

"Who's that?" Mae said, still peering into the gloom.

"The prodigal niece." Jodie could tell from the way he said it that he was enjoying himself. Enjoying the fact that not even her own family had recognized her. Enjoying the prospect of what would happen once they did.

Jodie shook her arm free of his grasp and glared at him. "It's me, Aunt Mae—Jodie," she said, hurrying up the two short steps to give her great-aunt a hug.

For a moment Mae Parker was perfectly still, then, pulling back, she looked hard at the younger woman. "Jodie?" she repeated. It took only seconds for the other shoe to drop. "*Jodie!* What in heaven's name have you done to yourself? Gib. *Gib!* Get over here!" she hollered. "Come see what your daughter's done to herself!" Then back to Jodie, "I *knew* it was wrong for you to be at such loose ends for so long. Idle hands always find trouble. You should've taken that job with

Mimi Henderson in Houston like I wanted you to. Then you wouldn't have had time to...to—''

"You don't know that, Aunt Mae," Jodie broke into her aunt's uncharacteristic sputtering. "I'd've probably done the same thing. I—"

"*Jodie!*" Her father rushed onto the porch, grabbed her and held her close. "I've missed you, gal. Missed you like the dickens! What are you doin' here so early? I thought you weren't gettin' in till tomorrow. If I'd known, I'd've..."

With her face pressed into her father's comfortably worn cotton shirt, it was impossible for Jodie to continue her protest. Instead, her nose twitched at the nostalgic scents of turpentine and oil paints. Her father might frustrate her frequently with his ineffectualness, particularly in his dealings with Mae, but she loved him. Loved him dearly.

Pulling back, Jodie smiled through a haze of tears. "You know me, Dad. I never do anything that's expected."

He'd changed little since the last time she'd seen him. A few more sprinkles of salt in his salt-and-pepper hair. A few more wrinkles to befit his sixty-three years. He beamed with happiness at her return, not seeming to care one whit about what she'd done with her hair.

Her cousins joined them on the porch. "Hey, little girl," Rafe said, plucking her away from her father to twirl her around. "I didn't recognize you!"

LeRoy stole her away from Rafe and continued the twirl. "You gonna find it hard to stay on the farm now that you've seen Paree?" he teased.

Jodie giggled at their antics—until Mae broke into the fun.

"What kind of trouble did you get yourself into on the way here?" she demanded. "Tate's a busy man. Got a whole county to look after. I'm sure he has more to do than round up strays."

Jodie glanced at Tate, who'd remained standing a short distance from the porch, his badge gleaming on his tan uniform. She wondered how he'd react if she fudged the truth.

Instead of abandoning her to her own devices, though, he said easily, "It's never any trouble to see a pretty young lady home, Miss Parker. It's one of the perks of the job. Now if you'll excuse me, I better be on my way."

His level brown gaze met Jodie's, and when it did, something inside her stirred.

"You sure you don't want to come inside, Tate?" Rafe invited.

Tate shook his head. "Better not."

Shannon pushed her way through the group on the porch. "Jodie? It *is* you!" she exclaimed. "Let me see what you did to yourself. Oh...your hair!" A slight pause. "It looks great. Such a change!"

"Looks like she's tryin' to be someone else," Mae grumbled.

"I'm still me, Aunt Mae," Jodie said.

As the others started to file into Mae's house, LeRoy said, "I'll go wake Harriet. She'll kill me if I let her miss this."

"The boys are asleep, too," Shannon confided to Jodie, "but believe me, we don't want to wake them.

They're like bears when they're disturbed. Typical Parker men.''

Jodie joined in the general laughter, but something made her look back at Tate. He was already at his patrol car pulling open the door. That same something made her break away to join him.

If Tate was surprised, he didn't show it. "Back in the bosom of the family," he taunted softly. "All safe and sound."

It had always been like that between them, him treating her like a spoiled brat! It wasn't her fault she'd been born into one of the oldest and most influential families in the area. She'd never traded on her name—expecting favors or asking for them. But he didn't seem to see it that way.

"Thanks to you," she returned with just as much mockery. "You never know what kind of pervert might be hiding behind a creosote bush."

"No, you don't," he agreed solemnly.

Jodie ran a finger along the rim of the car door. She had something to say and she needed to say it quickly before she got cold feet. "Thank you for not telling Aunt Mae you stopped me for speeding."

"You looked in enough trouble already. I didn't need to add more."

"Still...thanks."

His gaze flickered to her altered hair. "If you'd wanted to set the cat among the canaries, you couldn't have made a better choice."

"I didn't do it to cause trouble."

"You didn't?" he scoffed. Then before she could reply, he continued quietly, "It's good to have you home again, Jodie. The place hasn't been the same without you.''

The slight huskiness in his voice did odd things to Jodie's equilibrium. She took refuge in prickliness. "Why?" she challenged, "Because no one else keeps things stirred up?"

He smiled slightly. "You could say that."

His gaze remained steadily on her, and Jodie found she couldn't look away. It took a call from the police radio to break them apart.

As he slid into the driver's seat and reached for the hand mike, Jodie took an uncertain step backward. She listened as he made a clipped comment, then broke off. When he looked at her again, his expression was grim.

"There's been a knife fight over at Mike Newman's. One of his cowboys is hurt pretty bad. I have to get over there." He'd started the engine while still talking, but before pulling away he swept her with another look. "Guess I'll see you around again sometime soon, hmm?"

Jodie nodded. Her insides were still all quivery. Why? She'd gotten over her schoolgirl crush on him years ago. Years and *years* ago!

"Jodie!" Mae hailed her from the porch. "What are you doing out there? Everyone's wantin' to talk to you!"

"I'll be right there, Aunt Mae," Jodie called back, then with a tentative smile at Tate, she hurried inside.

CHAPTER TWO

JODIE LUXURIATED lying in bed the next morning, listening to the sounds she'd awakened to for most of her life. The distant harmony of men's voices, lowing cattle and, occasionally, cars and machinery starting up and moving off. A warm June breeze ruffled the window curtains, bringing with it the sweet smells of grasses and flowers and earth. With all the places she'd visited this past year, none had inspired this same swell of feeling. Which surprised her, because she'd seen some pretty amazing things.

There was a tap on her door, and her father came in carrying a tray. "I wasn't sure you'd be awake, but I took the chance. You still like a good strong cup of coffee first thing in the morning?"

Jodie struggled to sit up as he placed the tray on her bedside table. When she saw he'd included not only coffee but a piece of toast spread with her favorite blackberry jam, she protested, "You didn't have to do this, Dad."

"I know."

Jodie caught his hand. "I thought of you often, especially in Italy. So many wonderful art museums and so much beautiful scenery. It's completely different from here. I could just see you scrambling around, trying to paint everything."

"Here's not so bad," her father said mildly.

"I know, but—"

"Aunt Mae was real fired up when you turned down that job. She'd had to pull a lot of strings."

"I didn't ask her to pull any."

He smiled. "Then you took off, which was probably the smartest thing you could've done. What time does she want to see you this morning?"

"Eleven." Jodie frowned. "How's she doing, Dad?"

"Compared to what? A whirlwind?"

"I don't know," Jodie said, shrugging. "It just seemed, last night, as if she's suddenly...older."

"She *is* older! But she's the same Mae as ever. Cantankerous, determined, with a temper hotter'n a pistol when you don't do somethin' the way she wants." He looked at Jodie, the corners of his eyes crinkling as he teased, "You'll be able to see for yourself at eleven."

Jodie groaned. "Maybe I should have stayed in Europe!"

Her father ruffled her short hair. "She sure didn't like this very much, either. Every time she looked at you last night she ground her teeth. I swear, I thought she'd picked up termites in her house until I found out what that noise was." His fingers stilled. "Your hair used to be the same color as your mother's, the same bright copper that burns like a flame when the sun hits it."

Jodie moved her head away. Her mother was a subject they'd always avoided.

"Is it permanent?" her father asked.

"It's a rinse. It'll wash out in three or four shampoos. I did it in London because I felt like it."

"To get a rise out of us? Out of Mae?"

Jodie frowned. "Why does everyone automatically assume that?" First Tate, now her father. Couldn't a person just do something and not have everyone make a big deal of it? But then, on the Parker Ranch everything was a big deal if it went against the common thought. Against Mae's thought.

Her father patted her shoulder. "Drink your coffee before it gets cold. Aunt Mae wants to see me before she sees you. I think she has an errand for me to do in town, so if I'm not around when you come out— Say, how'd you like me to return your rental car, since I'll probably be goin' that way?"

"That would be great! But I'd rather she let you have the day off. I mean, it *has* been a year since we've seen each other."

He moved to the door. "I imagine she expects we'll have lots of time to catch up."

"What if I plan to leave again soon?" Jodie countered, irritated with her great-aunt for making assumptions.

Her father stopped dead in his tracks. "You plannin' on leavin' soon?"

Jodie shook her head. "No, no. I'm here for a couple of months at least."

He found his smile again. "Well, all right. For a minute there I thought..." His smile broadened. "I'm just glad to have you home again, honey. Real glad. We all are."

Her father's words rang in her ears as Jodie sipped her coffee and nibbled on her toast. Everyone *was* glad to see her. They'd welcomed her back into the family circle without a moment's pause. Harriet had even burst into tears.

A special family dinner was planned for tonight and, later in the week, on Friday night, a huge barbecue with friends and neighbors invited. Jodie had protested, saying she'd rather keep things low-key. But her wishes had been swept aside.

"Buck up, Jodie," Shannon had whispered when she'd noticed her tight expression. "Mae's been counting the days until you came back. Let her have her fun, then you can make a stand."

The trouble was, Mae had been riding herd on the family for so long that *making a stand* was nearly impossible. Her great-aunt thought it was her right to direct everyone's life.

Jodie sighed, checked the bedside clock, then hurried off to bathe and dress. The dreaded hour was fast approaching.

MARIE, MAE'S HOUSEKEEPER, passed on Mae's instructions that Jodie was to report directly to her private office. Before allowing Jodie to proceed to her fate, though, she confided that if she'd had the same opportunity to travel when she was young, she'd have done it no matter what.

"I think what you did was wonderful. And so would she—" Marie gestured toward Mae's office "—if she'd thought of it first. And your hair—I like it!"

Jodie's lips twitched. Marie and her camp-cook husband, Axel, having no children of their own, had formed a strong attachment to each of the Parker children living on the ranch. Jodie's early abandonment by her mother had especially pulled at their heartstrings. As she'd grown up, Jodie had spent many an hour in Marie's kitchen under the guise of helping her, while in reality they'd chattered endlessly about any and everything. "Thanks," she said softly, and kissed the housekeeper's cheek.

Then, carrying herself with dignity, she walked down the hall. She'd taken special care with her appearance, using a minimum of makeup and wearing her most conservative dress—a navy blue knit, buttoned fully to the neck. Nothing had been left to chance, from her tiny gold earrings to the delicate shell cameo that was pinned at her throat.

Last night's butterflies again took wing as she paused outside the office door. Then she opened it.

The room was exactly as it always had been: book-lined walls, a sitting area to one side and her aunt's highly polished rosewood desk positioned perfectly to assert dominance over anyone who entered.

Her aunt was seated behind the desk writing in a journal. She seemed unaware of Jodie's presence until Jodie murmured, "Aunt Mae."

The white head, hair caught on top in a smooth knot, snapped up. "You're late," she said tartly.

Jodie checked her watch. "Only a minute." Then, before her aunt could launch into further criticism, Jodie continued, "Aunt Mae, I want to apologize. I never did thank you for arranging that position for me with

Mimi Henderson. I thanked her when I turned it down, but I never—''

Mae cut her off. ''What good are apologies after so much time has passed?''

''It's better than nothing surely.''

''Not in my book.''

''Aunt Mae—''

Mae slapped the journal shut. ''It's one thing to turn Mimi down. It's another thing entirely to disappear for a year!''

''I didn't disappear!''

''What would you call it, then? We barely heard from you!''

''I wrote. I called.''

''When you felt like it—which wasn't very often.''

''Aunt Mae—''

''Don't 'Aunt Mae' me,'' Mae scolded.

Jodie shifted from foot to foot. She *had* been lax about keeping in touch. But it was for this very reason, to avoid what was happening now.

Mae's hawklike eyes narrowed as if she sensed a weakening. ''I raised you like my own daughter since before you could walk. I didn't teach you to be inconsiderate.''

''I didn't do it to be inconsiderate, only to avoid unpleasantness. *This* kind of unpleasantness.''

Mae's features tightened. ''Surely you didn't think you could just waltz home and no one would say a word?''

''No, I knew *you'd* be bound to say something.''

Mae glared at her. Then she motioned for Jodie to accompany her to the sitting area. As they settled on either end of the dark green couch, she asked stiffly, "Did you get anything of value out of your year away?"

"I believe so."

"What?"

"An appreciation of life outside Texas. Different people, different places, different ways of thinking."

"Better ways?" Mae demanded sharply.

"Sometimes, yes," Jodie replied honestly.

Mae shook her head and tisked. "How can a Parker say that?"

Jodie rolled her eyes.

Mae saw and demanded, "Are you still ashamed of who you are? Is that why you did what you did to your hair? But if that's the case, why'd you choose black? It just makes you look more like one of us."

The physical resemblance among the family members was striking—black hair, black eyes, strongly carved features. Jodie had always been the odd person out with her coppery-red hair, hazel eyes and gamine-like features. Her goal in London, though, hadn't been to look like a Parker. That had been the *last* thing she wanted.

Mae watched her keenly. "You are still ashamed," she said flatly, answering her own question. "I'd hoped…" She sighed. Then, shoulders sagging, she murmured, "I'm too old for this, Jodie. There's not all that much time left."

Her great-aunt seemed to undergo a transformation right in front of her eyes. The fierce matriarch changed to a tired, frail, overburdened woman who looked every one of her eighty-eight years. Then the illusion vanished. Mae's shoulders were back in place, her chin jutted forward, a defiant look in her eyes.

Had she only thought she'd seen something? Jodie wondered. Confused, she failed to register Mae's next words and stammered, "Wh—what did you say?"

"I said I'm disappointed," Mae snapped. "You're too old to behave so foolishly. But it's not surprising, considering that you always did jump into things without taking time to think 'em through. The best example I can come up with is that mess you got into with that young cowboy."

Jodie stiffened. "That was a long time ago, Aunt Mae."

"What was his name? Rio, wasn't it?"

An old mixture of shame and resentment burned through Jodie. "I was seventeen!"

"I tried to tell you what would happen. So did Rafe. So did Shannon and Harriet. But did you listen? No. You ran off with him, expectin' him to marry you. If Rafe hadn't gotten the truth out of Jennifer Cleary—" the daughter of the rancher whose property bordered the Parker Ranch and who'd been Jodie's best friend at the time "—Lord only knows what would have come of it!"

"Well, it wouldn't have been marriage," Jodie said bitterly. "That wasn't part of Rio's plans, remember?"

"He just let you think it was."

Jodie stood up, rubbing her arms as if they were cold. "Do we have to go through this again?"

"Then your change of plans at the university," Mae continued, undaunted. "First you wanted a degree in business. You took all the necessary courses, made excellent grades, then you decided business didn't interest you. Art history was your cup of tea. So you shifted everything to that, even though it meant adding another year before you could graduate. I tried to talk you out of it, but you were determined. Then, after I went to all the trouble to arrange a position for you at the Hofinze Museum—one of the most respected in the country, I might add—you ran off to play in Europe!''

"I've apologized for that," Jodie said tightly.

Mae tugged on Jodie's arm. "It's not me I'm worried about, Missy. It's *you!*" she said. "How old are you? Twenty-four? Twenty-five? When I was your age I'd already lived through one world war, the Great Depression and several terrible droughts—one so bad we almost lost the ranch! The way you're going, you're just wasting your life! Letting it trickle through your fingers. And what you let trickle through, believe me, you won't ever get back!" She paused, then asked, "What are your plans? Do you have any? Have you even thought about it?"

"No," Jodie admitted.

Mae sighed in exasperation. "You have to set yourself a goal and work toward it, Jodie. Would you like me to—"

"I don't want you to do *anything!*" Jodie interrupted her fiercely. "I'm perfectly capable of—"

"There aren't many art museums out here," Mae cut in. "Unless you've changed your mind about that, too."

Jodie's cheeks were flushed as she walked to a narrow table on which various old family photographs were displayed. An entire range of emotions was washing over her, from the shame she still felt at being duped by Rio to fury at Mae's scolding. "Do you want me to leave the ranch?" she asked stiffly. "Is that it?"

"No!" Mae said quickly. "You just got here. And contrary to what you might think, I—we all missed you! What I want, is for you to turn your back on your irresponsible ways. Have the backbone to pick something and stick to it. Make up your mind that whatever it is, you're goin' to see it through."

Jodie had a hard time meeting her aunt's eyes. If Mae was frustrated by what she saw as her niece's continuing inability to settle down, it was nothing to Jodie's own frustration. She, better than anyone, was aware of her restiveness, of her inability to decide what she wanted from life. Was that natural for someone of her age? Or was it because she was too much like her mother and ill suited for a settled life?

"Jodie?"

Jodie looked up.

Her great-aunt's expression changed as she crossed to her. "I don't want to be too hard on you," Mae said mildly, taking her hand. "Just hard enough to make you understand. You're the closest I've ever come to having a child of my own. Do your old spinster aunt a favor and tell me you'll try. You'll at least do that for me, won't you, Jodie?"

The Parker charm. Jodie knew it well. If you couldn't win a battle by direct confrontation, win it by persuasion. But something made her pause. That momentary sense of her great-aunt's frailty.

Jodie glanced away for a second, then looked back. "I'll try, Aunt Mae," she promised quietly, and when her aunt reached out to hug her, she let her love for this steel-hard woman break through in response.

THE HOUSE was quiet as Jodie made her way back to the front door. Marie must have taken off—she was probably hiding out at the ranch hands' cookhouse, visiting Axel. And the family, knowing of the command appearance, had stayed clear, as well.

That didn't mean they weren't interested, though. On her way past Rafe and Shannon's house, Jodie was waylaid by Shannon and Harriet, who, "coincidentally", were just coming out with their young children.

Both five-year-old Anna, Harriet and LeRoy's younger daughter, and Ward, Shannon and Rafe's four-and-a-half year-old son, looked inquisitively at Jodie before running off to play under the trees in the center courtyard, a golden-haired puppy gamboling at their heels. Nathan, Shannon and Rafe's three-year-old, showed no interest in Jodie at all as he hurried to catch up with the others.

"They don't remember me," she murmured, looking wistfully after them.

"A year is a long time in a child's life," Shannon said.

"Oh, you'll be back in their good graces before you know it," Harriet said. "All you have to do is pay attention to Shep, Jr. Someone wrote to tell you about him, right? The kids got together and named him in honor of old Shep. Shannon told them he'd already been given a name at the kennel, but they said it wasn't the right one. What was it, Shannon? Duke or Domino or something like that?"

"Duke," Shannon said, smiling.

"Rafe sided with them, and since the puppy was his present from Shannon, that settled it."

"I thought Rafe didn't want another dog after..."

"He said he didn't," Shannon replied, "but he never got over losing Shep. Even after three years I'd catch him looking around as if he expected Shep to be there. They'd been part of each other's lives for so many years. One day I just did it. His face lit up when he saw the puppy, then the kids wanted to name him Shep, Jr....It was really Gwen and Wes's doing." She named Harriet's older children. "Ward! Ward, stop it!" she called when she saw her older son thump his brother with the puppy's rope chew toy.

"If those two don't look like Parkers," Jodie said softly.

Shannon laughed. "They seem to have missed my genes altogether. *"Ward!"* she again warned her older son. "I'll be back in a second," she said in exasperation.

Jodie watched as Shannon went to administer justice, her wheat-colored hair swinging against her shoulders. It was hard to believe that seven years had passed since Shannon had arrived at the ranch. At the time she'd been a pale stranger in need of recuperation from a plane crash she'd barely survived—one in which everyone else on board had been killed, including her father and her fiancé. Now, the limp that once disabled her had all but disappeared. And she'd become a Parker—in every way that counted.

Harriet must have been thinking along the same lines, because she said quietly, "It's pretty amazing when you think about it, isn't it? Shannon coming here, she and Rafe falling in love, having kids. Terrible as it was, if it hadn't been for that plane crash, none of this would have happened. She'd probably have married that other man, Rafe would've had to keep putting up with Mae shoving women his way, and you and I would have been short a good friend.''

Jodie turned to look at Harriet. In her mind Harriet's influence at the ranch had been pretty special, too. Jodie'd been ten when Harriet and LeRoy married, and from that point on her new cousin had always been there for her—across the courtyard, ready to help out in tough situations or willing merely to listen.

Harriet, sensing her scrutiny, turned wide-spaced gray eyes on Jodie. ''What is it?'' she asked, laughing. ''Are you counting my silver hairs? If you find more than six, let me know and I'll dye those suckers brown again so fast...You're not the only one who can play with hair color, you know.''

Shannon rejoined them. ''Hopefully that's taken care of it.'' She gave the children one last glance, before turning curious blue eyes on Jodie and Harriet. ''What are you two talking about?''

''Hair dye!'' Harriet said. ''What do you think? How would I look as a platinum blond? I could buy one of those skintight dresses, then walk around like my knees are glued together.'' She struck a Marilyn Monroe pose, which went amazingly well with her lush figure, before bursting into giggles.

''LeRoy would have a heart attack,'' Shannon teased.

''Not to mention Aunt Mae.'' Jodie grinned.

"Which brings us back to what Shannon and I want to know," Harriet said. "How did it go? You don't look particularly the worse for wear. No singed edges."

"None that show at any rate," Shannon agreed.

Jodie smiled wryly. "Well, she wasn't pleased, but beyond that..."

"Oh, come on," Harriet said. "There has to be more."

"She wants me to grow up."

The stark statement, tinged with hurt, caused a silence, then Shannon asked, "Isn't that what you've already done?"

"It seems I haven't done it well enough. Not in her view."

"She's proud of you, Jodie," Harriet said quickly. "Proud that you graduated with honors from the university, proud that you—"

"She threw Rio in my face again," Jodie interrupted tightly.

The other two women shared a glance. "But Rio was such a long time ago," Shannon said.

"That's what I told her."

"So what does she want you to do?" Harriet demanded.

"Basically?" Jodie said. "The opposite of what I've been doing up till now. No more running away from...things."

Shannon shook her head. "Wouldn't you think that at her age she'd let up a bit?"

Harriet grumbled, "She probably only sees it as having less time to get what she wants."

"She truly does care about you, Jodie," Shannon

assured her. "She cares about all of us, but you most of all. It makes a difference that she practically raised you. Maybe that's why she expects so much."

A brightly colored ball bounced by, followed immediately by the puppy and three laughing children.

"We were just on our way to Harriet's house for lunch," Shannon said. "Would you like to come along?"

"The more the merrier!" Harriet said.

Jodie smiled her regrets. "No, I'm going to lie down for a while. My body still thinks it's somewhere else. And I sure don't want to be guilty of falling asleep during dinner tonight. Aunt Mae would never forgive me."

"She'd probably make you start taking afternoon naps." Harriet laughed.

After a few minutes spent playing with the puppy and talking to the children, Jodie continued to her father's house. It, too, was quiet. He must still have been in town on his errand or off somewhere painting.

For most of her life her father had distanced himself from her and from others. As she'd grown older, she'd come to understand that he used this distance as a defense. If he lost himself in his painting, he could get away from everything that bothered him, both in the present and from the past. Over the years his avocation was supposed to be a secret from Mae, but she'd known, as she always did.

Gib was remarkably talented. His scenes of working life on a ranch looked so genuine—the horses, the cowboys, the cattle—it seemed they might come to life and step off the canvas at any second. In the beginning he'd shown them to no one, not even her. Then, slowly, over the past few years, as he'd gained a little confidence, he'd begun to work out in the open in his spare time.

Where would he be now if he'd been encouraged from the onset, instead of discouraged? If Mae hadn't thought it a waste of time for a grown man to smear dabs of color on a canvas?

Jodie marched straight to the bathroom and, stripping off her clothes, stepped into the shower.

She did *not* want her darkened hair to make anyone think she was trying to look like a Parker. When Mae said that, it had stung!

Was that what Tate Connelly thought, too? Was that why he'd found the entire affair so amusing last night?

Jodie wet her head under the spray of water, poured a huge dollop of shampoo into her hand, worked it into a massive lather, then rinsed. She repeated the process until all traces of black had been washed down the drain and her hair once again gleamed with coppery-red highlights.

CHAPTER THREE

"TELL HER SHE'S GOT to stop hasslin' me, Tate! First thing I wake up, last thing at night, all the while I'm tryin' to do anythin'! She even calls me at work—*at work!*—to complain. I'm gonna get fired. She's gotta stop it. Tell her she's gotta stop it! You'll do that for me, won'tcha? Tell her she's gotta stop or…or you'll take her in, put her in jail. Yeah, that's it. She wouldn't like that, not a bit. 'Cause then she couldn't get at me! You'll tell her, won't ya? Won'tcha?"

Tate listened patiently as Jimmy Evers gave his side of the story. Before that, he'd listened patiently to Jimmy's wife, Eve, as she'd told hers. He and Jimmy stood outside the Everses' ramshackle house, the front screen door hanging loose on its hinges, trash scattered about the yard and several long-dead car hulks littering the driveway. Jimmy, dressed in dingy jeans and a torn undershirt, reeked of sour mash.

"She says you hit her, Jimmy," Tate said evenly.

"I never did!" Jimmy denied. "I pushed her, but she was comin' at me with a pot. One of those big heavy ones. If I hadn't pushed her, I'd be on my way to the hospital right now…this very minute…prob'ly dead! Then she couldn't hassle me anymore, could she?

Maybe I shoulda let her do it. Just let her haul off and—''

Tate cut into the torrent of words. ''She says you hit her before she tried to hit you.''

''That's not true!'' Jimmy blustered.

''Then why's she got that big bruise on her forehead?''

''She got that when she fell!''

''Fell after you hit her?''

Jimmy shook his head vehemently. ''No! No! I *pushed* her. After she came at me, I pushed her an'...an' then she fell.''

Tate took hold of Jimmy's arm while reaching for the handcuffs attached to the back of his service belt. ''I'm gonna have to take you in, Jimmy. You can tell it to the judge.''

Jimmy tried to back away. ''Uh-uh! I don't wanna tell nothin' to no judge.''

Tate swung the man around so he could lock his wrists firmly behind him. ''This has all happened before, Jimmy. No use you causin' trouble now.''

As Jimmy continued to protest, Eve appeared inside the screen door. She was a tiny woman, bone thin, old before her time. ''What's goin' on?'' she demanded.

''I'm takin' Jimmy to jail, Eve,'' Tate said.

''Why'd you tell him I hit you, Evie?'' Jimmy whined, twisting his head so he could see his wife.

'''Cause you did. But I don't want you to take him to jail!'' she told Tate as she pushed outside.

''I'm afraid it's out of your hands now.''

''Evie!'' Jimmy wailed.

''I won't press charges!'' Evie declared angrily.

"I still have to take him in."

"But he didn't hit me! I...I lied!"

Tate shook his head as he took Jimmy to his patrol car. "All I can go by is what you told me earlier and what I see with my own eyes."

"Evie!" Jimmy wailed louder.

Tate was bending to put the reluctant man into the backseat when Evie, undoubtedly suffering from a drink too many herself, attacked him.

"Let him go! *Let him go!*" she screeched. "You don't have any right! I'll file a complaint, all right, but it won't be against him. It'll be against *you!*"

For a small woman she packed a good wallop. Still, Tate ignored the blows raining down on his back until he had Jimmy secured. Then he turned to deal with the distraught wife. After a short scuffle he overpowered her.

Tears streamed down Evie Evers's cheeks as she stood with her arms pinned against her sides.

"Eve...Evie, listen to me!" Tate said urgently. "He's hurt you today. He's hurt you in the past. Just last week one of your neighbors called to complain that Jimmy was waving a gun at him and yellin' that he couldn't sit on his own porch. Your man makes a whole world of trouble for himself when he drinks. You know that!"

"But I love him," Evie moaned, her faded blue eyes pleading for understanding.

Tate suppressed a weary sigh. How many times had he heard that before? Not only here, but during the years he'd worked street patrol in Dallas. "Did you talk to those people I told you about?" he asked.

Her body twitched and she turned her face away.
"No."

"Do you still have their card?"

"I have it," she admitted. But she wouldn't look at
him, probably because she had no intention of using it.

"Give 'em a call, Evie. That's what they're there
for, for people like you and Jimmy. They can help."

By this time Jimmy had started to cry. They could
hear his blubbering through the closed window. He
wasn't crying for the misery he'd caused his wife,
though. He was crying for himself, because once again
he was in trouble.

As Tate settled behind the wheel, he watched Eve
Evers return to her house. Other eyes were watching,
as well, from behind the cracks in drawn curtains.
Something else for the neighbors to talk about.

THE BRIGGS COUNTY Sheriff's Office was located in
Del Norte, the county's largest town, population a
fairly even 1,200 souls. There were only two other
towns within the county limits and both were small
enough to miss if you blinked. The remainder of the
county's 6,000 square miles was mostly isolated ranch-
land, policed by Tate and his four deputies. Because
resources were spread so thin, an informal understanding had been worked out between the Del Norte police
force—a chief and two officers—and the sheriff's office, where they would each make themselves available
to assist the other when called upon. The jail, though,
belonged solely to the county, and as sheriff, Tate was
charged with its administration, a job that caused him
innumerable headaches. Some problem or other always

seemed to crop up, just as his predecessor, Jack Denton, had warned.

Jack had accomplished quite a bit during his long tenure as sheriff. He'd ushered Briggs County into modern times, pressing for and then overseeing the building of the new jail facility and the purchase of new patrol cars. He'd also demanded that the county provide uniforms for himself and his men. While the counties surrounding them were just now starting to think about changing from the good-ol'-boy, everybody-knows-who-we-are jeans and white shirts, the members of the Briggs County Sheriff's Department already wore professional-looking uniforms.

"Ain't nobody gonna mistake one of my men for somethin' they aren't!" Jack had decreed. And he was right. Today's population was very mobile. Lawmen weren't known by everyone in the county anymore. When they gave a command or drew a gun, it was to everyone's advantage to know that they were on official business, with all the appropriate authority.

Tate parked the patrol car next to the low stone building and took Jimmy Evers through to the jail facility in back.

"Let him dry out," Tate instructed one of the jailers, "then he can call whoever he wants. He's not goin' anywhere for a while."

He started to turn away, but was stopped by a hasty, "Sheriff? Doug Rawlings has been complaining he needs some pain pills for his back. Says if you don't do something about it soon, he's gonna file a lawsuit."

"Another one?" Tate muttered dryly. "Tell him I'll

see if I can get the doc to stop by. But he's goin' to have to wait his turn. Be sure to tell him that, too.''

Tate made his way along the connecting hallway to his department. In contrast to the new jail, the sheriff's domain hadn't been spruced up since shortly after the Second World War. The walls were painted an institutional green, and the lighting was an inadequate fluorescent. A long wooden bench that had been rescued from a derelict bus station was pushed against one wall, and across from it sat a faded couch of unknown age. This served as the holding area for people awaiting questioning or for those from the community who wanted to speak to someone in the office. A scarred wooden table stood in the opposite corner, on which was perched an ancient, though still functional, coffeemaker, a jar of creamer, a box of sugar cubes, a stack of cups and a few assorted plastic spoons. Above it was a map of the county and a bulletin board covered with notices and Wanted posters. The place had looked the same for as long as Tate could remember, and if anyone ever had the bright idea to change it, he'd put up one heck of a fight. He liked it the way it was.

"Tate?" Emma Connelly, still slim and in her early fifties with short silvery hair and the same brown eyes as her son, was a dispatcher for the sheriff's office and had been since before Tate was born. "A sheriff from up in Colorado's been trying to get hold of you for the past couple of hours. He left his number, wants you to call. I put it on your desk." His mother also did double duty as clerical help, assisting Rose Martinez, who'd been with the sheriff's office for almost as long as Emma had.

"Thanks," Tate said.

Her gaze ran slowly over him. "You want to come by for dinner tonight? You look like you could use a good meal. I'll cook you a steak."

He smiled. "I might just take you up on that."

Tate proceeded to his private office, a small room dominated by a huge walnut desk and lined with file cabinets. After hanging his service belt and hat on the prongs of the antique deer antlers a previous sheriff had contributed to the wall decor, he sat down and began a cursory look at the material awaiting his attention. But he couldn't concentrate on the paperwork and, instead, ended up assuming his favorite thinking position: his body stretched back in the chair, arms folded behind his head, boots crossed comfortably at the ankles and resting on the desk blotter.

Normally he liked to use these quiet moments to sort things out—evidence in a case, personnel problems, community relations and, of course, the latest problem at the jail. Today, though, his thoughts were purely personal. Drew Winslow, his former supervisor from Dallas, would be calling again soon, expecting an answer. An answer Tate didn't have.

It wasn't as if he hadn't been considering it. For the past week he'd thought of little else. Being asked to join a prestigious task force formed by one of the state's largest and most respected law-enforcement agencies wasn't something that happened every day. It was an honor, as well as a major career opportunity. A recognition of the skills he'd honed during his four years of service with the Dallas Police Department, his six years as a sheriff's deputy and the past year and a half running the county office. The invitation was a dream come true. Only…it wasn't as simple as that. There were certain realities to be reckoned with.

The first was his mother. If he accepted the position, it would mean moving away again and leaving her on her own. Most likely he'd be working out of Austin or possibly even Dallas again. There was no way he could commute. And even though she seemed to have her diabetes under control—which made it doubtful she'd experience another health crisis like she had years before, bringing him back home—as her only child and last remaining close relative, didn't he have a responsibility to her to stay?

Then there were the citizens of Briggs County. The dust had barely settled since his election as sheriff, and sheriffs grew old on the job here. He'd known that when he'd let Jack persuade him to throw his hat into the ring as his replacement.

Which brought him to Jack. How would he see the situation? Jack, the old friend who'd done so much to help both Tate and his mother in the years since Dan Connelly's death.

Tate's expression tightened as he thought of his father. Integrity and duty had been his watchwords. Not in a fanatical sense, but in the simple way he lived his life. What would *he* have done if presented with this same choice?

When Tate swung his feet to the floor, he still had no answer for Drew Winslow.

Then another thought pushed past all the others. It, too, was personal—highly personal. Because it involved Jodie Parker. Still as arrogant, still as spoiled, and now, irrefutably, back home.

Tate grabbed the message slip his mother had mentioned, reached for the phone and punched in the number. Work was what he needed. Something to keep his mind off everything else, particularly Jodie Parker.

"Bill Preston, please," he directed when the ringing telephone was answered. "This is Sheriff Connelly. I'm returnin' his call."

A moment later he was speaking to his counterpart in Clayborne County, Colorado.

As EXPECTED, the return of Jodie's hair to its natural color was noticed as soon as she and her father presented themselves at the family dinner that evening.

"Showing good sense at last!" Mae declared, the light of victory in her eyes.

"Oh, Jodie!" Harriet cried. "That dark color looked so nice on you!"

"Not that this isn't better," Shannon added quickly.

Jodie laughed off all the comments. "I got tired of it," she dismissed. "Now that I'm back home, I want to be me again."

"That's always best," Mae agreed.

"I wouldn't want to get lost in the crowd." Jodie fixed her gaze on her great-aunt. When Mae's lips thinned, she knew she'd made her point. It was imperative she not let her aunt think she'd won any ground.

Included at dinner that evening were the Hugheses, who lived in Little Springs Division, the closest of the nine divisions or territories, on the ranch. Dub Hughes, retired now, had been foreman at the ranch for most of his sixty-odd years, and he was there with his wife, Delores, as well as the current ranch foreman, his son Morgan Hughes, his son's wife, Christine, and their fourteen-year-old daughter, Erin. The Parkers and the Hugheses had always been close. Rafe and Morgan had grown up together like brothers, learning to work cattle, learning to run the ranch. The icing on the cake had come when Morgan married Christine, who'd proved to be a Parker herself, much to her surprise. Their union was a perfect blending of the two families, bringing them even closer together.

Fourteen adults and adolescents sat around the dining-room table, while the younger children were served at a small table nearby.

After considerable urging, Jodie shared all she could remember about her trip. What she'd seen and done over the past year, which towns and cities were her favorites, occasionally offering amusing anecdotes about some of the people she'd met. By the end of the meal everyone's curiosity was exhausted, as was Jodie.

Coffee was served in the living room, and following the custom, the gathering broke into smaller groups, some spilling out onto the front porch. Topics of conversation depended on the makeup of the group. The men talked mostly of weather and ranching, while the women talked of anything but.

It was from the latter group that Jodie learned her Aunt Darlene and Uncle Thomas were off on a cruise to Alaska.

Harriet grinned when she saw Jodie's surprise. "I know," she said. "The travel bug really bit Thomas hard. All Darlene has to do is show him a few bro- chures, he looks at 'em and off they go!''

Jodie shook her head. It was hard to imagine Uncle Thomas setting foot on a cruise ship, much less enjoy- ing it.

"Maybe he decided if you could travel, he could, too.'' Shannon laughed.

"Where are the babies?'' Harriet asked suddenly, looking around the room.

"I sent them outside with Rafe and LeRoy.'' Shan- non turned to Jodie. "Did you know that Rafe's al- ready got Nate started riding a horse? But then, he did the same thing with Ward.''

"You knew he would,'' Harriet said.

"I expected it, but—''

"Wesley's going on the fall roundup,'' Harriet of- fered. "He turns thirteen this summer. Thinks he's al- most grown.''

Jodie's eyes settled on the tall lanky boy who stood on the other side of the room talking with his younger sister, Gwen, and their cousin Erin. "From the look of him, he is,'' she said. "I couldn't believe it when I saw him earlier.''

"He's already as tall as his daddy,'' Harriet bragged.

"Gwen's grown a lot, too,'' Jodie said.

"I'm starting to feel positively old!'' Harriet grum- bled good-naturedly. "If it weren't for little Anna—''

Her words broke off as a very pregnant Christine Hughes joined them. Christine smiled at Jodie, her eyes aglow. "You look wonderful, Jodie,'' she said. It was the first time they'd had an opportunity for a personal word.

"I can definitely say the same for you," Jodie returned. She'd heard that Christine and Morgan were expecting their first child this summer, but she hadn't known how close to term the pregnancy was. It looked as if the baby could arrive at any moment. "You're so..." Her mind went blank.

Christine supplied a colorful image of her own. "I look like a watermelon about to explode!"

Jodie grinned. "When's the baby due?"

"In three weeks."

Morgan came up behind his wife and rested his hands lightly on her shoulders. "We're hopin' she decides to arrive a little early."

"She? It's a girl? You know for sure?" Jodie asked.

Morgan nodded. "My mother thinks it's terrible. Nature's supposed to surprise us. But we couldn't resist when the doctor asked us if we wanted to know."

"We're going to name her Elisabeth," Christine confided. "Spelled with an *s*. We'll probably end up calling her Beth."

"Is Erin excited?" Jodie asked, glancing at the pretty dark-haired teenager across the way.

"She can hardly wait."

Rafe came into the living room, herding the younger children before him. Little Nate giggled and ran to hide behind Morgan's legs. Rafe caught up with him and swung the child into his arms. It was easy to see that the two men were cut from the same cloth. Both were tall and lithe, except where Rafe was dark—dark hair, dark eyes, dangerous edge—Morgan was blond, with pale blue eyes that had a perpetual twinkle.

Mae looked away from her conversation with Gib

and the older Hugheses. "Did I hear a car drive up?" she demanded.

Rafe nodded. "That's what I was comin' to tell you—we've got company."

The company turned out to be Tate Connelly. When Jodie saw him step into the living room, she experienced the same leap of pulse she had the night before.

Tate was quick to realize what he'd interrupted. "I didn't mean to intrude on a party," he said.

His gaze scanned the room until coming to rest on Jodie. For a moment he seemed distracted, then he continued, "I can do this tomorrow. No use botherin' you all tonight."

"Nonsense," Mae declared. "You've come too long a way for it not to be important. Rafe? Morgan? Dub? Let's go to my office."

Jodie's accelerated heart rate refused to slow down. Was it the uniform? Crisp and official, a symbol of power? Or was it the man in the uniform, Tate himself?

"I wonder why he didn't just telephone?" Christine mused once the men had followed Mae down the hall.

Harriet nodded toward Jodie. "Maybe we don't have to look very far."

Shannon grinned. "I did notice where his attention lingered."

"He probably wants to arrest me," Jodie murmured.

"Or he could be surprised that your hair's red again. Harriet told me," Christine explained, since she herself hadn't seen Jodie with the dark color.

"It could be more than that. Didn't you have a crush on him a long time ago, Jodie?" Harriet asked, teasing. "Maybe he's finally come around."

"I was a kid!" Jodie defended. "Now I'm not. Neither is he."

"No, he's a hunk, that's what he is," Harriet declared.

Jodie was relieved when Delores Hughes joined their group and turned everyone's attention to Christine by saying, "If you're tired, we can leave. No telling what's going on in there. Rafe can bring Morgan and Dub home later."

Christine massaged her lower back. "What I'd really like is to sit down for a few minutes."

Harriet sprang into action, assisting Christine to the nearest chair. "Oh, my heavens! I don't know why I didn't think of that! Come over here."

The children began to make a lot of noise and run about the room. Shannon hurried to control them.

With everyone's attention elsewhere, Jodie wondered if she could slip out without notice. But before she could put her thought into action, Mae and the men returned—and for some reason they all looked straight at her.

What had she done? She'd just been kidding when she'd said that Tate might be there to arrest her.

"Jodie," Mae said, "Tate's come to give us some news. It concerns each of us, but you most of all."

Jodie felt a swift exchange of looks. Even the children grew quiet.

Tate's lean face was well schooled. "I've come to ask you to keep an eye out for someone. A cowboy who used to work on your ranch. He's wanted for questioning in the beating of the nineteen-year-old daughter of a rancher up in Colorado. The girl's lost the baby she was carryin', and it seems to be touch-and-go for her, too. The sheriff up there is notifying all the places this cowboy's ever worked to be on the lookout for him. His name's—'' a pause ''—Rio Walsh.''

CHAPTER FOUR

A SENSATION like raw electricity shot through Jodie as her gaze clung to Tate's.

"Rio!" The name moved across the room like rolling thunder.

Gib, Harriet, LeRoy, Shannon—their shock quickly gave way, and almost as one their attention jerked to Jodie to see how she'd taken the news.

"Rio?" she breathed in disbelief.

Tate nodded.

"But...but that's not possible," she said.

His expression hardened. "I'm afraid it is."

"Jodie!" Mae exclaimed. "How can you say that? After the way he treated you!"

"He...Rio just wouldn't do that!" Jodie said. "Get her pregnant, yes. But not— That's not the way he is! He'd never hit a woman, much less beat her."

"How can you know *what* he'd do?" Mae demanded harshly. "You misjudged him from the get-go, if I remember right. Which I do. And it's been years since—"

"Yes, it has," Jodie shot back. "I tried to tell you that earlier!"

"I warned him not to show his face in Texas again," Rafe said evenly, breaking into the disagreement.

"And I didn't put a time limit on it. He knows better than to come back here." Rafe was a hard man, accustomed to having his words heeded, particularly by someone who'd had the bad judgment to harm a member of his family.

"I still have to pass the information along," Tate said. "Sheriff Preston reckons he'll head for familiar territory."

"Well, he won't find any comfort here!" Mae declared. "Not from any of us. We'll turn him in faster'n a snake can blink."

Tate nodded as murmurs of agreement came from around the room.

"I still don't believe it," Jodie said stubbornly, setting her jaw.

"Not from *any* of us!" Mae snapped, her angry gaze fixed on Jodie.

Tate's attention also fell on Jodie. In response she lifted her chin. Then something happened she hadn't expected: he smiled at her. A small smile that disappeared as quickly as it came.

Mae broke the silence. "Have you had dinner yet, Tate? I'm sure Marie can make you up a nice plate."

Tate flashed his smile again, this time including everyone. "No, thanks, Miss Parker. My mom's expecting me for dinner tonight."

Mae nodded approval. Familial togetherness was one of her highest priorities. No matter how small the family. "And how's your mother doing?" she asked. "It's been some time since I've seen her, but she looked all hale and hearty when I did."

"She's doin' just fine, Miss Parker. I'll tell her you asked."

"Do that. And tell her I'll stop by the station the next time I'm in town and say hello."

Tate nodded, gave a slightly awkward salute, then left the house.

"Such a nice boy," Mae commented as the patrol car pulled away.

"He's not exactly a boy, Aunt Mae," Harriet said.

"From my perspective he is."

From *Jodie's* perspective too much was happening in too short a time. Her journey home, her reckoning with Mae, her first steps toward readjustment to life on the Parker Ranch. She'd been away for long months. Now she was home, yet not at home, just as in some strange way she'd never been completely "at home" here. She was the odd person out in the Parker clan, both in looks and in attitude. Very much a Parker, but different. *Wanting* to be different.

When the get-together broke up, Jodie tried to slip out with Harriet and her brood, but she didn't get farther than the porch.

"A word, Jodie," Mae commanded.

Jodie shifted the sleepy little girl she'd been carrying into LeRoy's arms and waited as Mae moved to stand beside her at the railing.

"A private word," she qualified, waving Gib on when he paused on the steps. "I won't keep her long."

Sounds carried easily in the night. Muted words and childish laughter drifted from the other houses on the cool breeze, as did the chirp of crickets and the sharp cry of a hunting bird.

Mae remained quiet, listening. Then she stirred. "I love this place, Jodie," she confessed softly. "I love it like it was a living-breathing thing. All my life it's been like a mother and a father to me. Whenever I have doubts, I go to the land. I touch it, I feel it, I rub it into my skin so I can make the connection. Parker land, Parker blood. Can you understand that?"

Jodie shrugged and looked away.

Mae sighed. "One day you will. At least, I hope you will. I don't understand what's happened to you, Jodie. Why you don't—"

"I really am tired, Aunt Mae," Jodie cut in. "I should go to bed. So if you don't mind—"

"I meant what I said about Rio," Mae interrupted sharply. "That girl could've been you!"

Jodie shook her head. "I wouldn't have gotten pregnant. I *didn't* get pregnant!"

"But for the grace of God!" Then, seeming to realize that their discussion had taken an unintended turn, Mae reverted to her previous reflection. "I don't want you to get hurt again, Jodie, that's all. That's why I—"

"It's like Rafe said, Aunt Mae. Rio knows better than to come back to Texas, much less this ranch, because if he does, he'll have Rafe after him, too. Not just Tate and that sheriff up in Colorado." She paused, searching for a way out of the uncomfortable discussion, and in the end fell back on humor. "And *you!* Sometimes I think Rio was more afraid of you than he was of anyone else."

Her great-aunt's dark eyes glimmered with satisfaction. "He had good reason," she said gruffly. "He still does."

JODIE KISSED her father good-night as they parted in the hallway. While preparing for bed she could barely keep her eyes open, but once she was stretched out between the sheets, sleep seemed a distant hope. Her thoughts continued to churn.

She'd been ''in love''—infatuation, attraction, flirting, having fun—a number of times over the years. Men liked her and she liked them. But only twice had she ever been in what she termed *love*—where her emotions had been deeply touched—and the first time didn't really count because she'd been so young. The second had counted, though. She'd truly believed herself ready to spend her life with a man—Rio Walsh.

The youngest of the cowboys living on the ranch, at twenty-two he'd been wild, reckless and bad-boy good-looking, with curly blond hair and light blue eyes. He'd first come to work for them the winter Jodie turned seventeen. Like many of his breed, he was as cocksure of his own attraction for women as he was of his skills working cattle. It didn't take long for the two of them to notice each other and start seeing each other. On the sly of course, because Mae had been adamantly opposed to any contact between them.

Jodie's feelings had gone deeper than rebellion, though. She'd truly believed she loved him. She'd dreamed of marrying him, of having his babies. They'd make a home together, a *real* home, somewhere faraway from her aunt's disapproval, where no one had ever heard the Parker name.

When it looked as if Mae would have her way— she'd wanted Rio dismissed and he finally was—Jodie had run off with him.

Only to be greatly disillusioned. His feelings didn't mirror hers at all. Her plans that they would marry were hers alone, and when confronted by the irate members of her family, he'd almost tripped in his haste to get away from her.

What followed was lost in a hazy cloud of humiliation and pain. Everyone had been kind to her, including Mae, but that did little to heal the hurt.

She knew she should hate Rio, but she didn't. Because all these years later she could look back and see what she couldn't see then: she'd been bored to tears on the ranch, as well as rebellious, and at seventeen, she'd been ripe for the kind of romantic adventure he could offer.

He was everything Mae and the others had warned her about: unprincipled, untrustworthy, a lothario who took advantage and moved on. But—and she was certain of this—he wasn't the sort of man to beat a woman. Particularly a woman carrying his child. There wasn't that kind of violence in him. He specialized in sweet talk to get what he wanted.

Seven years had passed since she'd seen him. He must still be working cattle, since the young woman Tate had told them about was the daughter of a rancher. Probably someone very much like she herself had been—young and vulnerable.

Tate could watch out for him all he wanted, but Rio would never show his face here.

Tate. The name caught hold of Jodie's thoughts. If she was just a little better at deceiving herself, she might have believed what Harriet had said earlier—that Tate was at last responding to her childhood crush. But what would make him suppose there was anything left for him to respond to?

Jodie rolled over and stared at the shadows on the wall, remembering the time she'd thought herself in *love* with him. When, with all the passion of her young and tender heart, she'd longed for a smile exactly like the one he'd given her earlier.

THE HOUSE where Tate grew up was a small two-bedroom structure that his father had built with his own hands in the months preceding his wedding, a gift for his new bride. It was simple of style and decoration, and not too long ago Tate had given all the woodwork a fresh coat of paint.

He parked the patrol car and walked up the stone pathway to the front door, where he tapped lightly and let himself inside. "It's me, Mom. And I'm starvin' as usual!"

His mother called from the kitchen, "Come on through. I was just waiting for you to get here to put your steak on."

Emma Connelly gave her son one of her lightning-quick looks. "Things go okay out at the Parkers?" she asked.

Tate lifted the lids curiously on a couple of bubbling pots. "Yeah. Probably wasn't necessary to tell 'em, though. Ol' Mae'll settle it herself with a shotgun if he shows up at the ranch again. She's still nursin' a grudge."

Everyone in the vicinity knew about Jodie's misadventure with the young cowboy. Most had felt sorry for Jodie. A righteous few thought she'd gotten exactly what she deserved.

"Can't say as I blame her," Emma said.

Tate leaned against the counter. "She sent a message for you," he said.

"Who did?"

"Mae Parker. Said to tell you she'll stop by to see you the next time she's in town."

"She will?" Emma said blankly.

Tate's smile was mischievous. "Yeah. She might even ask you out to the ranch for tea, too. How'd you like that?"

Emma quickly tumbled to the fact that her son was kidding her. "Actually," she said, "I might just like it. I'll put on my fancy duds and brush up on my manners."

Tate laughed. "It could happen."

"Not in my lifetime. We're town people, not ranch people. Not to mention being worlds apart when it comes to bank accounts."

Money had been tight after Tate's father died. Very little of the death benefits had been left once they'd paid off their debts. As a boy Tate had done numerous odd jobs for pocket money, then worked steadily in his off-hours throughout high school to help out. Jack Denton had done his best to help, as well, but Tate's mother was a proud woman, unwilling to take charity even from friends.

"Go wash up," Emma urged as she put the T-bone on the broiler. "This won't take long."

Tate did as he was bid and, on his way back from the bathroom, paused to examine the photographs arrayed on the piano. All were images from long ago, and all included his father. Some were of him with Emma, some were of him with Tate and some were of him alone.

Tate could see much of himself in his father's face. They shared the same cheekbones and brow, the same jaw and chin, but Dan Connelly's eyes were green. His expression was open and friendly. He'd been a good law-enforcement officer because he liked to help people. From grisly accident scenes on the highway to a family worried when a child was too long coming home from school—Dan Connelly had always been there to serve his community to the very best of his ability.

Emma had never remarried, not because she hadn't had the opportunity, but because she still loved Dan.

"If you don't get back quick, I'm gonna toss it out!" she threatened from the adjoining room.

"I'm coming!" Tate called.

His mother had to be careful with her meals, balancing her food with her insulin level and her amount of daily physical activity; as well, she tried to eat at approximately the same time each day. It was no surprise to Tate, then, that at this late hour she sat across from him and sipped a glass of iced tea, having already eaten.

"So," she said after a moment, "what does Jodie Parker have to say for herself? Does she seem any different?"

Tate's fork paused halfway to his mouth and he gave what he hoped was a casual shrug. "Seems pretty much the same to me."

"The whole town's curious. Everywhere I go some-one asks. You're the only one from here who's spoken to her, you know."

"She only just got back!"

"I know. A couple of their ranch hands came into town—J.J. and Cecil. They only saw her from a dis-tance, but they say her hair's black now."

"Not anymore."

Emma's eyebrows rose. "She took the color out so soon?"

"Mae didn't like it."

Emma shook her head. "It's a wonder the girl came back at all! She never did appreciate bein' told what to do."

Tate washed his bite of steak down with a long swal-low of chilled beer. "Hair looks better natural."

"So you noticed that, hmm?"

"Only in passing," Tate lied.

His mother sat forward, grinning mischievously. "You know, Tate, I've told you before I wouldn't ob-ject if you got busy and found me a daughter-in-law—only I never expected her to be a Parker!"

Tate knew his mother was teasing. Still, the subject was uncomfortable. "Me and Jodie Parker?" He laughed shortly, incredulously—as expected. "You don't have a thing to worry about there!"

His mother chuckled, then said, "Jack called. He said to tell you if you have time, he'd like you to stop by his place soon. He's got something he wants to talk over with you."

"Did he say what it was?"

"You know Jack. He always plays his cards close to his vest."

Tate nodded. Jack had been the sheriff in Briggs County for so long that being secretive with information was second nature to him. A gentleman rancher now that he'd retired, his time was at last his own. No more calls in the middle of the night, no more being dragged away from hot meals and interesting conversations. At first his old friend had seemed blissfully happy, assembling a small herd of cattle and fixing up his new place. It was only on Tate's last visit that he'd sensed a note of dissatisfaction.

Emma continued to talk, something about the fundraiser her women's club was planning, but Tate listened with only half an ear. He hadn't told anyone about the decision he was facing. Not even his mother—especially not his mother!—because she was one of his principal considerations. Maybe he could talk about it to Jack. Bring the subject up casually when he paid his visit. Then Jack could help him see his way through to the proper answer.

Again, another image pushed past the others. Jodie Parker, as he'd last seen her. Her delicate features set in spirited confrontation, her eyes gleaming like jewels from beneath the thick fringe of restored copper-colored hair.

All in defense of the cowboy she'd once loved.

A man whose behavior was totally reprehensible.

A man she hadn't seen in years.

Tate's slight smile quietly faded. Why had he felt that momentary burst of kinship with her, that flash of shared intimacy, as if he understood the forces at work behind her puzzling stance? Or could his response be explained by something much more elemental, a masculine reaction to a strikingly beautiful woman?

Up till now he'd never considered Jodie Parker in that light. To him she'd always been an irritatingly spoiled child. But she was no longer a child. She was a woman in every sense of the word—and undeniably beautiful.

His thoughts returned to his denial of any possible association between him and Jodie Parker. At this moment he wasn't so sure!

Emma Connelly continued to talk, outlining her part in the upcoming fund-raiser. She never seemed to notice that her son sat across from her in stunned silence.

THE PARKERS were united in their disapproval of Jodie's support for Rio. They didn't understand how she could overlook what he'd done to her and come to his defense.

First, Rafe: "You remember why I threw him off the ranch, don't you?" he demanded. "He was supposed to be your boyfriend, but not being satisfied with that, he tried to force himself on Shannon!"

"I'm not making excuses for him," Jodie said evenly. "I know what he did."

Then from Shannon: "Jodie, you don't still love him, do you?"

"No!"

Next, Harriet: "I thought you were more intelligent than that, Jodie!"

Mae: "Missy, I *despair!* That's the only word I can think of to describe how I feel. It's a good thing Rio was run out of Texas all those years ago! Otherwise you'd have taken up with him again. All he'd had to do was crook his little finger! Where's your pride, girl?''

Jodie had no answer, but neither did she back down. Not from any of them as one by one they stated their views.

By Friday night the worst of the storm had passed. Everyone knew where everyone else stood. But since the matter was moot—Rio Walsh was a memory and not an actual presence—ill feelings were put aside so that they could entertain their neighbors at the barbecue.

Once again Jodie found herself going through the events of her trip, this time answering more detailed questions from those who were either planning trips of their own or who'd already been to the same places she had but had missed something she'd seen or done.

Much to Jodie's teenage embarrassment, the Parkers had always actively worked their ranch, which meant they rarely left it. In contrast, most of their neighbors hired overseers.

The Clearys were a good example. Jim Cleary and his daughter, Jennifer, had lived in Dallas and come to West Texas mostly on holidays and for long weeks in the summer in their own private plane, treating their ranch more like a vacation spot than a home. To them, cattle were an afterthought.

It had been some years since Jodie had seen Jennifer Cleary. Once they'd been good friends, but the friendship had become strained after Jennifer divulged Jodie and Rio's secret destination when they'd run off; the friendship had cooled even more when Jennifer enrolled at a university in New England and Jodie chose Rice University in Houston.

Jim Cleary was the last guest to arrive at the barbecue. He was a large barrel-chested man in his mid-sixties, with a booming voice and bright blue eyes. He headed directly for Jodie the minute he saw her. "Jodie, girl! Look at you! You're all grown-up now, just like my Jenny." His eyes twinkled. "Must be something in the water out here that makes all the young ladies so pretty!"

"Mr. Cleary!" she returned warmly. "How are you?"

It had been several years since Jodie had seen him, too, and the lights strung across the center courtyard revealed that his only noticeable change was some additional weight.

"I'm retired now," Jim Cleary said. "Moved to the ranch for good—got fed up with all those trips back and forth. Now the only time I get in the plane is to go see Jennifer and Alan. They've set up house on the outskirts of Boston not far from the school where he teaches. They're expecting a baby this November—did you know?"

"No, I didn't."

"Been married for almost two years now," Jim Cleary said proudly. "Married right after she got her degree. She works at one of those public-broadcasting stations—as a production assistant, I believe it's called."

Jodie's smile stayed in place. She wasn't envious of the life Jennifer was building for herself, but it made her uncomfortable when she compared it to her own. Jennifer had moved to another level of maturity, while she was still floundering. "I'll have to get her telephone number so I can call her sometime."

"That'd be wonderful," Jim Cleary beamed. "She'd like that. And if you want to ride along next time I fly East, just let me know."

The Cleary plane. The last time Jodie had flown in it was when Rafe, her father and Shannon had reclaimed her from Rio in New Mexico. Jodie shook her head. "No, I think I'd better stay put awhile. Aunt Mae wouldn't like it if I left again so soon."

"Mostly I just visit for a few days. Think about it. I'm sure Jennifer would love to see you."

Jodie nodded and continued to smile, but was greatly relieved when Rafe and Morgan came to talk with Jim and she could slip away.

The barbecue dragged on. Everyone talked and ate and talked some more. Homemade ice cream was served for dessert along with Axel's special peach cobbler. After that pallets were spread on the grass for the younger children, most of whom, worn-out, fell asleep instantly.

Finally, nearing midnight, the last guest departed. But before the family members went to their respective homes, they helped clear the tables and chairs, making quick work of what would have taken Marie and Axel hours the next morning. Sleepy little heads bobbed as the children were then carried home.

Gib walked with Jodie to their house, his arm resting comfortably across her shoulders.

Jodie, enjoying the moment, said the first thing that

came to mind. "Jennifer Cleary's going to have a baby, Dad."

"I know. I heard."

"We're the same age."

"I know that, too."

She stopped on their front porch. From the soft glow of the lights that were still on in the courtyard—Axel was waiting for everyone to get home before he switched them off—she studied her father's face. She'd never thought of him as being a particularly handsome man. Over the years his classic Parker features had settled into a kind of blandness. But if you looked closely you could see he'd once been very attractive. Attractive enough to capture her mother's heart?

Jodie couldn't help but wonder about them. All she knew was that they'd met in an El Paso bar and married almost immediately, without Mae's knowledge. Had that been his idea or hers? Had the passion between them been so strong that Gib was willing to face what he knew would be Mae's certain displeasure? Or had it been the way Mae had told Jodie the one time they'd talked about it—that her mother had found entry into the Parker prosperity, and when offered a goodly enough sum to get out, she'd left without so much as a backward glance at Gib or her baby daughter?

Jodie suddenly burned to question her father about it, to see what he would say—but couldn't make herself do it. Instead, she inquired about another subject she'd been curious about over the past couple of days. "Why haven't you told me I'm wrong about Rio, like everyone else? I'd've thought you of all people... You didn't like him, I know that."

"I didn't like the way he treated you, that's for sure."

She tilted her head. "Daddy? Do you think he could have beaten that girl?"

While her father pondered his answer, the lights went off. Only the bright moon was left to cast its shadows. "I don't know," Gib said at last. "Do you...for sure?"

A quick defense of Rio tumbled from her lips, but the simplicity of her father's question gave her pause.

They parted again in the hallway, sharing a brief kiss, and Jodie quickly got ready for bed. She wasn't sleepy, though. So instead of climbing straight into bed, she curled up by the window that looked out onto the backyard.

How many times over the years had she sat there watching and waiting—restlessly—for something to happen? Gazing at the pasture that the night had turned into a moonscape but for the barbed-wire fence?

She pulled the curtain aside to relive another memory, one that had to do with Rio and their secret meetings. Rio had carried an old silver Mexican coin as a good-luck piece. It was drilled through and set in a metal loop, which he then clipped to his key ring. When he wanted to see her—when he knew he could snatch some free time from his ranch duties—he'd hang the silver coin from a loosened nail on the exterior window frame. When Jodie saw it, she'd collect it and bring it to their meeting place.

She smiled. How utterly romantic she'd thought the whole process at seventeen. Then she looked for the loosened nail to see if it was still there.

And saw a silver coin dangling from a metal loop!

CHAPTER FIVE

JODIE'S BREATH whooshed from her lungs. A coin? A silver coin? Had she become so wrapped up in her teenage memories that she'd started to hallucinate?

She shut her eyes, hoping that when she opened them the coin wouldn't still be there. But it was.

Was it *Rio's* coin? But how?

Her fingers trembled as she pushed the window open wider and brought the coin inside. They trembled even more as she examined it, because there was no mistaking. It was his! She'd spent hours when she was seventeen memorizing its every line.

Her first reaction was to fling it away.

The coin bounced and skidded across the hardwood floor before coming to rest on her bedside rug.

How dare he! How dare— She might defend him to the others, but not to herself. What on earth would make him think that she—*she!*—would be willing to meet with him?

Jodie shook her head. She didn't believe it. She *couldn't* believe it. He'd never come here! But if he did, if he had, wouldn't it mean he was desperate?

Her mind whirled. What should she do? Call Tate? Tell Rafe? If Rio had done what he was suspected of doing, he didn't deserve...

She crawled over to the rug, reclaimed the coin and sat with it, her back against the side of the bed. She'd defended him before her family, protested for his innocence. At the first provocation was she going to jettison everything she'd instinctually felt and said? Or was she going to give him a chance—one chance—to tell the truth?

She waited a half hour to make sure everyone was asleep, then, dressed in jeans and a light jacket, she slipped outside, across the gravel drive, through the courtyard and onto the path that led to the business heart of the ranch. The ranch office, the bunkhouse, the workshops and a large tack room all faced each other around a small clearing. Her goal was the storage room to the rear of the bunkhouse. It was there she and Rio used to meet.

Her heart beat rapidly as she paused outside the door. Not from any lingering attachment to Rio, but because she wasn't sure—if it *was* him—how deeply she wanted to get involved.

She rapped lightly on the wooden door. It jerked open and she was pulled inside. The windowless storage room, used mostly to secure the camp-cooking gear for the twice-yearly roundups, was in full darkness. Jodie couldn't see a thing, but she was highly aware that the grip on her wrist—hard and tight and urgent—belonged to a hunted man.

"Rio?" she asked, her voice low. "Is that—"

"Shh!" he hissed as the flint of a cigarette lighter scraped a low flame into life.

A moment passed before Jodie's eyes adjusted well enough to see in the flickering light. He hadn't changed that much. His face still had a boyish quality, even when sporting a mustache.

"Satisfied?" he grunted.

At her jerky nod the lighter flicked shut, plunging them back into darkness.

He reached past her for the door, peered out, then drew her after him as he crossed to the barn in a low crouch. Once inside, he pulled her over to the most distant stall.

When he seemed content to have their conversation in darkness, Jodie switched on the flashlight she'd brought with her. "Will this do?" she asked pointedly, placing it on its base on an upturned crate.

"I suppose," he returned.

His hair was longer than he used to wear it, falling in straggly blond curls almost to his shoulders. His eyes—older now with deep creases at the corners— kept darting toward the barn doors as if he was worried someone had followed them.

"You didn't tell anybody I was here, did you?" he demanded.

Jodie released an impatient breath. "I can't believe you had the nerve to do this! Are you crazy? The sheriff's looking for you!"

"Jodie, you can't tell a *soul!* 'Cause if you do—"

She cut him off. "I haven't made up my mind what I'm going to do yet. Anyway, why do you think you can come to me for favors? Do you remember what happened the last time we were together? When I thought you wanted to marry me and you—"

"I made a mistake!"

"—and you said all you'd wanted was to have a little *fun?*"

"I never said that!"

"You did."

He dragged a hand through his hair. "All that happened a long time ago. I was young, you were young—"

She crossed her arms. "And now you're in trouble again. I heard what happened, Rio. Tate Connelly— he's the sheriff here now—told us the other day. You've sweet-talked another rancher's daughter—only this one you got pregnant, then you beat her up!"

"I didn't!"

"I'm supposed to believe that? Me? When you told me one lie after another? You've come to the wrong person, Rio!"

"I never lied to you! Well, maybe once or twice, but never about anythin' important."

Jodie gave him a level look. "You lied about Shannon—about her wanting you to kiss her."

"I thought she did!"

"You're still lying. And you'd better start telling the truth!"

He shook his head and glanced toward the doors again. "You gotta help me, Jodie. You're the only person who can."

"You sure think a lot of yourself."

To her surprise he crumpled onto the straw, his shoulders hunched, his chin fallen. When he looked up, his expression was pleading. "I didn't do it and I can prove it! I was with some people when it happened!"

"Why didn't you tell that to the sheriff in Colorado?"

"'Cause he wouldn't believe me! 'Cause he and Crystal's daddy are some kind of special buddies."

"If it's the truth, he has to believe you."

Rio laughed hollowly. "That's not the way it works in the real world. Not for people like me. Lawmen act first, then check their facts—if they even bother to check. Sheriff Preston'd just hand me over to the Hammonds and let 'em take care of it."

"Who are the Hammonds?"

"Crystal's family. Real bad people to cross."

"So are the Parkers."

His eyes narrowed. "Not like this. These people will hurt you! Kill you even. Cripple you for sure. Make you wish they *had* killed you."

Jodie settled on the straw a short distance away. "Then why in the world would you get involved with...what was her name? Crystal?"

A muscle jerked along his jaw. "You won't believe me if I tell you."

"You love her," she mocked.

"I do! Not like...Not..." He shut up, obviously realizing that if he offended her, it would destroy any small hope he might have that she'd help him. When Jodie remained silent, he admitted, "Not like with all the others. Not like...with you. This time I really— I didn't see her until after I'd signed on at the Double Z, then I knew I was in trouble. She...she felt the same."

"So the baby was yours," Jodie said.

His head jerked up. *"Was?"*

She had never seen Rio so intent before. Never sensed in him this deep an emotion. When she realized he didn't know what had happened, she nodded slowly. "I'm sorry, yes. Crystal lost the baby."

He closed his eyes and began to rock back and forth, thumping the back of his head against the wooden stall separator.

Jodie didn't know what to say. She was under no obligation to feel compassion for him, but she would have had to be made of stone if she didn't feel something. She was quiet for a moment, then said, "Tell me what happened."

"I don't know! If I did I'd..." He stopped rocking. "The last time I saw Crystal she was fine. She'd told me about the baby the week before, and I was tryin' to find a way to work everythin' out. I saw her before I went into town for a ropin' contest. I went in early, the Friday evenin' before it started—last Friday, as a matter of fact, although it seems a lot longer." He shook his head and continued, "There were card games and such goin' on. This ropin' contest is a big draw. It has some nice prize money, and there's some big pots in the poker games. I thought I could win us some money to live on. Cowboys come from all over with their pockets full. One or two from Texas, even." He sat forward. "That's who knows I couldn't have done it! The fellas I was playin' cards with that night. All night! There's four of 'em. An' they'll remember me, 'cause I won! I took a bundle off 'em! Crystal was gonna be so happy—" His voice trailed off in misery and he began rocking once more, his head thumping against the separator.

"Why can't you tell that to the sheriff?" Jodie asked.

He looked at her. "'Cause I only know one of their names. This buddy of mine called Joe-Bob. The others—" he shrugged "—well, Joe-Bob knows 'em. They're his friends."

"Then all you have to do is produce this Joe-Bob."

Another hollow laugh. "I wish I could. Like I said, that contest pulled 'em in from far and wide. And by the time I found out Crystal was in a coma and that Sheriff Preston was lookin' for me, everybody'd scattered. Moved on back to the ranches they work on or to other places."

"And Joe-Bob?"

"He's one of the boys from Texas I told you about. He'd been workin' on a ranch up in Montana and was on his way back home. Said he'd made arrangements with a rancher in West Texas that was lookin' for extra hands. That's why I'm here—to find him."

"What's his last name?"

Rio gazed at her steadily. "All I know him by is Joe-Bob. Big ol' boy, about thirty. Could be part Mexican. Brown hair, dark eyes."

"If you show your face around here, you'll get picked up. Tate's telling everyone to watch out for you."

"That's why I need you. To help me find Joe-Bob. Please, Jodie! I know I don't deserve it, but you're the only person I can ask."

"Are you completely out of your mind?"

"I was afraid to turn myself in. Afraid what would happen. You don't know these Hammonds!"

Jodie could sense his fear. He might be lying about other things, but not that. "I don't know," she said slowly. "I have to think."

He grasped her by the shoulders. "Don't think too long, okay? I have to get this straightened out. When Crystal wakes up, she's gonna wonder what's happened to me. She'll think I ran out on her! I'm sure that's what her daddy and her stepbrothers are gonna tell her."

Only Rio Walsh would have the gall to ask an old girlfriend to help him retain the affections of a new one. Jodie gazed at him incredulously and wondered how in the world she'd ever been attracted to him. Even to the point of running off with him. Now she felt nothing but an odd kind of pity.

She wriggled against his hold. "Don't touch me!" she snapped.

He let go instantly.

They both got to their feet and looked at each other a little awkwardly. This wasn't the first time they'd had to brush the straw from themselves after being together in this stall. Only, years before, she'd been exhilarated after being with him.

"Where will you be?" she asked.

He shrugged. "Around."

She fished in her pocket for his silver coin. "Here," she said. "I'll make my decision tonight. When you're ready to meet again, put it out like you did before. *If* I agree to help, I'll be here within the hour." She cocked her head. "Did you do the same thing with Crystal? Leave the coin for her to find?"

When he didn't answer, she knew. He'd probably

used that signal many times before her and after. It wasn't anything special.

She started for the main doors of the barn.

"Jodie?" he said, still keeping his voice low. "You won't tell anybody until after you've let me know, will you? You'll at least give me a head start?"

She waited long seconds before replying. "You're just going to have to trust me about that, aren't you?"

Then she walked away.

SURPRISINGLY JODIE SLEPT soundly once she got into bed, and when she awoke the next morning, her mind was made up. She believed him. She would help. His feelings for the girl had rung true, and that was what had finally convinced her.

Of course they had to continue to keep his presence a secret. That he knew the ranch and the ranch hands' schedules like the back of his hand was an advantage. They would find some out-of-the-way place for him to stay while she… That was where her plans got a little sticky. While she what? How was she going to find this Joe-Bob? West Texas was huge. The ranch where this cowboy was employed could be nearer to El Paso than Del Norte. Or closer to New Mexico than the Big Bend area.

She checked for the coin after awaking, and checked again after she'd showered and dressed. It wasn't there. So it was with a mild start—part of her still wished his return had been a bad dream—that she saw it upon returning to her room after breakfast.

For years she'd felt somehow inadequate because Rio had rejected her. She knew it was silly—she had nothing to feel inadequate about!—yet still she had. Then last night, in that odd reality in which she'd seen him stripped bare of artifice, her lingering doubts about herself had disappeared.

She retrieved the coin, slipped it into her pocket, then started off for a seemingly casual stroll near the work area.

There was no need for stealth in the daylight. If anyone saw her, she'd stop and talk. Jodie, home from college and her year's vacation, exploring her old stomping grounds.

No one was about, not even Rafe in the office. From the sounds of activity in the corrals and pens beyond, some of the cowboys were there, but most were out tending cattle or seeing to the upkeep of the fence— both never ending activities. Still, she tapped lightly on the storage-room door, in case someone might hear.

Rio was waiting for her, looking more exhausted than he had the night before, as if he hadn't slept. He had a lot to think about, though he didn't know the worst. From what Tate had said, Crystal was in worse condition than Rio understood. Besides losing the baby, she was in a fight for her own survival, and Jodie wondered whether or not it would be kinder to tell him.

"First," she said, handing back the coin, "I've decided to help you." At his quick release of breath she cautioned, "Wait. You may not like what's coming. You know the old adobe schoolhouse? That's where I think you should hide. It's out of the way, yet close enough I can get to it on horseback in under an hour. It's—"

"It's rubble!" he burst out.

"It's a place where no one would think to look. That's what you want, isn't it? Until you can turn yourself in when you prove your alibi?"

"It doesn't have a roof! And the walls—"

"Forget it, then! I'll call Tate and he—"

"No, no. The schoolhouse'll be fine."

"Next," she continued, "you have to wait for me to contact you. No more of your coming here on your own. If you keep it up, someone's going to spot you."

"They haven't so far."

"Which could be pure luck." She frowned. "How did you get here, anyway? Did you hitch or drive or what?"

"I have a pickup truck."

"Where's it now?"

"Hidden away a mile or so from here. I borrowed from a friend up in Colorado. Brought my gear with me just in case. Sounds like it's gonna come in handy—sleepin' out and all."

"I'm sorry the accommodations aren't perfect," she murmured dryly. "How about supplies?"

"I have enough food to last a couple of days. After that…" He shrugged.

"I'll bring you more if this drags out." She hesitated. "There's something else. Last night when we talked about Crystal, I told you she'd lost the baby, but…her condition is more serious than you think."

"How bad is it?" he asked quickly.

"Tate said 'touch-and-go.'"

Rio groaned.

Jodie offered impetuously, "If you want, I'll go with you to see the sheriff up in Colorado. We'll make sure he listens. I can even get Rafe and Aunt Mae to—'' When she realized what she was saying, she stopped.

Rio laughed. "Yeah, right. Your cousin and aunt are gonna see to it that I get justice. Most likely they'll just find a nice strong limb and hang me themselves, save everyone else the trouble. The tree in front of the bunkhouse still looks pretty sturdy.''

They heard Axel whistling as he walked by on his way to the cookhouse, and they instantly lowered their voices. Jodie didn't want to be caught with Rio any more than he wanted to be caught himself. She could just imagine what the family would say if they knew. Especially Mae.

"What are you going to do?" she whispered, anxious to be back in her father's house. "Wait until night to make your way to the schoolhouse?"

"That's what I thought. I'll probably stay put here until then. Unless you think Axel'll come in. He hasn't started using this place for everyday storage, has he?"

Jodie shrugged. "I have no idea. I just got back myself. If you'd showed up last week, you'd've missed me. I was in New York."

"Ahh…so you finally got what you wanted. To escape from the Parker Ranch."

Somehow when Rio said it, the notion grated. She lifted her chin. "Actually I was away for a year."

"How'd you get Mae to let go for that long? Or did you just run off again?"

"Run off" was a little too close to the truth for Jodie's liking. She straightened to her full height, which was only an inch or so shorter than Rio's and chose not to respond. "One more thing," she said.

"Can you give me a little more information about this Joe-Bob? About the ranch he's working on? Are you sure it's in West Texas?"

"That's what he said. And that's all I know."

"His last name?" she tried again.

Rio shrugged. "Like I said, I don't know that."

Jodie grumbled, "What you're asking for is a miracle."

He smiled. Much like one of his old cocksure smiles. "If anyone can do it, you can, Jodie. You're a Parker. And that counts for somethin' out here."

Jodie frowned and shook her head, but she didn't try to convince him otherwise. The effort would have been futile. And maybe he needed that kind of faith in her to hold on to at present. The magic of the Parker name. Just ask and all doors open to you.

"I'll try to ride out in the next day or two to see how you're settling in," she promised.

He nodded and she turned away.

As she was about to let herself outside, he said quietly, "Hey Jodie…thanks."

And he sounded sincere.

CHAPTER SIX

TATE'S ORIGINAL PLAN to drop by Jack's place Saturday afternoon had to be postponed. Late in the morning, two teenagers, joyriding in a stolen car, had missed a turn and plowed straight into a parked eighteen-wheeler just outside the town limits. Both boys had been hurt, one seriously, and it had taken hours to get everything sorted out and the parents notified. Then a call came in from someone who thought he'd seen Rio Walsh a few days before. A deputy wasn't available, so Tate went to interview the man himself.

"Sure looked like him," Stan Dodson, a part-time gas jockey at one of the local service stations, said. "I'm pretty good at rememberin' faces. That and license-plate numbers. Not a lot else to do when I'm on duty. Didn't see him at the station, though. Wasn't actually in Del Norte, either. Off in Fort Stockton. I had to go up there to pick up a special order. And while I was there, I stopped by to visit a cousin of mine who works at one of those chain grocery stores. That's where I saw him."

"And you're sure it was him?" Tate pressed.

"Fairly sure. He has a mustache now, otherwise he's pretty much the same. He used to come in here to gas up that old pickup truck of his. The one with the cow horns for a hood ornament. When I heard you was on the lookout for him, I thought I better give ya a call."

Tate smiled. "You've been a big help, Stan. You, ah, didn't happen to see which way he headed when he left, did you?"

Stan admitted sheepishly, "My girlfriend says I'm too curious sometimes for my own good, but I stepped out to watch him leave. He took off this direction down the highway."

Tate clapped the man on the shoulder, thanked him again for his help, then went back to the office.

Several administrative matters had to be attended to, but once he'd dealt with them, he put a call through to Bill Preston in Clayborne County.

"Can't say for sure," he told the other sheriff, "but I think we've had someone spot Rio Walsh. Not in this county, but coming this way. Person knew him from before and recognized him."

Tate could hear the squeak of the other sheriff's chair as he sat forward. "Best news I've had all day!"

"We'll step up our activity, see if we can catch him for you. From what I know of him, he's not the kind of person to keep to himself. He may lay low for a while, but he'll surface sooner or later."

"That's what I think, too. Man, Rufus Hammond is gonna be glad to hear this."

"Rufus Hammond?" Tate echoed.

"Crystal Hammond's daddy—the girl Rio Walsh beat up."

A whisper of unease moved along Tate's spine. "It might not be a good idea to say anything to him yet.

Not until we know for sure…have your man in custody and all.''

"Girl's not getting any better," Sheriff Preston said gruffly. "In fact, she's failing fast. Got all kinds of complications. Do Rufus good to hear some positive news for a change."

Tate offered no further advice. It wasn't up to him to tell another sheriff how to run his county.

After hanging up, Tate composed a bulletin to be passed along to his deputies and to the Del Norte police chief, alerting them to the sighting. He also sent a notice to the law-enforcement agencies in the surrounding counties. If Rio Walsh showed his face anywhere in the vicinity, he wanted him detained.

Tate's thoughts swung to the Parkers. Their ranch would be a high-priority destination for the cowboy. Tate was in accord with the sheriff in Colorado that Rio might think he had friends there, at least among the hired hands. But unlike the Colorado sheriff, Tate had drawn no conclusions about the man's guilt. The fact that he was fleeing, though, spoke volumes. Out of curiosity Tate had run a check on Rio Walsh's prior record and been surprised there wasn't more. A few traffic warrants, a drunk-and-disorderly, participation in a couple of bar fights—pretty clean for an itinerant cowboy. Still, there was that trouble with Jodie, which showed a history of involvement with susceptible young women.

Tate stood up, retrieved his hat from the antler prong, jammed it on his head and strode into the hall.

"Get this out right away," he said, stopping by the dispatch office. "Top priority. I'm off to the Parkers."

He weathered his mother's raised eyebrow. "Read that and you'll see why," he instructed brusquely before continuing to his patrol car.

JODIE SET THE STAGE for what would be for her, as an adult, a new endeavor. Shortly after lunch she announced to Mae that she planned to start riding again. Like every other Parker on the ranch, she'd learned to sit a horse almost before she learned to walk. Riding had been like breathing to her. Then her favorite horse had died at about the same time she'd begun to question her place in the world, and she'd stopped. If she were to saddle up now, without preparation, it would be sure to draw attention. Exactly what she didn't want.

As it was, Mae looked at her suspiciously. "Why?" she demanded.

Jodie answered with clear-eyed innocence. "I thought you'd be happy about it. Aren't you the one who's been going on at me about connecting with the land? I thought I'd try, but if—"

"Are you up to something?" Mae countered.

"No. I just I used to love to ride, remember?"

"I remember."

Jodie shrugged. "I won't do it if you don't want me to. It was only an idea."

Mae continued to look at her, a woman who until recently had always been a full two steps ahead of everyone else. Now she was only one step ahead, and the shortcoming obviously irritated her. She could see no reason for Jodie's determination other than the one she claimed, so at last she gave her approval. "No, you're right. It'll do you good to get out and about. Help you to think. Figure things out."

Jodie felt a small easing of pressure. It was her plan to ride every day so that everyone would get used to it, and when she needed to contact Rio, her motives wouldn't be suspect.

"Would you like to have company?" Mae asked. "I'm sure there'd be any number of volunteers. Shannon loves to ride now, too."

Jodie shook her head. "I'd rather be on my own, Aunt Mae."

Mae nodded, then sighed. "I wish I could do what you're doing. Getting out on the land isn't the same from a truck."

Mae had ridden well into her seventies, until an old leg injury and advancing age prevented her. When she wanted to visit sites on the ranch, Rafe or Morgan, sometimes both, would drive her.

"Be sure to take a rifle with you," Mae directed. "You never know what you might run into."

"I will," Jodie promised. Shooting accurately was something else Jodie had learned at a young age, but that, too, was another ranch activity she'd put aside as she'd grown older.

Word must have filtered out about her decision, because when she went to the corral later that afternoon to pick out a horse, one was already waiting.

Cecil, the shyest of the ranch cowboys, said quietly, "Rafe told me to pick a good 'un for ya. This here's Tony."

He blushed as he spoke and shrugged with a loose-limbed awkwardness that belied his thirty-some years.

Jodie complimented him on his choice of horse, her practiced gaze going over the animal.

"Would ya like me to saddle 'im?" Cecil asked.

Jodie saw the saddle straddling a nearby rail. "No, I can take it from here."

The cowboy bobbed his head and self-consciously added, "Me and the boys are glad to have you back from those foreign places, Miss Jodie. Texas is where you belong, not out there."

He blushed even more when she smiled at him, then had to hurry away to recover. Jodie wondered if that was the most Cecil had ever said to a woman.

She took time to make friends with the horse, feeding him the carrot she'd brought and running her hands over his strong neck and back. It had been so long. *Too* long! What had been her purpose in denying herself this delight?

She'd just finished saddling up and was leading Tony out of the corral when a familiar white police patrol cruiser, one with a bright blue stripe down its side and the Briggs County insignia on the front door, pulled into the parking area abutting the pens.

Jodie's whole body went on alert.

Her first thought was of Rio—or actually her second. Because when Tate stepped out of the car, it wasn't fear or worry that caused a fine tremor to attack her limbs. There was something about him that made her overreact—the way he looked, the way he moved. Then apprehension about Rio swamped everything else.

She made herself greet him warmly. "Tate! Hello!"

Was that a little too warmly? She'd never spoken to him so enthusiastically before.

He looked a bit taken back, but recovered quickly. "Jodie," he said, closing the distance between them. "I didn't expect to see you out here."

Jodie now had some insight into how Cecil probably felt all the time—total and complete insecurity about what to say and do next. Every part of her felt awkward. The way she stood, how she held her head. Her fingers tightened on the reins as the big horse stamped impatiently at her side. "I...I was just about to go for a ride. Do you ride?" she asked, then laughed uncomfortably. "I suppose that's a silly question after having known you for so many years, but I never thought to ask before. I—"

She might have gone on forever if he hadn't cut in. "I ride some," he said, "but not like you. I never had much access to a horse."

"You should come out when you have some free time. I'll—we'll—we can go for a ride."

Tate looked at her oddly again, as if puzzled by her uncharacteristic chirpiness. She cleared her throat and tried for normalcy. "Is it Rafe you want to see? He's around somewhere. Cecil talked to him just a little while ago. He probably knows where he is."

Tate glanced at the slim cowboy, who had bent to check the shoes on a horse. "I'll ask him in a minute. I wouldn't mind havin' a word with you, though, if you're not in too much of a hurry."

Her stomach tightened. "Is here all right?" she asked. "Or...or we could go over there." She motioned to an old wooden bench that some of the cowboys had long ago propped against the workshop wall. Wild grasses struggled for survival along its base, but they'd been beaten down so many times by booted feet that they'd just about given up.

"Over there's fine," Tate said, and after waiting for her to tie the reins to a post, fell into step behind her as she nervously led the way.

Did he know? Had he somehow found out that she was helping Rio?

Jodie perched uneasily on the rough bench. She wasn't surprised when Tate continued to stand. The better to interrogate her? He'd been a big-city policeman in Dallas. Was that the way they taught their officers to intimidate a suspect?

"I came to tell you Rio Walsh was spotted in Fort Stockton," he said. "And he's headed this way. In fact, he's probably somewhere around here right now." Tate paused. "You knew him pretty well." Quite an understatement, Jodie thought. "What do you think he'll do?"

He didn't know! He didn't know that she— "Ah..." She had to answer before too much time passed. "The Rio I knew would keep going. He'd cross the border at some point and hide out in Mexico. That is, if he actually did what you're accusing him of doing."

"I never said he did a thing. All he's wanted for is questioning."

"Someone obviously thinks he did it."

Tate had left his hat in the car. To signal he was on a friendly call? He sounded very official, though, when he replied, "No charges have been filed yet."

Since the moment had presented itself, Jodie decided

to make use of it. "You know I don't believe he hurt this girl. Who says he did, anyway? Her family? And who are they? What are they like?" She fired off the questions as nonchalantly as she could. One slip and Tate would pick up on it. But she had to be sure that at least some of the things Rio had told her were true. And Tate was the perfect person to ask. "I mean," she continued, "are they like us? Like the Parkers?"

He smiled slightly. "Would you be disappointed if they weren't?"

"Not in the least," she denied, her chin lifting.

"They're people of influence, I'd say," Tate answered seriously, frowning. "Sheriff up there seems pretty tight with 'em. I don't know much more than that."

"What about the girl? Is she…"

"It looks worse for her now than it did before."

There was a small silence as Jodie lowered her eyes. To her surprise she felt Tate reach out to lightly smooth the hair at the crown of her head. Her breath caught until his hand moved away.

"You don't have anything to feel badly about, Jodie," he said quietly. "You didn't know the kind of person he was. He fooled you, like he's probably fooled a lot of people over time."

Jodie was afraid to look up, afraid of what he might read in her eyes. "That's what you don't understand. I'm sorry for the girl, but I still don't think Rio hurt her."

"If she dies, he'll have to answer for it," Tate said firmly.

Jodie's head lifted. "What if he could prove he

didn't do it?'' The instant the words popped out she wished them back. She attempted a hasty repair. ''It's called an alibi, isn't it? Wouldn't it only stand to reason that he *might* have been somewhere else when the assault occurred? Just because he was seeing her doesn't mean—''

''He's not doing himself any favors by disappearing. If he has an alibi he should tell Sheriff Preston. Running away is the act of a guilty man.''

Jodie did all she could to keep her gaze steady. But as she continued to look at him, she became lost in the intricacies of the tiny flecks of amber scattered through the dark caramel of his eyes. And the way those eyes drew attention in an already handsome face. A face that reflected strength of character and strength of will. Firm jaw, straight nose, serious mouth. She wondered what it would take to tease that mouth out of its seriousness and into passionate life.

A horse whinnied, making her start. It was Tony, calling her to their ride. He'd grown impatient waiting.

She jumped up and in her haste collided with Tate. He reached out to steady her. His hands were on her arms, his chest against her chest, his thigh against her thigh.

Their closeness lasted only seconds, but Jodie's mind carried an imprint of everything about him. His compelling warmth, the hardness of his body—all coiled muscle and sturdy bone—the light fresh scent of his aftershave. Coming so soon after her earlier thoughts, she couldn't prevent glancing at his mouth. Or speculating that all she needed to do was rise up on tiptoe and...

He smiled—warm, yet controlled—and Jodie pushed away from him.

"I...I have to go," she managed inarticulately. "Tony..."

His smile disappeared. "Of course. I didn't mean to delay you. Tell Tony I was the one who made you late."

Tell Tony? Jodie looked at Tate in confusion, then realizing his mistake, motioned to the waiting gelding. "That's Tony," she said with quiet amusement.

Tate followed her gaze, stiffened slightly, then laughed. "Still, offer my apology," he said. And with a nod he went to check on Rafe's whereabouts with Cecil.

TATE'S HOUSE was only a few blocks from the station, making it easy to get back and forth. Convenience had been one of its selling points, but since becoming sheriff a year and a half ago, he might just as well have commandeered a cell in the new jail for his use. He seemed to spend more time at the station or out on calls than he ever spent at home. Something was always happening. Something always needed his personal attention.

He let himself into the small two-bedroom house. He hadn't changed the place much since moving in seven years ago. The same curtains that had come with the house still decorated the windows; he'd hung a few pictures, but had stopped with the intention of finding some he liked more. He'd added a comfortable chair, a TV, a kitchen table. One bedroom was properly furnished, the other set up as an informal office. Not exactly warm and welcoming, but familiar.

He left his hat and service belt on a table by the door and shucked everything else on his way to the shower. One of the joys of life, he now deemed these precious moments of solitude, when hot water and soap could wash away the frustrations of his office, the inconsistencies of man, and the sometimes downright meanness shown by one human to another. Keeping the peace was his life's work. But sometimes, for a few minutes, it was nice to get away from such weighty responsibility. No phones, no radio calls, only the hot soap-scented water.

He stood with his back to the shower head and let the stinging spray ease the tightness in his neck and shoulders, keeping his mind purposefully blank. Steam filled the room, and when after ten minutes he shut off the water, it was like waking up in a warm all-enveloping cloud.

Slowly the mist cleared and along with mental clarity came a symbol of his day-to-day life—a ringing telephone. It was the station. He was needed.

With methodical care Tate donned a fresh uniform. Had Jack found the routine as wearing as he did? On patrol in Dallas, then later as a deputy here, his free time had pretty much been his own to spend as he wanted. There were call-ins, but not every hour, every day, seven days a week. Jack seemed to have thrived under these conditions. For Tate it was beginning to chafe.

Because of the new position he'd been offered?

Because he was having a hard time reconciling himself to such a Spartan existence?

Jodie Parker had offhandedly invited him to go riding with her. Even if she'd been serious, would he ever have found the time to actually do it?

Jodie.

His hands paused while adjusting his dark brown tie. He remembered what it had been like, for a fleeting moment, to hold her close. She'd always seemed so exotically out of place in a harsh land like West Texas. With that abundant copper-red hair—even if it was now short—her pale skin and jewellike yellowish-green eyes.

He remembered her from the time she was eleven or twelve and rode the school bus he drove the semester before he enrolled in college. A gangly little kid with major attitude.

In his arms that afternoon, she'd been all soft and warm and, though still delicately made, rounded enough to interfere with a man's thought processes. Which she very well knew. Which she'd very well known since adolescence!

Only, she'd never tried it with him before. Not that she had today, either, he corrected himself. Today she'd been...what? Her reactions could be described as a bit on the questionable side, if he had a mind to be suspicious.

The problem was, he couldn't read her the way he could other people. Was it because he had to fight through his own emotions before he could even begin to touch on hers?

He laughed again as he thought of Tony. The horse!

But what wasn't funny was the flash of jealousy he'd experienced when he thought Tony was a man.

Why would he be jealous? He had no claim on Jodie and no reason even to press for one.

As his mother had said, they were town and the Parkers were ranch. The Parkers had a history in the area longer than almost everyone else who lived here. They *were* West Texas!

Still he'd felt it, which was something he was going to have to examine more closely in the none-too-distant future.

He pinned his badge just above the left pocket flap of his shirt. An old-fashioned five-pointed Texas star that Jack hadn't been able to bring himself to replace. Tradition still had merit, Jack had said, even in a modern world with modern uniforms.

After collecting the rest of his gear Tate strode out to his patrol car and drove to the jail, where trouble brewed once again.

JUST A FEW SHORT DAYS ago, Jodie reflected as she rode slowly back to ranch headquarters, she'd had two principal worries: dealing with Mae and resolving her own lack of direction in life. Now, two unexpected new difficulties had been added to the mix: she was undeniably attracted to the local sheriff, *and* she was harboring someone he and others might soon label a murderer.

If she dies, he'll have to answer for it. Tate's words rang in Jodie's ears.

What would Mae and the other members of her family say if they knew what she was doing? Probably swear that she was beyond all hope. But now that she was committed, wasn't it important to see it through? Mae had urged her to turn her back on her irresponsible ways, to have the backbone to pick something and stick to it. Well, this wasn't something she would have picked voluntarily, but did that make it any less profound? An old friend needed her help. An old...friend.

To that end she needed a plan, and while riding she'd come up with a scheme she hoped would work. It all hinged on her ability to retrieve a listing of the ranches in the West Texas Regional Ranching Association from either Mae's office or the ranch's business office. She couldn't go in and just ask for it. She'd have to "borrow" a copy.

Tomorrow. Early.

Slip in, slip out.

And pray she went unnoticed.

DUSK HAD FALLEN by the time Jodie reined Tony in at the corral. The cowboys who'd been out all day were coming in, as well, hungry as bears for the dinner Axel had prepared for them. Plenty of meat and beans, fried potatoes and chili peppers, topped off with corn bread or sourdough biscuits, and a dessert of cake or cobbler.

The cookhouse had a long trestle table that the four cowboys who called ranch headquarters home clustered around to eat. Sometimes Rafe and Morgan joined them, sometimes not. This evening Jodie saw neither.

Was it because of what Tate had told them about Rio?

After replacing the saddle on the rail, Jodie glanced toward the bench where, earlier, she'd talked with Tate.

And she relived again those moments of closeness, when she'd gazed into his eyes and wondered what it would be like to kiss him.

Her hands paused in their rubdown of the horse. Taking advantage of her distraction, the big gelding shook his great head, gave a spirited snort and trotted off to join the other horses at the far end of the corral.

Jodie glanced from him back to the bench.

She still wondered what it would be like to kiss Tate.

CHAPTER SEVEN

JODIE DECIDED to search the ranch office before taking on the more difficult and dangerous job of entering Mae's private lair. She'd stand a far better chance of talking her way out of discovery by Rafe than by her great-aunt. And if she played her cards correctly, she wouldn't get caught at all.

That this was a Sunday was of monumental help. Ranch activity knew few days off, but Sunday mornings were typically slow to begin. Particularly since Rafe and Morgan had started families.

She slipped through the unlocked door and into a room that was surprisingly spare for such a large and successful ranch operation. A worn desk, a well-used chair, a four-drawer metal file cabinet. On the wall behind the desk was a calendar and a painting of a prize red-and-white Hereford bull that had hung there since the thirties.

For the first time Jodie felt the chill of a true outsider. She was in a place she'd known all her life, but as an intruder, not part of the unit. In the past she'd always seen herself as different from the others, but she'd always had the safety net of knowing she did belong. Now, by entering this office so furtively, was she symbolically cutting herself off from the rest? And if that was so, was it what she really wanted?

She shook herself free of the disturbing thoughts. All she was here for was the ranch listing. A simple thing. In another day and time she would be teased for wanting something so dry and innocuous.

The top drawer of Rafe's desk was locked, so her search moved to those remaining. Phone books and folders were scattered among blank notepads and cattlemen's magazines. One drawer was filled with supplies. She was just about to give up and move to the file cabinet when, among a stack of brochures in a bottom drawer, she found what she wanted. Her satisfied smile increased when she thumbed through the narrow booklet and saw the array of telephone numbers.

Easy as pie, she thought as she tucked the booklet safely into her back jeans pocket. Then, after insuring that everything was exactly as she'd found it, she slipped outside and started toward the path to the compound.

Only, Rafe was standing in the doorway of the tack room, his gaze steadily on her, even as he talked with one of the ranch hands. How long had he been there? she thought in near panic.

Jodie proffered an offhand wave and decided the best thing she could do was go talk to him. If she didn't, he would really start to wonder.

"Morning," she said, forcing a smile. "I was just looking for you. You weren't in the office, so I thought, well, he's got to be around somewhere!" She was very careful to face him, so he wouldn't see the booklet protruding from her back pocket.

"What do you need?" he asked. "Mighty early in the mornin' for you, isn't it?" He squinted at the rosy light of the new day.

Jodie shrugged. "I'm still on London time. Hours ahead of everyone else. Night is day, day is night—it's a mess." She tried a laugh, but it sounded fake.

The cowboy Rafe was talking to was the man who'd years ago taken Rio's place. He was older, far less attractive and undoubtedly did the job just as well. Rafe nodded to him, ending their conversation, then stepped off the narrow porch to take Jodie's arm.

The golden-haired puppy scrambled out of the doorway and did his best to rollick at their feet as they walked. Rafe laughed at his antics. "It sure must be nice to have that kind of energy," he murmured.

"How long have you had him?" Jodie asked. She knew she was only prolonging the inevitable. Rafe was too much like Mae to let go of an unanswered question. He would return to it.

"About three months. Shannon gave him to me. She thought I was lonely for Shep."

"And were you?"

Rafe's dark eyes reflected lingering pain at the loss of his loyal companion. "Yes," he said simply. "I was."

"Are you going to use Shep, Jr., as a cowdog, too?"

The pain lessened as he watched the cavorting puppy. "Probably not. I can't get him away from the kids long enough to train him."

When they arrived at the gravel drive, Jodie glanced at the house she shared with her father and wished herself already there.

"Well...Daddy's probably holding breakfast for me," she murmured, easing away, yet still careful not to turn her back to him.

"You never told me what you wanted," Rafe said, stopping her.

Jodie had yet to come up with a good answer, so she grabbed the first thing that sprang to mind. "I was wondering if Tate told you about Rio being spotted."

Rafe frowned. "You're trying to find me this early in the morning to ask that?"

"I've been awake for *hours*," Jodie claimed. And this time she wasn't fibbing. She hadn't slept much at all last night. She'd been unsettled about everything—from Rio to Tate to her prospective clandestine visit to the business office.

Rafe's expression was doubtful. "Tate told me," he said.

Great. Make two strong-minded men suspicious of her motives. She shrugged. "I was just wondering what you thought, that's all."

"I think he's a fool if he comes back here," Rafe said tightly. "Better he keep going, cut across the border."

Jodie nodded. "That's what I think, too. That's what I'd do. Cross into Mexico and keep going until I hit the Pacific. Put as much distance between me and everyone here as possible."

Rafe's frown darkened. "You aren't plannin' another long trip anytime soon, are you?" he demanded.

"Good heavens, no!" she said forcefully. "I've traveled all I want for a long time. Like I said, I haven't even gotten over my jet lag yet.'' She tried another laugh. This time it was more successful.

His scowl lessened, but Rafe still watched her.

Jodie gave a parting wave and turned to go to her house. As she did, she slipped the booklet from her back pocket to the front. She didn't think Rafe noticed.

HALFWAY THROUGH the afternoon Jodie fell back against the rear cushion of the couch. She'd started with the nearest ranches, disguising her voice from those who might recognize her—from Jim Cleary in particular—then worked her way down the alphabetized list.

Not one claimed a ranch hand by the name of Joe-Bob. Not even when she hinted that the "cash prize" he'd been awarded and she was calling about was considerable.

Her head throbbed and her throat felt scratchy from talking. She had a few calls yet to make and a few recalls to those who hadn't answered previously, but so far no luck.

What if it continued? What should she do next? What *could* she do?

She had to talk to Rio. If he was afraid of the sheriff in Colorado, maybe he'd talk to Tate. Tate would have far more resources to find this Joe-Bob than she had. He'd have access to *all* the ranches in the area, big and small, whether or not they were members of the ranching association. Also, when questions were put by a sheriff, they held greater weight.

She made herself dial the next number, and as soon

as the ring was answered, she started again on her practiced spiel.

JACK DENTON was sitting in a rocker on his front porch when Tate pulled to a stop at the end of the driveway. At his approach Jack slowly unfolded his bulk. He'd always been a substantial man, impressive both in character and in size. A good six feet, he tipped the scale at over two hundred pounds. Pounds that had been solid muscle in his younger years, but at sixty-two had softened.

"Well, would ya look at what the cat just dragged in!" he exclaimed as Tate approached the porch.

"It hasn't been that long, Jack." Tate smiled ruefully as his old friend came to greet him.

"It has, but who's countin'?" Jack looked him up and down as he thumped him soundly on the shoulder. "They been runnin' you off your feet lately?"

"Same as always," Tate said. "You know how it is."

"Sure…yeah. Sit down…sit down. Would you like somethin' cold to drink?"

Tate took a slat-back chair. "Somethin' cold sounds real good."

Jack went to rummage around in his kitchen and came back with two bottles of diet soda. "Diet's all I got. I been tryin' to take a few pounds off lately, not that it's doin' much good." He handed a bottle to Tate before dropping back into the old rocker.

The two men sat in companionable silence, and as he took several long satisfying swallows Tate's gaze moved over his old friend's property. When Jack had first bought the place, it had needed a lot of work. Now the modest house was in tip-top shape, as were the outbuildings and the fences. In comparison to some of the neighboring ranches, the spread was quite small. But the thirty or so head of cattle that Jack ran on his hundred acres were just as important to him— possibly more so—than the bigger herds of the large ranchers.

Tate's gaze moved to the man himself. Besides having the reputation as one of the fairest, most ethical and toughest sheriffs the county had ever known, Jack was also one of the most reticent. As Tate's mother had said, Jack played his cards very close to his vest. He always had. It was hard to know whether it was because he was the county's first African-American sheriff and, as such, felt the need to be cautious, or because it was just his nature.

"Place is lookin' better every time I see it," Tate said to Jack finally. "You've just about got it the way you want it, haven't you?"

"Almost. Barn could use a little more work inside. Everything else..." He shrugged.

Tate's eyes narrowed. "What's the matter, Jack? Last time I was out here I thought somethin' was botherin' you. Do you need some help? You know all you have to do is say the word, and you'll have more volunteers than you can shake a stick at."

Jack shifted in his chair. "It's not that," he said.

Tate set his half-empty soda on the wooden floor planks. "Something's not gone haywire with your health, has it?"

Jack remained silent.

"Dammit, Jack!" Tate burst out. "If you can't talk

to me, who can you talk to? You've known me all my life. You've known my family. You and my daddy were best friends. You cradled him in your arms when he lay dyin' on the highway. You're the one who caught the two bastards who murdered him! You're the one who cried when you testified about him at their trial. You're the one who did the best you could to see my mom and me through the worst of everythin' afterward. So, Jack, what is it?''

Normally when Tate got exercised about something, Jack smiled in tolerant amusement. Today his gaze remained steady. ''I might say the same thing to you. Why didn't you tell me about that task force you've been asked to join? Why'd I have to hear about it from someone else?''

Tate's eyes widened. Jack had heard?

Jack set his soda on the floor next to Tate's, then leaned forward, gripping the rocker's armrests. ''How do you think it felt hearin' something like that from a stranger? I didn't believe it at first. No, I said, Tate woulda told me! I've known that boy since he wore diapers. Hell, I've *changed* his diapers! He'd *tell* me if he was thinkin' of leaving again!''

''I only got asked a week or so ago,'' Tate defended. ''Anyway, I thought it was supposed to be a secret until everything was settled.''

''Some people don't believe in secrets,'' Jack said.

''Some people?'' Tate shot back. ''That sure doesn't include you, then, does it? A possum has less secrets than you!''

Jack leaned even further forward. ''Are you callin' me a possum?''

The two men glared at each other, then slowly the sparks in their eyes changed to amusement, and both started to laugh. Tate, young and strong. Jack, old and wise.

Jack continued to chuckle as he settled back in his seat. "A possum!" he repeated.

Tate grinned. "It was the only thing I could think of. I knew you'd take exception if I compared you to a polecat."

"Good thing for you that you didn't!"

Tate moved restlessly to the edge of the porch. "Actually that's one of the reasons I stopped by," he admitted. "Hell, Jack, I don't know what to do! Drew Winslow's gonna call back for an answer soon, and I'm just as far away from making a decision as I was when he first talked to me. You remember me tellin' you about Drew Winslow, don't you? My old supervisor in Dallas?"

"Actually he was the one who called me," Jack said. "He wanted me to persuade you to accept. When I got over my surprise, I told him it was your decision and yours alone. That I wasn't about to influence you either way."

"What'd he say to that?"

"Said you were gonna miss a great opportunity if you turned him down. And that state law enforcement was gonna miss a great cop." Jack was silent a moment before asking quietly, "What do *you* want to do, son?"

Tate shook his head. "I don't know. Part of me wants to go, the other part thinks I should stay."

"Because of your mother?"

"That and other things." Tate was sure Jack knew

he meant the sheriff's job, but neither man said the actual words. "What do you think my dad would say, Jack?" he asked. "What do you think he'd tell me?"

"Your daddy was one of the finest men I ever met, Tate, and I'm not exaggerating. It broke my heart when I couldn't do anything to help him that day. It was the worst time of my life, up to that point."

Tate's gaze dropped. He knew Jack was thinking of his wife, Maureen, who'd died a few short years ago. She'd always dreamed of owning a ranch, but she hadn't lived long enough to realize it.

Jack cleared his throat. "I promised your daddy somethin' that day. I'm not sure if he heard me or not, but I said it. And I stuck by it. I swore to him that I'd watch out for you and your mother for as long as it took. I never told you that, because I've always believed actions speak louder than words." He released a breath. "Now I'll tell you this, too, because it's somethin' I think he'd say. First and foremost you have to be true to yourself. You may have to dig deep to figure out just what it is, get down to the bare essentials, but you'll know it when you see it."

Jack had given him numerous bits of advice over the years, probably more than Tate had been aware of, but nothing quite as frustrating as what he'd just said. Tate had already tried digging deep down inside himself and he'd gotten exactly nowhere.

Truth be told, he wanted Jack to give him more than simple direction. He wanted him to point to the answer and give him a hard push. But it wasn't going to be that easy. Jack was refusing to either point or push.

Tate squared his shoulders and straightened his

spine. He'd come to Jack like a hopeful boy. Jack was sending him away a man, with the message that only he could make such an important choice.

"Guess I'd better get goin'," Tate said easily, then added with genuine feeling, "Thanks for your wisdom, Jack. I'll let you know as soon as I decide."

Jack got to his feet. "How're those two boys that hit that truck yesterday? I heard one was hurt pretty bad."

"His chest was crushed, but the docs were able to fix him up. Gonna be in the hospital awhile, though. The other one ended up with some nasty bumps and bruises and the holy hell scared out of him. Hopefully they both learned a lesson and won't steal any more cars."

Jack nodded. "I also heard somethin' else..."

"Your antenna's certainly plugged in," Tate teased.

"I like to keep up," Jack said. "I heard," he began again pointedly, "that Jodie Parker is back at the ranch and that you've been out to see her several times."

A flash of memory burned through Tate—the warmth of her breasts pressed against his chest, the feel of her hips and thigh against his, her waiflike beauty. He clamped down on his body's immediate response and answered, "I saw her because she was there. Nothing else. You know, Jack, one of the first signs of gettin' old is lettin' your imagination run away with you."

"Well, she always was a pretty thing. And I had the idea you'd noticed even though you wouldn't admit it. Red hair, yellow-green eyes..." Jack paused, then, "You gonna ask her out?"

"No!"

"Why not?"

Tate moved uneasily. "Because... Since when would I have time?" he demanded.

"I always found time for Maureen," Jack said.

"You two'd been married for ten years before you got to be sheriff. And she was always shooin' you out the door because you kept trying to tell her how to do things, remember? It's not the same thing as—" He stopped himself.

"Courtin'?" Jack supplied with a twinkle. "Seems like you been givin' this a lot of thought."

Tate shook his head in exasperation. "I haven't! I—"

Jack laughed. "I always did like that word. Courtin'. It sounds so much nicer than what kids call it today."

"Kids today sure don't court," Tate said wryly.

"How about grown men like you?" Jack persisted.

Tate stomped off the porch to the patrol car. "I'd've never guessed you were a secret romantic, Jack. But then, I suppose that's what possums have those pouches for—not just to carry around their little ones, but to keep their secrets in!"

"You're gettin' dangerously close to that polecat territory again," Jack warned with a widening grin.

"You take care, Jack," Tate urged fondly, before settling in behind the wheel of the patrol car.

As luck would have it, the instant he started the engine a call came over the radio. A call that caused him to give a quick wave to his old friend before he started off down the hard-packed dirt road, careful not to raise too much dust until he was a distance from the house.

Then he floored the gas pedal, unmindful of the billowing cloud that trailed behind him.

TATE WENT STRAIGHT to his office and sat at his desk, not taking time even to hang up his hat. It sat on his blotter, a sign of his irritation, as he reached for the telephone and dialed the now familiar number in Colorado.

When Sheriff Preston answered, Tate demanded, "What's this message you left me about Rufus Hammond and his two sons bein' on their way to my county? Why would they want to do somethin' like that?"

"'Cause Rio Walsh was spotted there. I told you I was plannin' to tell 'em."

"Why didn't you stop 'em, then? The last thing I need around here is a bunch of angry men goin' off half-cocked, lookin' for someone who might or might not be in the vicinity. That's why I didn't want you to pass the word on until we knew for sure and had brought him in."

"I *had* to pass the word on!" There was a small pause. "Crystal Hammond died this morning…just before dawn."

"This morning?" Tate glanced at his watch. It was a few minutes after four in the afternoon. "Why are you so long tellin' me this?"

"'Cause I had my hands full up here, that's why. All hell broke loose after the girl died. Crystal was my goddaughter, and my wife's niece. And she didn't take it very well. Then Rufus went berserk. I did everything I could to calm him down, but he wouldn't listen. Neither would those two boys of his. They all jumped into their truck and took off. And I know for a fact they have a huntin' rifle with 'em.''

Tate bit out angrily, "Dammit, I won't stand for any vigilante action in my county!"

"They've got good reason, for God's sake! He's killed one of the sweetest little girls I ever laid eyes on. Just beat her to a pulp. Kicked her in the stomach repeatedly. It was sick!"

It *was* sick, Tate thought. Still, he said sternly, "I'm the law in my county. I don't care what the provocation. If a warrant's been issued for Rio Walsh's arrest, I or one of my deputies will take care of it. And if any of your relatives misbehave, they'll find themselves takin' up jail space right alongside him!"

"Bastard deserves to die!" the Colorado sheriff growled.

Tate strove to overlook the other man's emotionalism—the girl had been a part of his family, after all. But it didn't change the law. "In my book a man's still considered innocent until he's proved guilty in court, Sheriff," Tate said tightly. "My job isn't to pass judgment and neither is yours. We'll find Rio Walsh if he's here and we'll bring him in. Then the justice system can take over."

The other sheriff swore mightily, and Tate remembered his previous whisper of unease when dealing with Preston—the man's quick assumption of undeniable guilt. As Jodie had questioned, what tied Rio Walsh to the crime other than the fact that he was the girl's lover? How much investigation had been carried out?

"What kind of proof have you got on him?" Tate asked curtly.

"Enough," the other sheriff snarled. "Are you questionin' my methods? 'Cause if you are..."

"It was a simple request."

"Well, just believe me when I say I got all I need."

The phone was slammed down. Tate hung up, as well, but his reaction was much more measured, and the frown on his brow deepened.

JODIE WAS TOO disheartened even to sit back. She'd actually found a couple of Joe-Bobs toward the end of the list, but neither matched the description Rio had given her. One was too old, the other a carrot-top with blue eyes.

She had one number left to call, not yet having gotten an answer. She planned to give it one more try before going to see Rio.

The phone rang, the jangle cutting straight into her nerves.

It rang twice before she reached for it.

"Hello?" she said cautiously.

"Jodie?" A man's voice. And not just any man—Tate!

"Tate?" she asked, even though she didn't need to.

"Where is everyone?" he demanded irritably. "I've tried the ranch office, I've tried Mae, even Rafe's house..."

"Rafe and Aunt Mae are out driving somewhere on the ranch. And the others went to spend the afternoon at Little Springs. I don't know where my dad is—probably off painting."

She heard his impatient release of breath. "When will Rafe be back?" he asked.

"I don't have any idea." She frowned. "Why? What is it?"

She could almost feel his reluctance to tell her. "That girl up in Colorado died this morning," Tate said. "A warrant's been issued for Rio Walsh's arrest."

"No," she breathed, her body tingling in alarm.

"'Fraid so. And to top it off, some of her family's on their way here to mete out a little justice of their own."

Jodie made no sound. She couldn't let herself. She had to pretend that Rio hadn't told her about the family's nasty disposition.

"If they can find him," Tate added. "And if they think they can get around me."

Jodie strained to make her voice natural. "Has anyone seen him again?" That would be a logical question, considering the previous sighting.

"No, but I doubt that'll stop the Hammonds from looking. Which means they'll head straight for the Parker Ranch. They know he worked there. They probably don't know about you and him yet, but it won't take 'em long to find out."

She gripped the receiver more tightly. "But—"

"Someone needs to get hold of Rafe. They left Colorado shortly after dawn, driving a pickup. It'll probably take 'em a good twelve hours to get here. And…they're armed."

"That won't worry Rafe."

"I'll try to head 'em off here in town, but they could

slip through,'' Tate said as if he was thinking out loud. "Good thing Morgan has law-enforcement experience. I'll call him, get him to come over and take care of things while Rafe's away. Or is he out with Rafe and Mae?''

Jodie shrugged. "I don't know." Her fear was starting to build.

Tate must have picked up on her unease because he said, "Whatever happens, this is gonna be contained, Jodie. *I'm* goin' to contain it. Rufus Hammond has lost his daughter in a particularly horrible way and he's not thinkin' straight. What we have to do is convince him it's in his best interests to let the law take care of things."

"How...how many of them are coming?" Jodie asked. She would have to tell Rio, and God only knew how he would react. Both to the news that Crystal had died and that some of her family members were coming to find him. He *had* to talk to Tate now, turn himself in.

"The father and two brothers," Tate replied.

Jodie swallowed tightly.

"You don't have anything to worry about, Jodie," he continued. "These people are after Rio, not you."

Jodie wanted to believe him, but how would the Hammonds react if they learned she was hiding Rio?

"No one will hurt you, Jodie," Tate promised. "I won't let them."

Her reaction to the intimacy of his tone temporarily overtook her worry.

"I..." She tried to speak, but couldn't.

He said nothing for a moment, as well, then rang off.

Worry returned with a vengeance after Jodie hung up. Her hands began to tremble, then the trembling spread with lightning speed through the rest of her body.

Rio was wanted for murder. *Murder!*

What had she gotten herself into?

CHAPTER EIGHT

THE OLD ADOBE SCHOOLHOUSE was little more than a weathered ruin, leaving no sign of the children of a bygone era who'd studied there. The roof had either fallen in or blown away years ago and the walls had started to crumble. One corner was missing entirely.

Jodie secured Tony to the lone scraggly tree growing in front and made her way to the open doorway. "Rio?" she called as she stepped inside. "It's me, Jodie. Where are you?"

A figure emerged from the shadows, causing her to start.

"You frightened me," she said.

"Who were you expectin'? Jack the Ripper?"

She dropped the saddlebag she carried in front of him. "I've brought you a few things—bread, cheese, some roast beef, water."

"I saw you comin'," he said. "I've seen a couple of other people, too—Gene and Cecil. It sure was hard not to call 'em over and say hello. It gets real lonely out here." He watched her intently. "Have you heard any word about Crystal, how she's doin'? I know it's not easy for you to find out, but—"

"Things have gotten a lot worse, Rio. That's why I'm here."

"A regular bluebird of happiness," he said under his breath.

"I can leave this second if you like," Jodie said stiffly.

"No, I'm sorry. I'm sorry. It's just…I'm used to bein' on my own, but I always have somethin' to *do!* Cows to look after, fences to mend. Not hidin' out like some mangy coyote—cringin' from my friends and jumpin' every time I hear a noise. My mind keeps turnin' and turnin'—thinkin' of Crystal, wonderin' how she is, wantin' to be with her—"

"Rio," Jodie interrupted him tightly.

He rushed on, "I don't want her to think I've deserted her! It bothers the hell out of me that she'll wake up and I won't be there! I'm tellin' you this, even though I know you won't believe me. But I've changed my ways, Jodie. I've—"

"*Rio!*" she repeated sharply.

Rio's mouth snapped shut and he glared at her. He wasn't accustomed to being spoken to like that by a woman. Then his glare dissolved as he read the terrible truth on her face.

"Crystal's dead, Rio," Jodie said quietly. "She died this morning."

For a long time all he could do was stare at her, as if he'd heard the words but was having trouble understanding their meaning. Then he turned away, his arms rigid, his hands curled into fists. A visible shudder passed over him, and when he turned back, a trail of tears ran from his tortured eyes into his beard stubble. "I want to find out who did this to her," he said slowly, unevenly. "And when I do—"

"There's even more to worry about," Jodie interrupted him again.

"Whaddaya mean?" He swiped at his cheeks.

"A warrant's been issued for your arrest. And Crystal's father and her two brothers are on their way here to find you."

"They're not her brothers," he corrected her flatly. "They're Rufus Hammond's boys. They don't share a drop of her blood. Crystal's shy and sweet, and they're—" His words stopped and he looked at Jodie with dawning horror. *"They're coming here?"*

"Tate called to tell us they're on their way from Colorado. He said they'd probably storm out to the ranch first thing."

Rio looked around, his body crouched, as if he imagined himself caught in the crosshairs of a rifle scope. "You didn't tell him about me, did you? You didn't tell him where I was?"

"No, I didn't tell him, but I think we should! He's the only person who can help you, Rio. I was going to come anyway and suggest that, then—" She stopped. She didn't want to mention Tate's call again. Once seemed more than enough to terrify Rio. "Tate's not like the sheriff in Colorado. He'll listen to you. He won't—"

"They're all alike! Each and every one. I *told* you how it is!"

"Not Tate!" she contradicted stubbornly. "Rio, I've talked to every ranch but one that I have a listing for. The Joe-Bob we're trying to find doesn't work at any of them. I don't know what else to do! If we tell Tate, he can contact each and every ranch in this section of the state. Even the ones not listed with the ranching association. And just in case someone I talked to brushed me off, he can make them tell the truth. Then you'll have Joe-Bob to back up your story.''

Rio shook his head, his long blond curls jerking. ''They'll kill me! They'll kill me before anyone here can draw two breaths!''

''Tate won't let them!''

His pale eyes pinned her. ''What is this?'' he demanded. ''Who is he to you? You seem to think he's some kind of—''

''I've known him for years. Longer than I've known you. I know what he's like, and he won't—''

''He's young and good lookin', ain't he?'' Rio challenged. ''Are you sleepin' with him?''

Even at such a tense moment Rio had picked up on something in her voice when she spoke of Tate. But this wasn't the time to be defensive. She had to get Rio to see reason. She issued her own challenge. ''Would it make a difference if I was? Don't you think, if it's true, it might go a long way to making everything better for you? If I tell him I believe you, it'll carry some weight!''

''Uh-uh. No way. Not this time. Not when it involves the Hammonds.''

''He's going to *stop* the Hammonds!''

''You don't know them,'' Rio muttered, and started to pace the dirt floor.

''Then what are you going to do?'' Jodie demanded.

He stopped to look at her. ''You say they're on their way. They're not here yet?''

"Not at ranch headquarters. At least, not when I left."

His lips thinned. "I still have time to get away."

"Where to? If you run now, you're going to be running for the rest of your life—from the law, from the Hammonds. Is that what you want? Do you want to go on like you have these past few days? You were complaining a few minutes ago because you couldn't talk to your friends."

"I'll make new friends."

"Where? Across the border? That might stop sheriffs like Tate, but it's not going to stop the Hammonds. If they're so terrible and so determined, don't you think they'll find you eventually? Then what will you do? You won't have anyone to help you."

His lips curved into a tight smile. "I didn't know you still cared."

Jodie ignored that. "If you've told the truth, you have nothing to worry about. We'll find this Joe-Bob."

"I thought you said—"

"Leave that to me."

"I can't stay here!" he asserted. "It's too close. Someone's liable to come up on me when I'm sleepin' or somethin'."

Jodie racked her brain. "I agree," she said. "You have to get farther away. What do you think—out in the rough country, in the foothills? I won't be able to contact you as easily, but that's not something we'll need to do again until everything's settled."

"I'm not waitin' around forever. Not even in the foothills. I'd rather take my chances in Mexico than have the Hammonds find me off in some lonely canyon.''

"Give me until sunset Wednesday. If I haven't contacted you by then, leave. I don't know exactly what I'll do yet, but I promise—I won't tell *anyone* where you are.''

He considered her proposal, obviously torn between the desire to run away and the desire to have his name cleared. For the old Rio there'd have been no question. He'd already have hopped on her horse and ridden away to the pickup truck he had stashed, then been off to Mexico, leaving her to find her way back to the compound as best she could. The new Rio, though, the one who claimed to be innocent of murder, the one who claimed to have truly loved the murdered girl, stayed firm.

"All right,'' he said. "Wednesday, sunset. You know the canyon with the old trapper's shack in Big Spur?''

Jodie nodded. She knew it vaguely. Big Spur was one of the outer ranch divisions, very remote, with only one cowboy living in a trailer assigned to tend stock. The trapper's shack, remote even within the remote division, had been used years ago by an employee of the federal government who trapped coyotes and bobcats.

"That's where I'll be, and I'll keep an eye out for you,'' Rio said.

Just then Tony let loose with a high piercing whinny, as if he'd seen another horse. Rio instantly ducked, hiding himself again in the shadows.

Jodie cautiously went to check if someone had come

upon them. In the distance she saw several horses, grazing wild and free on a hillside. She patted Tony. "You want to be with them, boy?" she murmured.

The horse made a soft sound that might have been agreement.

Jodie returned to the schoolhouse. "It wasn't anybody," she said. "Everything's clear."

"This time," Rio said ominously.

Jodie had nothing to offer in reply. She went back to the horse and remounted.

At first she'd thought she might have brought too many supplies. Now she was glad she had. As things turned out, Rio would at least have enough to eat and drink for the next three days.

She gave the schoolhouse one last look. All was quiet. No one would suspect that a wanted man was secreted inside, even if only for a short time longer.

WHEN JODIE RETURNED to the compound, it was to find Morgan Hughes camped out in a chair on Mae's front porch, the rifle he normally carried with him when he rode the range resting across his lap.

"Where've you been?" he asked. "Tate called, told me I should get myself over here PDQ, to protect you and the ranch, and then I find you gone."

Morgan had always been a favorite of Jodie's, almost like another cousin.

"I had to go out," she said.

"You know about these people who're coming?"

"Tate told me."

"Then you picked a pretty strange time to disappear."

That was the only trouble with Morgan. As Tate had said, he was a trained law-enforcement officer, a commissioned Texas Ranger, who'd once worked for a private state-wide organization of ranchers to combat cattle theft. He'd gone off active duty, though, since taking over the foreman's job for his father. Yet his instincts were just as keen. She had to tread carefully.

He got up to stand at the porch railing, the rifle hanging casually from one hand, the muzzle pointed at the floor. At least that was something she could feel good about, Jodie thought. If the Hammonds did show up right away and try to cause trouble, Morgan was perfectly capable of holding them off.

"I had an errand to run," she claimed. She knew a way to take his mind off where she'd been. "How's Christine?" she asked. "Almost another week down. Any signs of the baby coming?"

Morgan's chiseled features creased immediately into a smile. "She felt a little twinge this morning, but it turned out to be a false alarm. I don't know who was more disappointed—Erin or her."

Jodie tucked her fingers into the back pockets of her jeans and rocked on her boot heels. She smiled. "Or you, too, right?"

"I have to admit I'll be relieved when it's over. When little Elisabeth's with us all safe and sound and Christine's through the delivery."

"Are you going to be in the delivery room?" she asked.

"You bet. Wild horses couldn't keep me outta there."

A car engine caught their attention. Both looked toward the front of the compound to see who was turning into the long drive. It was Mae's big black Cadillac, old but in perfect running condition, LeRoy at the wheel. With him were most of his family and all of Rafe's.

LeRoy stopped to let everyone out before taking the car to the garage at the side of the barn. Harriet and Shannon were laughing as they supervised the younger children's exit. They'd just come from a pleasant afternoon of visiting, and neither seemed to have a care in the world.

Jodie glanced inquisitively at Morgan, who answered quietly, "I didn't want Christine to worry, so I just said I was needed over here, not why."

Shannon caught part of his explanation and looked from Jodie to him—and then down to Morgan's rifle. Her eyes widened. "What's up?" she asked.

Harriet, who'd just turned from waving her husband away, did a similar double take, her gray eyes on the rifle.

The children started to scamper off, but both women ordered them to stay put.

Morgan said easily, "We could have a little trouble come our direction in a bit. That girl Rio Walsh beat up in Colorado died this morning. And now Tate says her father and brothers are on their way here to find him. The Parker Ranch is where they're gonna want to start lookin'."

"We'd hand him over with bells on if we knew where he was," Harriet said.

"I know that, you know that, but they don't. It's somethin' we'll have to get across to them."

"Rafe will never let them have free run of the ranch," Shannon said.

Morgan patted the rifle. "That's what I'm gonna tell 'em. Unless Rafe gets here first. Then he can."

"She died!" Harriet exclaimed, shocked and looked at Jodie. It must have just hit solidly home with her that what had happened to the other young woman could just as easily have happened to Jodie.

Jodie tried to offer a reassuring smile, but her emotions were in such turmoil she failed. She was the only person who knew where to find Rio. She couldn't betray him. Then again, didn't she owe her family her first loyalty?

Rafe and Mae walked up the pathway from the work area, and when they spotted the group clustered by the front of Mae's house, their steps quickened. It took only a moment for them to receive an explanation.

"No-good cowboy's still causin' us trouble," Mae snapped fiercely. She looked tired, as if spending most of the day out on the ranch had been hard on her, even from the relative comfort of a pickup truck.

"Tate say what time they might turn up?" Rafe asked.

"Probably not before six," Morgan replied.

Everyone who had a watch checked it.

"It's six now," Rafe said.

Morgan merely nodded.

Rafe lifted his younger son, who'd been trying to gain his attention, into his arms. Little Nate gurgled with three-year-old pleasure. "Ice cream! Ice cream!" he demanded shrilly, which provoked the other children to join his chant.

Rafe turned the boy over to Shannon and rubbed the top of his older son's head as he hopped up and down at his elbow. "Why don't you and Harriet take 'em over to our place and give 'em what they want?" he said to his wife. "Jodie, you help Aunt Mae."

"Help me!" Mae exploded. "What's she gonna do? Sit me down in my rocking chair and cover me with a lace shawl?" She looked around. "Where are Wesley and Gwen?"

"They're staying the night at Little Springs," Harriet said.

"Good. Now you keep those babies inside. Don't let 'em out unless you come with 'em." She was more direct with her orders than Rafe had been. Her attention moved back to her great-nephew. "What do we know about these people?" she demanded.

While Rafe gave his limited response—he knew very little about them, unlike Jodie who had Rio's assessment—Jodie edged away from the group, then escaped to her house. She had a lot to think about. She had to find a way to warn her family about the Hammonds without them learning how she knew. Also, there was her continuing problem with the elusive Joe-Bob. She'd promised Rio they'd find him. Now it was even more important!

She peeked through the curtain, to where Mae, Morgan and Rafe still stood in a tight group in front of her great-aunt's house.

Her only consolation at that moment was that her family weren't good people to cross, either. They were Parkers, on Parker land. And the Hammonds would be wise to respect that.

THE PATROL CAR'S powerful engine ate up the miles of the narrow two-lane highway as Tate raced to what he hoped would be a quiet setting. He'd decided that his best bet to prevent mayhem was not to try to intercept the Hammonds in town, but to be present himself at the Parker Ranch. And the sooner he got there, the better.

He doubted that the Hammonds had already arrived. It was a long hard drive south from the Colorado border—a twelve- to fourteen-hour undertaking that the men were performing in a highly emotional state. There was no way to tell how many unbroken hours they'd been awake before the girl died—she'd been hovering near death for more than a week. No way to tell how much they'd eaten—or drunk. Their tempers would be raw, easy to provoke. They'd be like powder kegs, ready to explode in their quest for vengeance.

And at the Parker Ranch they'd hit resistance head-on. When they demanded to search every nook and cranny of the place, they'd be refused. Then...*KABOOM!*

Rafe Parker and Morgan Hughes were on Mae's front porch when Tate arrived, their rifles a hand's reach away. Within seconds Mae and Jodie had joined them.

Tate parked his patrol car front and center before Mae's house. He wanted it to be an emphatic statement to anyone who saw it that the law in Briggs County wasn't to be taken lightly.

"Rafe, Morgan," he said to the men, then turned to the women. "Hello, Mae...Jodie."

Rafe and Morgan stepped to the porch railing. They

didn't look especially glad to see him, but neither were they hostile. Both were imposing individuals. Strong of will, unified in their determination to protect what was theirs.

"You have any new word on the Hammonds?" Rafe asked.

Tate shook his head. He'd left his hat on, content for the moment to let their business remain official. "Not a thing."

"Then why are you here?"

He'd known it wasn't going to be easy. These big-time ranches were like feudal strongholds. They had their own rules and regulations, their own procedures, which usually boiled down to "Don't bother us and we won't bother you." For an outsider to come onto their property, even someone they'd known for years, and try to tell them what to do wasn't something they took to very well.

Tate kept his poker face. This was serious business. He was aware of Jodie on the fringe of the assemblage but couldn't let his gaze wander toward her. "I think you know why. My job is to prevent trouble. They're comin' lookin' for it, and you'll give it to 'em if they push you too hard, which they'll probably do."

"Damn straight," Morgan agreed softly.

"So I'm plannin' to be here to prevent it."

Rafe's dark eyes narrowed and his jaw tightened. "You don't think *we* can do that?"

Tate answered carefully. "I'm sure you'll want to, but they may not let you. From what Sheriff Preston tells me, they went berserk when the girl died. They're not goin' to want to listen to reason. Think how you'd feel if the same thing had happened to someone you love."

Jodie made a soft sound that Tate steeled himself not to respond to.

Rafe's jaw set even harder. "I'm still not giving 'em free run of the ranch."

"I don't expect you to. All I want is for you to let me hang around and help keep the lid on things when they get here."

Rafe's dark eyes bored into him. A prototypical Parker, the strength of his will was awesome. Through sheer nerve, hard work and fierce determination the Parkers had carved a place for themselves in this rugged and often hostile land the previous century. That same determination carried through to this day.

Tate returned Rafe's gaze unflinchingly.

"All right," Rafe said after another moment passed. "You can stay. We'd rather not have this meeting get out of hand, either. Like you say, these people are hurtin'."

"It's that danged Rio Walsh!" Mae spit. "I knew the first time I set eyes on him that he was gonna be trouble. I should've put my foot down right then."

Rafe relaxed a bit as a slow smile tilted his lips. "That must be the first time in history you ever kept your feelings to yourself."

Morgan smiled, too, but wisely didn't comment.

Mae sputtered even as Rafe continued, "Rio was a damn fine cowboy—that's why he got the job. If he'd stuck to that, he'd probably still be here."

"A skunk can't hide its true colors for long," Mae declared.

"Shouldn't that be 'smell'?" Rafe countered teasingly.

Mae lifted an eyebrow. "Hush up, boy. We have business to attend to." She turned to Tate. "You're welcome to stay as long as it takes, Tate. Now, first order—have you had anything to eat lately? Rafe and I haven't. I was goin' to get Marie to put some sandwiches together for us before all this came up. She can easily make more."

Tate couldn't remember the last time he'd eaten. "A sandwich sounds good, thanks."

"She'll make enough for everyone. Jodie, go tell her."

Jodie didn't move. She didn't seem to have heard. Suddenly she gave a start and apologized, "I'm sorry, I—"

"Go tell Marie to make some sandwiches," Mae repeated. "Enough for everyone. And maybe some of that potato salad we had yesterday. It could be a long evening."

A tinge of pink lent color to Jodie's cheeks. Her hair was beginning to grow out, soft curls starting to feather and fluff. She'd always had wonderful eye-catching hair, both the shade—flaming copper—and the sheer abundance. Tate wanted to touch her hair again now, only this time not lightly as he had yesterday. He wanted to thread his fingers into the soft silkiness, then pull them through and watch as the late-afternoon sun turned the strands into fiery rivulets of red and gold.

Their eyes met and for a second Tate lost the ability to breathe. The way she looked at him—did she know what he was thinking?

She turned away to do her aunt's bidding, and the world settled back into place, leaving, it seemed, only Tate shaken.

"Tate?" Mae said his name as if she was repeating it. He moved his gaze. "Are you plannin' on staying the night?" she asked. "Because if you are, you can have one of the guest rooms in my place. They both overlook the driveway."

"No, thank you, Miss Parker. I'll stay in the patrol car."

"I won't hear of it!" Mae exclaimed. "You couldn't be comfortable there!"

"I've done it before," Tate replied, smiling.

"Well, I wouldn't be able to sleep a wink thinkin' about you. At the very least let us set up a cot in the living room. You'll be just a few steps away from anything that happens. I won't accept less."

She'd said it and she meant it. As gracefully as he could, Tate accepted her autocratic hospitality. *If* he had a need for it. Personally he hoped the Hammonds would just show up and get the whole affair over with. He was planning to escort them into Del Norte and house them at the town's lone motel overnight. That is, if they behaved. If they didn't, the county would pick up the tab. They couldn't get up to much mischief from the inside of a jail cell. And tomorrow they could all start over.

JODIE SLIPPED into a downstairs bathroom after delivering Mae's message to Marie and ran a cool damp hand over the back of her neck. She had to stay focused. She'd already set her course of action—tell

Tate. And Tate was even here, removing her need to seek him out. All that remained was to get him off by himself and—

A quiver of emotion played along Jodie's spine, an excited little trill of anticipation. She'd caught the look he'd given her moments before and recognized it for what it was. That it had happened in the midst of all this turmoil surprised her. But very little had ever been as expected in her life.

—and tell him. About Rio, about Joe-Bob, and all she knew about the Hammonds! She—

She wanted to do more than talk to him. She wanted to look deeply into his eyes and watch as they ignited with desire. She wanted to feel his arms go around her and pull her close. She wanted to feel his lips press hungrily on hers.

—she had to beg for his help! Only, would he help when she refused to tell him where Rio was hiding?

She looked at herself in the mirror. At the short hair, pale face and serious expression. She was changing. Somehow, somewhere deep inside herself a shift was taking place. She could sense it even though she didn't understand it—or even begin to grasp the implications. Did it have something to do with Tate?

She forced the thought away. There simply wasn't time at present to search for an explanation. The Hammonds could be here any moment.

She took a bracing breath and stepped back into the hall. Mae would want to know that she'd accomplished her mission.

CHAPTER NINE

JODIE SAT ON PINS and needles all evening, desperate to talk privately with Tate, but the opportunity never presented itself. Finally, at midnight, the watch was called off until morning, and she had no other option but to go home with her father, who'd eventually joined the gathering.

"You coulda knocked me over with a feather when I found all of you at Mae's," Gib said with a chuckle as they walked down the long driveway to their house. "I thought I'd missed a command performance or somethin'. I thought, *Uh-oh, Mae's gonna have my hide!* Then it turns out to be more stuff about Rio." He gave Jodie a considering look. "You okay with that?"

Jodie shrugged. There wasn't much about any of this she was truly okay with. "I'm fine," she fibbed, then changed the subject, "Where were you earlier? Off painting?"

He opened the screen door to their house, switched on the overhead light and saw her inside. "Mmm. That and thinkin'. Here, I have somethin' to show you." He moved past her to retrieve an envelope from a side table.

"What is it?" Jodie asked.

"It came in yesterday's mail. Read it," he said.

Jodie did as he instructed, then looked up, smiling. For a moment she was able to slip free from the worry that had gripped her all evening. "They want you to show some of your work? At a cowboy-art exhibition? Dad, that's wonderful! You must be so excited."

He nodded diffidently.

"You're going to do it, right? I mean, you wouldn't refuse, would you?" From her father's body language she could see he was considering doing just that. "Oh, Dad, don't! You're good. Really good. People have nothing but praise for your work—when you let them see it. Didn't you have some paintings on display in San Antonio early this year? And weren't they a success? You wrote me about it, remember?"

"That was just a little gallery," he said uncomfortably. "Friend of a friend, that kinda thing."

"Daddy!"

He continued to look uncomfortable as he folded the letter back into the envelope and returned it to the table. "Well, that's what I was thinkin' about most of the day—whether to do it or not." He cocked his head. "You really think I should? It's a big show. Lots of big names. I'll probably get lost in it."

"Your work is good, Daddy. It'll stand on its own, proudly. I'm not just saying that, either. I'd tell you that even if you weren't my father."

"Wonder what Mae'll say if I do," he mused.

"For once, don't care," Jodie advised, seemingly flippant, yet actually serious.

Gib nodded, but Jodie knew he was only agreeing to consider what she'd said, not necessarily to act on it.

JODIE COULDN'T WAIT. She *had* to talk to Tate. If someone saw her sneaking back over to Mae's house, they'd just have to wonder at the cause. She doubted that either Rafe or Morgan, who was staying the night at Rafe's place, would get much sleep. They'd probably stay dressed and in chairs near the front door, their ears fixed for any unusual sounds. Now would be as good a time as any for her to seek out Tate.

Jodie slipped into her lightweight jacket and left the house, her stomach doing its usual flip-flops the closer she got to Mae's. What she was planning to do could get her into a *lot* of trouble, not to mention make everyone in her family angry if they found out.

She swallowed as she started up the porch steps, her gaze fastened on the front door. She doubted Mae had locked it—she seldom did. Jodie was just about to test it when a hand clamped down firmly on her shoulder.

"Jodie?"

Tate! He wasn't inside the house as she'd expected or as Mae had directed. Instead, he'd camped out on the front porch, evidenced by the light blanket thrown hastily across the arm of one of the high-backed chairs when he'd gotten up.

Tate was the person Jodie had come to see, yet she was hesitant to face him. Everything about him stirred her senses, even his voice. She'd met many handsome men over the years, had even dallied with a few. But not one had affected her this way. Made her feel instantly—

"Jodie?" he said again.

She quickly collected herself. "You startled me!" she exclaimed, taking care to keep her voice low.

"What are you doing here?" he demanded, his voice as hushed as hers. "Sleepwalking?"

Jodie decided not to prevaricate. "No. I...I need to talk with you."

"What about? It couldn't wait? Or you couldn't have said it earlier?"

She shook her head.

He glanced at the door, then at the chair next to his. "Where?" he asked. "Inside or out?"

Jodie thought of Mae. Better to keep this outside. She gestured at the chairs. "Over there."

They both sat, but he seemed determined not to relax with her or to put her at ease. "Okay, what's up?" he said.

Jodie had prepared what she was going to say and how she was going to say it. But now that the moment had arrived, it was far more difficult than she'd imagined. The words she'd rehearsed in her head evaporated, and she was left to pull the story together as best she could. "I...I think you all should be very careful with the Hammonds."

"And why do you say that?" His face didn't give anything away, but Jodie had the impression she'd surprised him.

"Because...I've heard they're bad people."

He moved slightly. "What do you mean by 'bad'?"

"They hurt people when they don't get their way."

"Where did you hear that?" he asked.

"Just...from someone."

"Someone who knows them? And who might that be? I didn't think anyone around here knew the Hammonds. If they do, why haven't they said something to me?''

The barrage of questions increased Jodie's nervousness. To combat it, she dug deep inside herself for a little of the Parker hauteur. ''Does it matter who told me?'' she snapped.

''It might,'' he shot back, and waited.

Jodie stood up. This wasn't going the way she'd wanted. They were already off on the wrong foot.

His fingers curled lightly around her arm. ''You know something, don't you? What is it?''

He was perceptive. Too perceptive. She wanted to break loose and fly away. Why had she ever agreed to help Rio? Especially, as Mae so often reminded, after the way he'd treated her? She must have been temporarily insane. Tate was going to figure it out before she could say anything, and then she'd be the one moldering away in jail, while Rio, after three days, would be off to Mexico and freedom.

She tugged at her arm, trying to gain release. ''Just forget I ever came back. I'm sorry I bothered you. I only thought—''

His grip tightened. ''Tell me.''

There was very little light that night. Some high clouds had veiled the moon and the stars. Still, she could see he was watching her levelly, intently. ''What...What if I don't?'' she breathed.

Even the chirping crickets stilled. Not a muscle moved in Tate's face, not an eyelid quivered. Finally he bit out, ''Who?''

''Rio,'' she choked out. ''I wanted him to tell you himself. I told him he should. But he thinks that all sheriffs are alike, that he won't have a fair chance to tell his side of the story. He didn't do it, Tate! He was somewhere else when it happened, playing cards with—''

He let go of her arm so suddenly she nearly lost her balance.

"If I had a dime for every criminal who claimed he didn't do what he's accused of, I'd be a rich man! And you fell for it!''

"I didn't *fall* for anything. I believe him!''

"Why? Because you used to sleep with him? Or because you still do?''

Jodie gasped. She hadn't expected his attack to be so personal. "No! I believe him because—''

Rafe's front door jerked open and he stepped off his porch, his long lithe body tense. Morgan was right behind him. They'd heard their raised voices. "What's goin' on?'' Rafe called.

"Nothing,'' Tate said. "Jodie and I are havin' a little talk, is all.''

"Jodie?'' Rafe repeated, surprised. "What's Jodie—'' Morgan put a hand on his friend's shoulder and said something close to his ear. Rafe looked at Morgan hard, then his tension drained away. "Morgan says we need to stay out of this. So…night, folks.'' The two of them disappeared back inside.

Jodie took several deep breaths. Something else she'd have to deal with in the future!

Tate turned back to her. "Go on,'' he said tightly. "Why do you believe him?''

Jodie wished she'd never started this. Not any of it. When Rio had left his coin outside her window to summon her, she should have ignored it. And today she should have let him run away. Not stop him, not offer to continue to help. Then she thought of the girl. Of Crystal Hammond. Someone had murdered her and the child she was carrying. If it wasn't Rio, it was someone else. Someone who shouldn't be allowed to get off scot-free because law enforcement's attention was directed at the wrong man.

Jodie straightened her shoulders. "He says he was playing cards with four other cowboys that night—all night. But he only knows one of them. A man named Joe-Bob, who's supposed to be working on a ranch somewhere in West Texas. The others are friends of this Joe-Bob. So it's Joe-Bob we have to find."

"*We?*" Tate said sharply.

"You're the only person who can help us, Tate! I've already called all the ranchers who belong to the regional association. None of them admit to having hired this Joe-Bob. But I have no way of knowing if they're telling the truth or how to contact the other ranches—the ones not in the association. You do."

"What's this Joe-Bob's last name?" Tate asked.

"Rio doesn't know," she said simply. She knew this was a weakness in her argument.

"Was it his baby?" he asked suddenly.

"He says it was."

"That must've hurt."

Jodie had had enough of his baiting. She flared, "Look, I'm not doing this because of what once happened between Rio and me. He...I—"

Tate broke in. "You're just doin' it out of the goodness of your heart."

"Actually? Yes, I am. I don't think it's fair that he—"

Tate moved with the speed of a big cat, his strong lean body pressing against hers while his arms took her captive. "And I don't think it's fair that you're wastin' your time on someone like that. Jodie, wake up! The man's probably a murderer, and the story he's told you is just that—a story."

Jodie struggled to break away.

"That's what he's countin' on," Tate continued. "Tricking you again. Can't you see?"

They continued to grapple. Then something in the intimacy of the moment caused the atmosphere to shift. Tate seemed to lose touch with the need to explain the behavior of people outside the law, just as Jodie no longer responded to the need to escape.

One look into his glittering eyes and her breath caught.

Slowly his fingers threaded into her hair. He seemed fascinated by the way stray moonbeams gave a milky wash to the copper-and-red strands.

All she wanted was for him to kiss her. She *ached* for him to kiss her.

She didn't wait. She caught his face in both hands and pulled his mouth to hers.

An electric charge arced between them. The sweetness, the fire, the first fierce urgings of desperate need. It was a powerful combination. Jodie had never felt desire in this same way before. In comparison, everything else had been child's play. Tate created feelings in her that frightened her at the same time as they thrilled her.

When she tried to draw away, he wouldn't let go. His arms engulfed her, his mouth devoured hers...until she was shaken completely to her core.

"Tate," she murmured brokenly. "Tate."

Something, a semblance of memory, must have pierced his thoughts when she said his name. He lifted his head to look at her, looked at where they were, and his body stiffened. But even then he seemed reluctant to let her go.

Jodie pushed away and steadied herself. What had happened between them was a shock—the fantasies in her mind played out in real time! She smoothed her hair and settled her clothing into place, trying to think what to say next.

Tate must have been going through a similar introspection. He cleared his throat as he tucked the loosened tail of his uniform shirt into the back of his pants. "Um...Jodie..."

She shrugged, her cheeks hot. Always before in this kind of situation she'd been sure to keep the upper hand. Now she didn't know where the upper hand was, much less who could claim it.

Tate insisted on having his say. "I didn't intend for that to happen."

An awkward moment passed.

Then, "If you know where he is, Jodie, you have to tell me."

"No."

"I could charge you with aiding and abetting."

"But you won't."

A muscle twitched in his jaw. "No," he said, "I won't."

"He needs your help, Tate. He's afraid of the sheriff in Colorado. Afraid he'll hand him over to the Hammonds, then look the other way." She stepped closer to him again, drawn. She rested her hand lightly on his arm. "I told him you're not like that. That you'll listen to reason. That you'll help." She paused. "That you'll at least check out his story."

The instant she'd edged closer to him Tate's body tensed. Was he afraid to trust himself near her again? Jodie was secretly delighted. She moved even closer and caught the lightest scent of sandalwood left over from his morning shave. What would it be like to be with him in the morning, she wondered, to watch as he went through his usual routine? Showering, shaving—

His arm jerked away.

Undeterred, she smiled softly and touched his badge. "This *means* something to you. You don't want to see the wrong man pay for what he didn't do. I'll tell you everything Rio told me. Word for word. Then you can see what you think. Is that a deal?"

She was aware of his quickened breaths and the growing heat of his gaze. She was tweaking the lion's tail and enjoying it. So far.

"Why are you doing this?" he asked huskily. "Because you still love him?"

"Because I think he's *innocent!*"

"You're taking a big risk, then."

Seconds passed.

Finally Tate relented. "All right. Tell me what you know. But from over there." He pointed toward the chairs.

Jodie gave an impish grin. "Why? Is somethin' botherin' you, Mr. Sheriff?"

"You know damn well what's botherin' me! Now if you want my help..."

Jodie slipped into the chair she'd used earlier and repeated, seriously, everything she knew about Rio's alibi.

THE HAMMONDS arrived early the next morning. When their pickup truck slid to a stop only inches behind Tate's patrol car, it sprayed gravel and dust all the way to the porch, where the lineup of Parker men, Mae and Tate waited. Not an hour before, Tate had received word that the Hammonds were in town and on their way.

Jodie had been told to remain in the house, but when no one was looking, she'd slipped outside, staying in the background behind the others.

The father and two sons bailed out of the truck. All three were big and burly, with heavy shoulders and heads of thick curly dark hair. The father wore a full beard that was graying, while the brothers, in their mid-thirties, had several days' growth of stubble. One brother, probably the older, shared the same rough features as his father. The younger had a softer rounder face. None looked the least bit friendly.

The father was the first to speak. "I wanna talk to the man in charge," he said curtly.

Jodie, standing directly behind Mae, saw her great-aunt's shoulders flex. "Well," Mae said before anyone else could answer, "you're just gonna have to make do with me. I'm Mae Parker. How can I help you?"

Rufus Hammond's eyes narrowed. "You know who I am?" he demanded.

Mae nodded.

"Then you know why I'm here."

"We're sorry for your loss, Mr. Hammond," Mae said levelly.

The man arrogantly spit on the ground. "The only way I'm gonna believe that is when you hand over Rio Walsh." The two sons shuffled menacingly.

"We don't have him," Rafe said.

"That's not what we heard."

"Then you heard wrong," Rafe replied.

"We wanna look for ourselves!"

Rafe reacted instantly to the insult. "Are you sayin' you don't trust our word?"

"I guess that's what I'm sayin'!" Rufus Hammond replied.

Tate inserted himself between the two factions. He was back in full uniform—badge, hat, service belt with holstered gun, pepper spray and handcuffs. "Now that's enough!" he directed sharply. "There's not going to be any trouble here. Mr. Hammond, I'm Tate Connelly, sheriff of this county. I've spoken with Sheriff Preston a number of times. I've told him, like I'm tellin' you, if Rio Walsh is in the vicinity, we'll get him. You don't have to worry about that."

"Do you think we're stupid?" the older brother challenged. "We know how it works! You're all protectin' him because he's one of yours!"

"Like hell he is!" Rafe snapped back.

"Then why won't you let us look?" the younger brother demanded.

"Because Parker land is Parker land," Mae decreed.

"My little girl is *dead!*" Rufus Hammond exploded.

"That doesn't change a thing," Mae said.

The older brother bellowed and rushed the porch. Tate, already on the steps, grabbed him, gave a compact twist, and before the man knew it, his arm was locked into place high on his back, a pained look on his sweaty face.

"You cause any more trouble and I'm takin' you in. All of you!" Tate said through clenched teeth. "I don't know how it is in Colorado, but down here in Texas we take this kinda thing pretty seriously. There're certain rules and regulations I'm sworn to uphold. And anyone who breaks 'em—anyone!—is gonna have to answer for it. Do I make myself clear?" A pause. "Property rights also count pretty high down here. If the Parkers don't want you on their spread, you aren't on it! Is *that* clear?"

Rufus Hammond's tiny eyes glittered with rage, but he also had enough sense not to continue the challenge after taking into account the rifles held at the ready by Rafe, Morgan and LeRoy. "Yeah," he said ungraciously.

Tate let the brother go and gave him a shove.

"What about the girl?" the man snarled after almost staggering into his kin. "What was her name? Joanie? Jobie?"

"Jodie," his brother supplied.

"Yeah, that's it. Where's she? Is that her back there?" He pointed straight at Jodie. "The one with the short red hair?"

Jodie's blood went cold. She hadn't expected them

to spot her. Otherwise she'd have stayed indoors. She felt the disapproving glances of her family, as well as Tate's irritated look.

"Are you Jodie?" the older brother demanded.

Before she could answer, Tate said shortly, "If you want to talk to her, you have to make arrangements through me. We'll do it in a civilized manner, not like somethin' out of a Wild West show."

"She's not talkin' to *anyone!*" Rafe grated, contradicting Tate. "You got any questions, you talk to me. Jodie stays out of it."

The older brother looked at him. "From what we heard in town this mornin', I'd've thought you had plenty of reason to hate Rio Walsh yourself. Seems you'd want to help us string 'im up."

"There's not gonna be any stringin' up!" Tate said coldly.

A nasty smile. "So you say!"

Rufus Hammond's hand shot out, striking his son in the face. "Shut up, Tom, 'fore you get us into worse trouble."

"All I'm—"

"I said, *shut up!*" Another threatened backhand and Tom grew quiet.

Jodie felt the older man's malevolent gaze latch on to her, and she had to stave off a chill. She saw exactly why Rio was afraid of him. She sidled over a space, so that his line of vision would be blocked by Tate and Mae.

"I think maybe our business is over, don't you?" Rafe murmured with deceptive ease.

Morgan motioned with the barrel of his rifle, which

he'd partially raised, for the men to be moseying along. It had the authority of years of practice.

Tate stood steadfastly on the porch steps, like a rock, not intending to be moved.

Even LeRoy, whose quiet soul was happiest when he was working on a car engine, was up to the threat, united with his kin. His jaw was clenched, his lips a thin line.

And Mae...Jodie could feel the waves of hostility directed from her to the Hammonds.

Rufus Hammond grunted a command to his sons, who climbed back into the pickup truck. "All right," he said as he, too, climbed in. "We'll be goin'. But you haven't heard the last of this!"

He gunned the engine on the final word and the truck took off, leaving, as it had arrived, in a swirl of dust and sprayed gravel.

Those on the porch watched as it raced out of sight. Then all eyes turned to Jodie.

"I thought I told you to wait inside," Mae grumbled.

"Aunt Mae..." Rafe cautioned.

"Well, I did! And if she had..."

"All her presence did was get things out in the open." Rafe turned to Tate, who'd rejoined them on the porch. "What do you make of it, Tate?"

"A bad bunch," he replied. "I wouldn't want to be in Rio Walsh's boots if they catch up to him."

"I *hate* that we're put in this position," Mae continued. "Having to defend that no-account—"

"I'm not overfond of it myself," Rafe interrupted his great-aunt's tirade.

Jodie wanted Tate to look at her. Wanted him to give

some sign he remembered what they'd talked about last night—his agreement to help find Rio's card-playing friend. But he studiously avoided looking at her. Because of what had happened between them just before he'd agreed?

It had taken her hours to go to sleep last night. Hours to settle down. To be able to deal with her feelings. She wasn't sure about anything, except that she wanted to spend more time with Tate. Had he come to the opposite conclusion?

She gave a start when she heard him say her name.

"Jodie should probably stick close to the compound for the next few days," Tate said.

"She will," Rafe assured him.

"She'd better!" Mae asserted.

When Jodie looked up, Morgan winked at her and murmured to the others, "Don't you think maybe y'all should do a little askin'?"

"If she has any sense, we won't have to ask," Mae snapped.

"She's seen what they're like," Rafe agreed.

Jodie's jaw tightened. She hated to be talked about like she wasn't there. It reminded her of the treatment she'd received as a teenager. And now even *Tate* had done it! "Excuse me," she said tightly, and slipped around them to walk away.

"Jodie!" Mae called after her. "Don't you dare leave this ranch! Not without one of the men coming with you!"

Jodie kept walking, her body stiff.

"Jodie!" Mae called again.

A small fuss broke out on the porch, but Jodie refused to turn around. Footsteps pounded after her, accompanied by a rhythmic metallic clinking. Tate, the equipment on his service belt rattling, soon caught up with her.

Jodie wouldn't look at him. She was angry, she was frightened, and he had played a major part in it all.

He fell into step at her side, not saying anything until they arrived at her door. "Mae's right," he said, reaching out to keep her on the narrow porch. "Don't go anywhere alone."

"I'm not planning to," she returned.

He was standing close to her. So close they seemed to share the same ripple of awareness. His hand lifted, a butterfly caress to her cheek. Jodie looked away. She was aware that members of her family still remained on Mae's porch and were, in all probability, watching them.

His hand fell back to his side, as if he, too, realized they were on display. He glanced over his shoulder at Mae's house, then back at her, his expression a confirmation.

"This changes things, Jodie," he said tautly. "You have to tell me where Rio is."

For a wild and crazy moment Jodie had thought he'd meant things were changed between the two of them—the madness of an attraction that wouldn't go away. "I don't believe I do," she said.

"You saw the Hammonds. You saw what kind of people they are. You could get hurt! We need to end this *now*."

"I told you what the Hammonds were like last night, remember?"

"How can I forget last night?"

"You said you'd help."

"That's not what I was talking about!"

"It's what *I'm* talking about!"

It was so hard to look at him and not give in. The temptation to take the easy way out was strong. Tate would see to Rio's safety—for as long as he was in his jurisdiction. But what would happen afterward? When he had to turn him over to the Colorado sheriff? No, she couldn't do it. She'd given Rio her word and she had to see it through.

A muscle jumped in Tate's cheek. He knew she wasn't going to back down. "I hope you know what you're doin', Jodie," he said tightly. "And that you don't come out of this like you did the last time—the worst one off."

"I survived," she said flatly.

"And hopefully, if things go wrong, you can do it again." He wheeled around, ready to leave, until Jodie stopped him.

"Tate? You will help—right?" she asked, needing to hear him say it once again.

His eyes glittered at her from beneath the rim of his hat. Several seconds passed, then he said quietly, "Yes, God help me, I will."

CHAPTER TEN

TATE LEFT THE RANCH in a far worse frame of mind than when he'd arrived the evening before. Not only had his worst fears about the Hammonds been confirmed, but so had his doubts about the judgment of his counterpart in Colorado. There was an unprofessional closeness between the sheriff and the grieving relatives, a closeness that had hampered the investigation. If what Rio Walsh had told Jodie was true.

Tate's fingers tightened on the steering wheel. That was a mighty big *if.* Still it needed to be checked out. By him, not by anyone connected with Clayborne County.

If Rio Walsh had a confirmed alibi for the time of the assault, particularly one that was independently corroborated by the other participants in the card game, he would have to be ruled out as a suspect. Not railroaded into jail because it was convenient.

Tate's lips thinned. *Someone* had killed that girl. Some sniveling coward who took grim delight in attacking a far weaker person.

Tate wanted to be the man to get him. He'd love to root him out and make him face what he'd done. And if it did turn out to be Rio…

Jealousy seared through him in a white-hot flame.

He couldn't put aside something he'd overheard that morning when he'd gone into Mae Parker's kitchen for a cup of coffee. The housekeeper, while preparing breakfast, had been talking to her husband. *I only hope Jodie doesn't still have feelings for that Rio Walsh. You don't think that's why she's stayed away from the ranch for so long, do you? I always thought it was because she was enjoying her independence, but it's possible it might've been—* Then she'd seen Tate and stopped talking.

Tate had been back in Del Norte for only about six months when the Jodie-Rio thing happened. He, like everyone else, had known about it, but it hadn't really touched his life. He'd been too caught up in trying to adjust from big-city policing to being a deputy sheriff in the lightly populated county, and in his concern for his mother, who'd been having difficulty stabilizing her diabetes.

Through it all, though, he could remember he'd felt a gnawing irritability every time he thought about Jodie and her gigolo cowboy. She'd always had a way of getting under his skin.

He laughed dryly. *Getting under his skin!*

That kiss! Holy God! It had taken every speck of discipline he'd had in him to stop kissing her. And then not to kiss her again. But she hadn't made it easy. She knew the effect she had on him. She'd reveled in it. Edging closer, touching him...

He groaned. She been like a cat playing with a defenseless mouse.

There were people he knew who would laugh at that

description. Jack, for one. He'd guffaw and tell him he didn't look or act the least bit defenseless.

Only, that was the way he felt when he was with her. Completely at a loss to understand anything except the basics of elemental human biology.

A call came over the radio. A possible breaking-and-entering at a house on his way into Del Norte. Within seconds Tate's thoughts refocused on his duties, and he switched on the overhead lights and accelerated down the highway.

Five minutes later an old woman, nearly as old as Mae Parker but far frailer, met him outside the long metal gate that barred the way across her drive. She rushed up to the car, waving her arms, and barely let him get out before she exclaimed, "I saw him! In my back room! He was big. Huge! And he *growled* at me!"

Tate tried to calm her. "You live here alone, don't you, Mrs. Johnston?" He'd recognized her instantly as the widow of Del Norte's one-time postmaster.

"Yes! Just me—and my dog!" She indicated a small black terrier snuffling around at her heels that looked at least her equal in dog years.

"And this intruder growled at you?" Tate asked.

"Yes! It was terrible. Terrible!"

"You stay here while I check things out. If you want, you can sit in the back of the patrol car."

Mrs. Johnston shook her head, her eyes wide, her parchmentlike cheeks flushed.

Tate unsnapped the narrow strap that secured his gun, slipped through the gate and walked down the drive. Alongside the house, he carefully checked each window before moving past. He heard and saw nothing unusual inside. Then at the rear of the house he found a door ajar. Drawing his gun, he flattened out beside the door frame, hugging the aluminum siding with his back.

"You inside! You've got ten seconds to show yourself!" he called briskly.

There was a sound and his muscles tightened. Then a small furry head thrust through the narrow opening.

"Meow?" A young cat looked up at him.

Much of Tate's tension drained away, but his training had taught him to check further. He stepped past the cat, noticed that she was very pregnant and proceeded to check each room, particularly the back rooms, to insure they were empty.

Only when he was completely satisfied did he put away his gun and scoop up the young tabby. "Are you the criminal responsible for all this?" he asked, rubbing her under the chin, making her purr in response.

Tate brought her out to the old woman. "Here's your trouble, Mrs. Johnston," he said easily. "Seems like someone's lookin' for a place to have her babies. Does she belong to any of your neighbors?"

The house was closer to town than the far-flung ranches. One among a cluster.

"Not that I know of." She frowned. "Are...are you sure everything's...?"

Tate smiled. "I've checked it out, but I'll be glad to come inside with you and do it again if it'll make you feel better."

She shook her head. The dog moved around, sniffing, finally taking notice of the cat.

"Do you want her?" Tate asked. "She looks like she could use a good home."

"Not really," the woman said quickly, then relented. "I do like cats, though. So does Sophie." She glanced at the dog. "We had one up until a couple of years ago when our Isabelle ran off."

She took the cat away from Tate and stroked it lovingly. "What should we call you?" she wondered aloud as she started down the drive toward her house. "Pixie? Because you caused so much trouble? And next, we'll have to think up names for all your babies!"

She never thought to look around and say thanks, but Tate didn't mind. This was the kind of breaking-and-entering call he preferred. One where everyone was happy in the end.

In ten minutes he was back at the sheriff's office. He might have been gone a week, rather than merely overnight, from the number of important matters that "just couldn't wait" and the blizzard of telephone calls that "had to be returned right away." He cut straight through it all, though, with the matter he considered of highest priority.

He set his mother and Rose Martinez to calling all the ranches in Briggs County, while he contacted his fellow sheriffs in the other counties. If this Joe-Bob character was working on a ranch anywhere in the western part of the state, he was going to be found, and as soon as possible, because Tate put an urgency in his request.

He was determined to get this situation resolved quickly.

JODIE DIDN'T TAKE WELL to waiting. Particularly waiting while being kept in the dark. She reached for the telephone any number of times that afternoon to call Tate to check on his progress, but she hung up before punching more than three numbers.

What was happening? What was he doing? Had he had any luck yet in finding Joe-Bob?

She paced from room to room, glad her father was out. Life seemed to be going on much as usual around the ranch. The men continued to do their jobs, although one always seemed to be within easy calling distance. Each time she flipped the curtain aside to look out, someone noticed. They were watching her, protecting her. And it was starting to drive her batty!

She hadn't told Tate about the deadline. Should she have? Should she still? But how would he receive it? She was already skating on such thin ice with him. She didn't want to complicate things.

She gave a small wry laugh. As if everything wasn't already sufficiently complicated.

One thing was sure, however. She couldn't stand to be alone any longer. She had to find someone to talk to.

Shannon was seated at the dining-room table sorting through several packets of material when Jodie knocked on the door.

"Hi! Come on in," Shannon called, motioning for her to join her. "I was just going through some of the papers Jack Denton sent over. Did you know his grandfather fought alongside Teddy Roosevelt during the charge up San Juan Hill? And before him *his* father was one of the original Buffalo Soldiers? He joined the

Tenth Calvary shortly after the Civil War and was sent to help tame the frontier. He ended up stationed in West Texas at Fort Davis.'' Her eyes shone. ''Look! Here's a picture of Jack's great-grandfather...and this is his grandfather. Rafe told me Jack's family had been in the area almost as long as the Parkers, but I didn't realize— And something else! When he finally had enough of army life, his great-grandfather worked on a ranch—*this* ranch!—until he could support himself with the kind of work he really wanted, which was making furniture.''

She finally noticed Jodie's pinched features. ''Sorry,'' she said, pushing the papers and photographs aside. ''I get carried away. These family histories just take hold of me. I love learning about the things people did and how they match up to their descendants today. In Jack's case I'd say the genes run true to his ancestors.'' She grimaced. ''I should apologize again, shouldn't I?''

''No, it's me,'' Jodie said quickly. ''I'm interrupting.''

''The boys are taking their afternoon naps and I'm indulging myself. You aren't interrupting a thing.''

''But this...'' Jodie swept a hand over the paperwork.

''Can wait. Jack's not in any hurry. He just wants it all put together in a book one day. Would you like coffee or an iced tea or something?''

Jodie shook her head.

''What's up?'' Shannon asked after a small silence. ''Is it those men from this morning? Rafe told me they want to talk to you.''

''They think I can tell them something about Rio.''

"They looked pretty rough. I was watching from the window," Shannon explained. "I know they've been through a lot, but...well, I was glad Tate was here. It made everything more...official."

"I was glad, too."

Shannon hesitated, then said, "Jodie? You don't have to answer if you don't want, okay? But is something going on between you and Tate? I mean, *really* going on? Not just kid stuff?" When Jodie stiffened, Shannon continued in a rush, "I shouldn't have asked. It's that darned Parker directness I've caught from Rafe and Mae. Forget I said anything, okay? It's just that I've been worried about you. First about why you stayed away for so long, then if you still had feelings for Rio, and now..." She took a breath. "Oh, forget all this. Please! I'm embarrassing myself."

Jodie smiled tightly. It seemed to be her purpose in life to make people worry. "It just means you care," she said quietly.

"We all do!" Shannon exclaimed. "Right down to Shep, Jr."

The puppy was sprawled, sound asleep, on the floor at his mistress's feet.

Shannon laughingly amended, "When he's awake, that is."

Jodie moved to the window. Shannon had unknowingly struck another chord. A moment before, she'd said that Jack's genes ran true to his ancestors. Did hers, in relation to the Parkers? Where did she fit in? She'd been running away from "being" a Parker for so long she no longer knew. She loved them deeply, each and every one. And they—as they'd proved this morning and were still proving now—were willing to lay their lives on the line to protect her. And how was she repaying them? By harboring a suspected criminal. A man who, from the beginning, they'd warned her to stay away from.

A whisper of panic moved through her. What if Rio had made up the story? What if he truly was responsible for Crystal Hammond's death? And now she'd involved Tate in what could easily prove to be a lie!

She jerked her hand to her mouth to keep from crying out.

Shannon, who'd continued to watch her, came over to brace her shoulders. "Whatever's going on," she said quietly, "I have to tell you, it'll work out. I'm the all-time expert on that, remember? Things can look pretty bleak for a while—" she was obviously referring to the tragedy in her past, the plane crash she'd spent long months recovering from "—then when you least expect it, sometimes from a source you'd never *ever* expect, the bad is replaced by good. I love the life I have now with Rafe and the boys. I wouldn't trade it for the world. And at one time I thought my life was over. I wanted it to be over."

Jodie said huskily, "I'm not so sure this can work out. It's all such a..." She shook her head, unable to go on.

"Just give it time," Shannon urged.

Jodie nodded, but she knew that time was a commodity she didn't have. If Tate's search went past Wednesday, she'd have to admit everything—and then suffer the consequences.

TATE'S SENSE of urgency increased as the day wore on. His mother and Rose had received the same negative responses as Jodie. So far, no one they'd spoken to had hired a person fitting this Joe-Bob's description in Briggs County. Their only hope, it seemed, would lie with the sheriffs of the other counties.

Tate pulled a couple of his deputies from their accustomed routes to patrol the public roads near the Parker Ranch. He wanted to be sure, in case Rio Walsh decided to leave whatever hiding place Jodie had devised for him and make a break for town or beyond, they'd catch him before he got very far. Tate also had asked Chief Lovell to help him keep an eye on the Hammonds. At last report they'd yet to leave the town limits, and Tate had given instructions that he be notified the second they did.

Their stubborn determination to talk to Jodie worried him. Would she be able to keep quiet about everything she knew? Or would that feisty redheaded Parker temper get the better of her and she'd tell them exactly what she thought—and in the process divulge information she could have received only from Rio? Then they'd know, and press even harder.

She'd looked frightened this morning standing on the porch. His heart had twisted at the sight of her and he'd wanted to do something—anything—to take her fear away. Then again, maybe a healthy dose of fear was a good thing if it kept her on the ranch and kept her quiet if accosted.

Tate smiled weakly. Jodie Parker keeping quiet. That had the proverbial snowball's chance in hell!

CHIEF LOVELL called a couple of hours later. "Just thought you'd wanna know. They're still at the Waterin' Hole, orderin' beer after beer. Jimmy says they're holdin' it pretty well, not stumblin' around or causin' any trouble. But if they get in that truck of theirs and try to drive off, I own 'em! Not a doubt in the world they're over the legal limit. You got a spot for 'em to sleep it off, right?"

"You bet. I'll tell the deputy on duty to fluff up a few pillows just in case."

Chief Lovell hooted with laughter. "You do that!"

Tate cleared the remaining administrative work from the day before by meeting with several citizens. Two were officials of his mother's women's club who were there to request a contingent of deputies be on hand during the fund-raising fair they were holding the following weekend. They'd used the county park for the past two summers, but this year they were worried about adequate protection.

"The world seems to have gone crazy lately," club president Marybeth Hardy said. "Troublemakers everywhere. Even here! There are so many people we just don't know anymore."

"When I was a child we *never* had to worry about something terrible happening," vice president Wanda Brinks, an energetic sixty-year-old like Marybeth, contributed. "It's those drugs everybody's putting up their noses or into their arms or swallowing like there's no tomorrow. It makes them do crazy things. Decent people can hardly step out of their homes anymore!"

Tate listened patiently, then said, "Our drug problem's pretty low. It's around, but limited. If I believed what the people on TV said about how awful everything is everywhere, *I'd* be afraid to come out of my house." The women tittered. "So don't worry. Have your fair. One uniformed deputy will be plenty. You never had trouble in the past and you won't this year, either." He shook each woman's hand as he saw them out.

The next citizen was far harder to deal with. Harvey Stevens seemed to think that owning the town's largest car dealership gave him special rights. "Dammit!" he exploded, pounding his fist into his hand. "It's just not right! I pay my taxes—more than my share in fact. So when I need a policeman, I expect to find one, not have him off doing double duty to help the county! You have deputies. You have a budget. Use them! Stop poaching from Del Norte!"

Tate sighed inwardly. This wasn't the first time the car dealer had come to complain. "The last time you were here, Mr. Stevens, I explained how our mutual-assistance pact works. Is there something about it you still don't understand?"

"The whole damned thing actually!" Stevens shot back.

Tate launched into a replay of his previous explanation.

The car dealer listened, then at the end, after Tate had outlined all the advantages, he stubbornly maintained, "I still don't see where it's to my benefit."

Tate's temper snapped. "It benefits both the county *and* the town, Mr. Stevens. It's not about poaching money or personnel. It's about stopping crime while being chronically underfunded and understaffed. My deputies and I help Chief Lovell, and he and his officers help us.''

"There! See? That's what I'm talking about. The whole sordid affair isn't balanced. I'm sure you call for help much more often than Chief Lovell calls you.''

"The jail is a *county* lockup.''

"Which I helped pay for with my county taxes!''

Harvey Stevens was a stupid and argumentative man, who seemed to like nothing better than a good fight. Tate wished he could just deck him and get it over with. Instead, he dug deep inside himself for a wellspring of icy calm and said levelly, "I'll tell you what, Mr. Stevens. I'm going to make you a promise. If we get a call that someone's causing trouble out at your car lot and the town police need our help, we won't respond. I'll cite everything you told me just now. Then everyone can be happy. Does that sound good to you?''

The car dealer sputtered.

"In fact,'' Tate continued, dragging out a sheet of paper and a pen. "Why don't we formalize it? Your town tax money is to be used exclusively in town, and your county tax money in the county. It's not to be comingled. Of course if the need arises at either your home or your business, you're forfeiting your right to have the town police call the county for assistance. And you'll in no way hold either agency responsible.''

He slid the paper and pen across the desk and dared the other man to use them.

Anger flashed in the car dealer's eyes as he scrunched the paper into a tight ball and threw it into the wastepaper basket on his way out.

"Do I take it, then, you *do* want us to respond?" Tate asked as the door slammed shut.

Tate chuckled dryly, then indulged in a few moments of highly uncharitable thought.

It was at times like this that the task-force job looked mighty appealing. He loved police work, not politics. Not dealing with ill-tempered boors who caused almost as much irritation with their complaints as the criminals they employed him to arrest.

He went home, changed out of his uniform, heated a frozen dinner and ate it watching a sitcom on TV—all the while trying to relax. But the tension he'd lived with for the past day and a half wouldn't let him. He kept thinking of Jodie and the Hammonds—and what would happen to her if they ever learned she knew where Rio was.

He muttered a curse, collected his off-duty gun, clipped the short holster to the belt looped through his jeans and hid it under the cotton shirt he wore loose over a black T-shirt. Then he climbed into his own Ford sedan and headed for the Watering Hole on the outskirts of town.

The place was relatively quiet on Monday nights, as if trying to recover from the weekends, when cowboys from the surrounding ranches and workers from town converged to let off a little steam. Chief Lovell never let things get too far out of hand, though, and for the most part the participants respected his rules.

A juke box was playing an old Patsy Cline tune as Tate strode in through the old-fashioned swing doors. He was immediately hit by the scents of perspiration and stale beer.

The only lighting came from naked bulbs hanging weakly here and there, but it was enough for him to spot the Hammonds sitting at a table near the far end of the bar. A few other patrons were scattered about, and when one recognized him, he waved him over.

"Hey, Tate! Long time no see! C'mon—lemme buy ya a beer!"

Tate slid into a chair with the best available view of the Hammonds and smiled at his tablemate. "It's been a long time, Dale. What you been doin' with yourself?"

"Oh, this and that...this and that."

Tate was on speaking terms with everyone in town—from oldest resident to freshest newcomer. He knew their names, where they worked, how many kids they had or didn't have. Dale Travers was a hard-luck kind of guy he'd gone to high school with. Over the years he'd never seemed to get anything in his life together for long enough to make it count. Still, he had a good heart.

Tate spent the next hour nursing a lone beer and commiserating with Dale, while the Hammonds continued to drink steadily. From time to time other people joined Dale and him at their table, and from time to time Rufus Hammond looked over and frowned, as if their loud laughter annoyed him. But he didn't recognize Tate. And why should he? Out of uniform Tate knew he looked very different.

He heard only bits and pieces of the Hammonds' conversation, but it was enough to confirm what he'd suspected—they'd spent the better part of the day working themselves up into an even finer fury. Their anger was now all-inclusive, aimed not only at Rio Walsh, but at the Parkers, himself and anyone in town who they thought had gotten in their way.

Only when they began to make threats did Tate decide to intervene. He got slowly to his feet and walked to their table.

Considering the number of empty bottles littering it, none of them appeared any worse for wear. They looked just as mean and just as determined as they had that morning.

"Whaddaya want?" Tom Hammond, the older son, snarled.

"I couldn't help overhearing," Tate said evenly. "And it seems to me that maybe you boys should hang it up for the night. Before some of these good ol' boys behind me hear what you're sayin' and take exception. You're way outta your territory, in case you've forgotten."

Tom Hammond jerked to his feet and in the process knocked over his chair. "Just who the *hell* do you think you are, comin' over here to tell us—"

His words were cut off by his father's sharp order. "Right your chair and sit down, Tom!"

Tom stared at him.

Rufus Hammond hooked a foot around his son's leg and swept it out from under him. Tom crashed to the floor, and as he struggled to fight his way back up, his father murmured to Tate, "Where do we know you from? You look familiar."

"We met this morning. At the Parker Ranch. I'm the sheriff."

A whisper of a smile touched Rufus's mouth. "Yeah. That's it. I remember."

Tom Hammond needed help from his brother. Tate was fully aware of what each man was doing, where his hands were, what his eyes were saying. "Like I said," he repeated quietly. "I think you boys should call it a night."

The younger son's round face was flushed from alcohol and outrage. "No one tells us what to do!"

"And just in case you're thinkin' of driving, don't!" Tate added. "Motel's not that far from here and the walk'll do you good. Maybe it'll help sober you up."

"Like *I* said—" the younger son growled.

His father lifted a silencing hand. "You think you're really somethin', don't you, Sheriff?" he said to Tate. "When all you are is a..." He used a string of words that would have provoked a less disciplined man.

The other voices in the bar grew quiet as one by one the occupants realized what had been said and to whom. Their narrowed gazes moved from Tate to Rufus and back to Tate.

Dale was instantly at Tate's side. "Did he just say what I think he said?" he demanded, his whipcord body taut as he bounced on his toes, ready for battle. "Look-a-here, you! This is my *friend!* And nobody talks to one 'a my friends that way!"

Tate put a restraining arm across Dale's midsection. "I'll overlook what you said this time, Mr. Hammond. Takin' into account the circumstances. Just remember what I said earlier. You mess with anybody in my county and you're gonna pay for it. You're not in Colorado now. Sheriff Preston isn't in charge."

His overshirt moved during the restraining action and revealed that he was armed. A smile pulled at Rufus Hammond's lips as he slowly got to his feet. Then without saying another word, he walked away, not seeming to care whether his sons came or not. Like trained dogs they quickly followed.

The music played on, a wailing voice lamenting the duplicity of a one-time lover.

Once the show was over, the other occupants of the dimly lit room went back to their conversations and their drinks.

"Way to go, Tate!" Dale cheered. "If you ever need help with those SOBs, you just let me know. I'll be ready."

Tate patted him on the back, told him to take care and followed the Hammonds outside.

CHAPTER ELEVEN

BY THE NEXT DAY waiting had become intolerable for Jodie. She *had* to know what was happening. But when she placed the call to the Briggs County Sheriff's Department and it was answered by Tate's mother, her first instinct was to hang up.

Jodie had never really gotten to know Emma Connelly. The difference in their ages and circumstances had prevented it. But she knew the older woman was admired in the community for the way she'd handled herself the day her husband died. While on dispatch duty, she'd taken the call from the mortally wounded Dan Connelly, who'd dragged himself back to his patrol car to pass on whispered information about his assailants so they could be apprehended. Then she'd talked steadily to him, encouraging him to hold on until help arrived—only to learn later from Jack that her husband had died with her name on his lips.

"Mrs. Connelly? It's me, Jodie Parker. Is, ah, Tate in?"

"Jodie Parker?" Emma Connelly repeated, surprised.

"Yes."

A pause followed, then Emma asked, "How are you? I suppose it feels pretty good to be home again."

"Yes. Yes, it does."

Another slightly awkward pause, then Emma said, "Tate's in his office. I'll put you through."

The line clicked before Jodie could say thanks.

"Sheriff Connelly," Tate said briskly.

Jodie pushed a lock of hair behind her ear. "Tate, this is Jodie. I couldn't wait. Have you found anything yet?"

He took several seconds to reply. "Nothing so far."

"Nothing at all?"

"Nope."

"But you have started—"

"We're doing all we can, Jodie."

Short. Sweet. To the point. It was obvious he didn't want to talk to her. She felt at a disadvantage for having called him. "Well I guess I should let you go. You're probably very busy and—"

"I'm busy, but not that busy," he cut in. His voice softened. "I always have time for…constituents."

She laughed lightly, her heart rate accelerating. "I didn't vote for you."

"But you would've, wouldn't you, if you'd been here?"

"Who were you running against?"

"No one."

She laughed again.

"So I suppose that makes you a constituent."

He'd never spoken to her like this before—almost flirtatiously. She held the phone closer to her ear. "Did you make any campaign promises?"

"One or two."

"What were they?"

"Well, one was to continue Jack's—"

A voice intruded in the background. Someone had entered Tate's office and was in a rush to be heard. She heard Tate reply, then reply again. A brief time later, in a tone she now recognized as his official one, he said, "Jodie, I have to go. Somethin's come up. I'll try to give you a call later."

"That's fine," Jodie murmured, and before she got the last word out, he was gone.

Jodie set the phone back in place. She felt bereft at having been cut off from him so abruptly, just when they were on the brink of moving beyond their pasts to...To what exactly? Where did she want this to go?

She stepped out onto the porch and gazed at the courtyard, wishing that she could ride—do something!—to help make the time pass more quickly.

Mae, sitting on the porch of the big house, waved her over.

Jodie didn't want to talk to anyone. But she couldn't ignore her great-aunt's summons.

"You look like you need something to do, Missy," Mae said bluntly. "And I've got just the thing."

Jodie braced herself. With Mae you never knew.

"I've just got off the phone with Delores," Mae continued. "Seems Erin's been invited to one of those birthday/pool parties young kids like so much. She hadn't told anyone about it because she's concerned for her mom—doesn't want to leave her with the baby so close to being born. But the girl's mom called Christine to find out why Erin couldn't make it—her daughter was really looking forward to her coming—and that's when Christine found out. Now Christine wants

Erin to go. Thinks she should have a little fun—you know how serious the girl is. Only there's no way for her to get there. Dub and Morgan are off tendin' to a problem at Indian Wells and someone needs to stay with Christine—"

"I could take her," Jodie volunteered, perking up.

Mae immediately shook her head. "Oh, no. You're not leaving the ranch. Not by yourself."

"Erin would be with me."

"Not on the way back. No, I have a better idea. You go stay with Christine and keep her company while Delores takes the girl."

Jodie needed action, not more sitting. But at least Little Springs was a change from the compound, and Christine was as much a friend as a relation. "All right," she agreed, "I'll do it. When?"

"Right now. The party's already started."

Jodie nodded and, thinking that would be the end of it, turned to go back to her house to collect her purse.

"I'd say take the Cadillac, but your dad's got it. Take one of the trucks, instead."

"All right."

"And Jodie—"

Jodie turned fully.

"—take care."

"Don't worry, Aunt Mae. I will."

THE SHORT DRIVE to Little Springs gave Jodie a taste of the freedom she craved, enough to make her question how she could have allowed herself to be so at the mercy of other people's discretion. She longed for the year she'd spent in Europe. Not having to answer to anyone. Not being told what to do or how to think.

Yet her agreement to help Rio had been made freely, because she *believed* him. She couldn't conceive of him hurting anyone lethally. In particular, not Crystal. The qualms she'd been suffering were due to pressure and worry. But then, why was she worrying so much? Tate would find Joe-Bob, Joe-Bob would straighten everything out, then Rio would be free and she'd be proved correct. Her fingers twisted on the steering wheel. *She hoped!*

The new house sitting catercorner to Dub and Delores's house was of similar design, equally low to the ground and with the same redtile roof. It had been built the year after Morgan and Christine's wedding.

Jodie pulled the truck to a stop in front and hopped out. Hearing soft laughter from within, she tapped lightly on the door and called, "Hello! It's me—Jodie."

Footsteps hurried from the back of the house—Erin, in a bright red one-piece swimsuit with a white cotton coverup shirt. She looked as if she'd never suffered from the normal gaucheness of a young teenager. She had a natural grace and maturity that belied her tender years.

"Jodie! Hi! Everyone's on the back porch. Come on through."

Jodie followed the girl to the back of the house and smiled as she saw Christine ensconced like royalty in a white wicker chair cushioned with colorful pillows. A pitcher of lemonade and a book were close at hand,

and the air around her was cooled by a gently rotating ceiling fan.

"Now that's the life," Jodie teased, leaning close to hug her. "I didn't know that all you had to do was get pregnant to get such special treatment."

"Ahh! I don't feel very special right now," Christine protested. "Mostly I feel huge."

Delores solicitously fluffed a pillow and repositioned it behind her daughter-in-law's head. "It won't be long now," she assured her. "In a couple of weeks it'll all be over."

"Mom," Erin said, "I really don't need to do this. I don't care about pool parties or birthdays. Megan understands I'd rather be here with you."

Christine folded one hand over her swollen belly and reached for her daughter's hand with the other. "It's boring waiting. There's no reason you can't go to the party and enjoy yourself. I'll still be here when you get back. When I had you, I had plenty of warning. And once I got to the hospital, it took another twelve hours before you decided to put in an appearance. Everyone's going to get tired of twiddling their thumbs!"

Mother and daughter smiled at each other, alike but not alike.

"So go," Christine urged. "Then come home and tell me all about it."

Delores spoke up. "Thanks for coming over, Jodie. I won't be long—an hour at the most."

"Take all the time you need," Jodie said.

Delores patted her adopted granddaughter's arm. "We'd better get you there soon or it'll all be over. Don't forget your gift for Megan."

Erin nodded, even as her expression remained doubtful.

Christine squeezed her fingers. "Go," she said again softly. "This'll give Jodie and me a chance to gossip. She can tell me all the things about her trip she didn't want to mention in front of Mae."

Everyone laughed, then Delores herded Erin through the house, and within minutes, the car started and pulled away.

Christine wiped perspiration from her brow. "It would help if it wasn't so darned hot," she complained.

"Do you want a cool moist cloth for your neck? Aunt Mae swears by them when anyone's sick in summer."

Christine declined and patted the wicker chair next to her. "How about a glass of lemonade?"

Jodie agreed, then settled into a chair. For a time both women were content just to sit in the relative coolness and sip their drinks.

Christine sighed. "As you saw, I practically had to twist Erin's arm to make her go. She's so intent on helping me have this baby. It's almost as if she's still afraid we won't stay here. I thought she'd have relaxed by now, that she'd have stopped worrying, but I guess she hasn't."

Erin and Christine had lived a hard life before arriving at the ranch. They'd shifted from post to pillar until being taken in by Ira Parker at his home in Houston. Ira was the first person to take an interest in them and to help. Then he'd left them a share in the Parker Ranch.

Jodie had been eighteen at the time, old enough to

see all the layers in what had happened next. Christine's determination to hold on to that share for the sake of her daughter, the Parkers' stubborn insistence that only a Parker could inherit. Then the astounding news that Ira Parker was, in fact, Christine's father. Christine had wanted to leave after the discovery. But Erin, who'd fitted the ranch as if born to it, hadn't wanted to. She was a Parker through and through, emotionally, as well as legally.

A Parker on Parker land.

The same as Jodie.

Yet the sentiment Erin responded to so readily seemed to be missing in her. She was more like Christine than the other Parkers, because Christine hadn't been raised steeped in her lineage. She'd come to it later, an outsider. An outsider like she herself had always felt.

Jodie wanted to ask Christine if, after all this time, she'd grown into being a Parker. Or did she still feel an invisible divide?

Only, Christine spoke first. "You're very quiet," she said, "and you seem tense. I don't think I've ever seen you like this before. What is it, Jodie? Is there any way I can help?"

Jodie blinked. She looked down at her white-knuckled hands clasped tightly in her lap and immediately broke them apart. "Oh, no, it's nothing," she lied. She wasn't about to tell Christine about Rio. Christine might understand more readily than the others, but she didn't need to hear anything so upsetting. She had enough to think about with the coming baby.

"Is it something? Or someone? Like Tate?" Christine guessed.

Jodie jumped as if she'd been shot, causing Christine to chuckle. "Good heavens! I'm sorry. I didn't mean—"

Jodie stood up and paced a little, which she tried to disguise as interest in a blooming plant, then a half-knitted baby sweater that Delores had put aside. "This is pretty," she said, nervously fingering the soft pink yarn.

She could feel Christine's hazel eyes following her. "So it *is* Tate," she said softly. "Morgan thought so. He told me you two were—"

Christine stopped abruptly. So abruptly Jodie's head snapped up.

A light film of perspiration had broken out on Christine's forehead and upper lip. But it wasn't the continuing heat that made her smile with dawning delight.

"What is it?" Jodie whispered, already having a good idea.

Christine winced, held her side, then started to smile again. "I think...things are starting to happen."

Jodie hurried closer. "Are you sure?"

Christine nodded. "But we should wait. Something like this happened over the weekend and it was a false alarm. I wouldn't want to—" She winced again.

"Do you want me to get Delores back? I can. I'll call—"

Christine struggled to her feet. "Jodie, I'm sorry," she apologized. "But I think we should get going. Something tells me this isn't a false alarm, and it's not going to be at all like last time. This baby's anxious to get here!''

Jodie stared at her. She'd been too young when Gwen and Wesley were born, then away at college when her newest cousins had arrived. She had no experience with childbirth!

"You think we should go?'' she murmured blankly.

Christine chewed her bottom lip and nodded.

Jodie burst into action. "Do you have a bag packed? Do we need to bring anything else?''

Christine motioned as they moved toward the door. "My case is in the front hall. We put it there on the weekend.'' She caught her breath and had to stop walking.

Jodie grabbed the bag and, as soon as Christine was able to move again, saw her outside and into the truck. "We're going to make it to the hospital, aren't we? I mean, you aren't...''

"I hope so.''

Jodie groaned as she ran around to the driver's side and jumped in. "We'll stop by the compound,'' she said as they started off. "Maybe Dad will have gotten back with the Cadillac. It'll be easier on you than this old thing. We can also get some help. Harriet...Shannon. And someone should tell Morgan.''

"I probably should've made plans to give birth here, but I wanted the hospital in Del Norte, even though it's small. Erin had a little trouble breathing at first and I didn't want...''

Christine continued to talk, as if it was comforting to her, and Jodie listened, though most of her concentration was on the road ahead, trying not to hit too many bumps or dips.

They created an uproar at the compound. All the women came running out as the pickup eased to a stop behind the Cadillac, now parked in front of Mae's house. One look told everyone what was happening.

Mae, as usual, took charge. "LeRoy," she said to her nephew, who'd drawn guard duty at the compound, "go find Morgan. Shannon, go call the hospital, alert them and the doctor that Christine's on her way. Harriet, you go with 'em. From the looks of things, this is gonna be tight." Her sharp gaze moved to Jodie. "And you just keep doin' what you've been doing. I'd have your daddy drive, but Lord knows where he is. The man can disappear quicker than a flea on a monkey!"

"Who's gonna watch for the Hammonds?" LeRoy demanded.

"I am," Mae said fiercely. "Now get going! All of you!"

They transferred Christine into the Cadillac as Mae gave her orders. But before starting off, Christine had a request of Shannon. "Be sure to call Erin and Delores. Tell them..." She didn't finish the sentence. "They're at Megan Cantfield's, or they will be soon."

"I'll find them. You just take care."

Jodie started the more powerful engine and the car leaped forward.

The miles melted away as Harriet sat in the backseat with Christine, doing her best to keep her comfortable and offering encouragement. It seemed to take forever to get to Del Norte. Once or twice toward the end Jodie wasn't sure if they'd make it in time, and she gave special thanks for Harriet's calming presence.

The hospital was a small one-story structure set back off the town's main street. It was able to handle minor to serious emergencies, but for anything requiring specialized or prolonged intensive care, patients were transferred to hospitals in larger cities.

Jodie pulled the Cadillac into the emergency entrance, and Christine was whisked away quickly by the waiting attendants. Harriet went with them, leaving Jodie to follow after she'd parked the car.

Away from prying eyes Jodie finally gave in to her anxieties. One tension-filled situation had been piling on another, and it was too much. She started to shake and tears rolled down her cheeks. Rio, Tate, the Hammonds, her place among the Parkers, her unexpected responsibility for a mother and child's well-being.

Moments later she dried her cheeks. One situation at least had already been solved. Or was in the process of being solved. Christine was now safely at the hospital about to have her baby.

Jodie hurried inside, only to find she had to stay in the waiting room. Harriet was the only family member allowed to be with Christine until Morgan arrived.

"Is she having the baby yet?" Jodie demanded of the nurse.

"We'll let you know."

Jodie took a chair and restlessly flipped through a dog-eared magazine. Minutes later Harriet hurried in. "Jodie, after all that rushing, it seems little Elisabeth isn't as anxious to arrive in the big bad world as we thought. It looks like Morgan and Erin are going to have time to get here, after all. Isn't that wonderful?"

"Yes, wonderful," Jodie echoed.

"I'm going back in. I just had to come out and tell you...'cause I knew you'd be wondering." She glanced around the austere room. "Not exactly a cozy place, is it?"

"It's fine," Jodie said.

Harriet squeezed her hand. "Why don't you go get a cup of coffee or something? Nothing's going to happen for the next half hour—at least, that's what the nurse says."

"Tell Christine I love her."

Harriet beamed. "I will."

Jodie thumbed through the magazine some more, then tossed it aside. Maybe coffee would be good.

Only, the small cafeteria the hospital boasted was closed and the remaining option was machine coffee.

Jodie grimaced and went outside. When she'd parked the car she'd seen a café a short distance down the street. She was sure she could get a cup to go and bring it back to the waiting room.

She made her way to the café, received her order and was on her way back when a pickup truck that had just passed screeched to a halt, made a violent U-turn and raced back. Jodie froze as the occupants jumped out and rushed toward her.

"It's her! I told you it was her! Can't miss that red hair!" a rough voice cried.

Someone grabbed her arm, making her spill the coffee. The hot liquid scalded her fingers and she gave a small squeak of pain.

Other hands grabbed her, as well, trying to pull her off her feet.

Her survival skills kicked in. She twisted and turned, and when that didn't do any good, she threw the remaining hot coffee into one of the men's faces. By now she'd recognized them—the Hammonds!

Her action was met with a howl of outrage, and this encouraged Jodie to continue resisting.

"Catch hold of her!"

"Get— Don't let her—"

"Stop it, bitch! All we want to do is talk to ya. Not..."

Another car sped toward them, one with flashing lights and a wailing siren. Curses were snarled and the fingers on her arms tightened. Then she was let go, but not before someone gave her a hard shove that sent her sprawling to the ground.

She banged her knee and her hip painfully, then rolled over just as the Hammonds leaped back into their truck and took off down the street.

The front of the patrol car dipped as the brakes caught. The driver was out in a second. Tate!

He was on his knees beside her as she struggled to sit up. "Don't move. Does anything hurt?"

Jodie was sputtering, her temper temporarily getting the better of her. "It was them! Did you see? All I was doing was walking along and—"

"Jodie! Don't try to stand up. You might be hurt more than you think."

"I'm not hurt, just dented," she snapped as she got to her feet. Her knee and hip stung and throbbed, and the fingers on her left hand were tender.

"Come on, give me your arm. Put it around my shoulders. The hospital's just—"

"I don't want to go to the hospital," Jodie said.

"You're limping."

"I'm *not* going," Jodie said. "Christine's having her baby there!"

Curious eyes peered at them from the occasional car that passed by. A few people stood in the doorway of the café, the siren and flashing lights drawing their attention.

Jodie knew she only needed time to collect herself. No bones were broken, or she wouldn't be able to hold her weight, but after everything, this was just about the last straw.

"C'mon," Tate said. "We need to check out that knee. *Not* the hospital," he added quickly when she held back.

He switched off the patrol car's emergency signals, then drove them to a small house not far away.

The interior of the house had as little to offer as the exterior. It looked like a place someone used part-time. There was very little reflection of personality, except that, for the most part, it was neat and clean.

"Is this your place?" Jodie asked.

"*Mi casa es su casa,*" he said with a wry smile, picking up a discarded newspaper and an empty soft-drink can.

My house is your house, a Spanish courtesy. But it had been said in such a way that Jodie felt uncomfortable. As if Tate expected her to judge him poorly because of a perceived gap in their social standing.

"It's…nice," Jodie said.

"It's somewhere to sleep," Tate replied, removing his hat and setting it on a table by the front door. "Sit down. Can you pull up that pant leg?"

Jodie hitched up the blue denim of her jeans, noticing as she did the bright spots of blood. She didn't tell him that her hip felt worse than her knee. She didn't want him demanding to inspect it.

He made a sound deep in his throat and walked into what she guessed was the bathroom. She heard a medicine chest open and close, just before he returned with cotton balls, antiseptic and a large Band-Aid.

Without further words he knelt at her side and attended to her injury, gently cleansing it and covering it.

Jodie couldn't look away. Not from the closely clipped brown hair that still held the imprint of his hat, not from his hands that touched her with seeming indifference, when before they'd ignited her body to such wonderful... She turned her head, grimacing as she rejected the disturbing thought. She didn't need to add to her troubles!

"Sorry," he apologized gruffly.

She smiled grimly. He thought he'd hurt her.

"No, it's not—"

"Anywhere else?" he asked.

Jodie shook her head.

He stood up, as if relieved to have finished the job. "I know you want to get back to the hospital, but I need just a minute or two of your time."

Jodie gazed up at him, torn between desire and tears. Because of the way he was distancing himself? Because of the way he had always held himself aloof?

She didn't understand—either why he did it or why it was important to her that he stop.

She saw his jaw grind and realized he'd asked her a question, one she had yet to respond to.

"I asked if you're willing to press charges against the Hammonds. I've just been waiting for something to bring 'em in on. What they did to you qualifies as assault and battery, possibly even attempted kidnapping."

Jodie shook her head. "No. I don't want to do that."

"They scared the daylights out of you, didn't they? And they knocked you down."

"I still don't want to do it. It'll only make everything worse. Aunt Mae will go ballistic if she learns I've been hurt. She and Rafe could go after them. I don't want to cause any more trouble than I already have."

Tears again threatened as she struggled to her feet. But she didn't want to cry in front of him. She was Jodie Parker. Jodie...*Parker!* Listen to her! As if she was somehow better than anyone else because of her last name! That wasn't *like* her! She *never*—

Tate grabbed her hand to keep her from stumbling on her first step—her left hand, with the burned fingers. She gave an instinctive mew of pain.

"What?" he demanded sharply.

"It's nothing."

He turned her hand over and examined it. When he saw the redness and the light blistering, he demanded, "How did this happen?"

"Hot coffee. I threw the rest in Tom's face."

A frown and a smile jostled with each other, and the smile won. "The hell you say!"

She nodded. "I did. Right before you drove up."

"Maybe I should have left you to it, then. You might've whupped 'em all."

Jodie's smile was wobbly. "I might've."

He smoothed an escaped tear away with his thumb. "It's not really very funny, though, is it?"

She shook her head again, unable to speak through a too-tight throat. He was being kind and thoughtful and concerned.

"That's why I think you should press charges. These people are loose cannons. And until we get the final word on Rio's alibi, they'll be better off in jail. It'll be safer for them, for you, for your whole family—for everyone."

They remained close. Him holding her hand, her looking up.

Their gazes locked for a long time, and slowly he bent to kiss her.

Then someone rang the doorbell.

CHAPTER TWELVE

"TATE! I WAS JUST on my way to the station when I saw your car out front and I wondered—"

Emma Connelly's words halted the moment she stepped into the house and saw Jodie. She looked from Jodie to Tate and back again, disbelievingly at first, then with her cheeks flushing crimson.

For the first time in years Tate was annoyed with his mother. Or rather, with her timing. Five more minutes, *one* more minute, and they might've...He couldn't remain annoyed with his mother for long, though, in view of her obvious embarrassment.

"Jodie had a little accident, Mom," he explained. "She, ah, I was helping her."

Jodie's pant leg, still hitched up, revealed the wide Band-Aid. She, too, appeared ill at ease in the situation. "Tate's been very kind, Mrs. Connelly."

"What happened?" Emma asked.

Tate felt Jodie's quick look. He knew she didn't want to advertise the altercation. He also knew his mother's propensity for gossip. She'd never say a word about anything that happened on the job, but events outside it were fair game. Unless he asked for her silence, which, in this case, would only bring on more questions. "She fell," he said simply.

His mother raised a skeptical eyebrow, but didn't pursue it. "Are you hurt bad?" she asked Jodie.

Jodie shook her head and bent to roll down her pant leg. As she straightened, she said, "I should get back to the hospital, Tate." Then to Emma, "Christine Hughes is having her baby. We had to rush her into town, but now it looks as if it's going to take some time. Still, I'd like to be there."

Tate looked at his mother. "Did you need something special?" he asked.

"I just saw your car, that's all. And I know you usually—" She broke off, gave her head a little shake, then turned to Jodie. "Christine Hughes is expecting a little girl, isn't she?"

"Yes, ma'am," Jodie replied.

They parted company moments later, Jodie having limped back out to the patrol car, while his mother returned to her car.

Jodie didn't miss the long look Emma gave them as she pulled away. "She's not convinced," she said evenly.

"No," he agreed.

"Will it cause problems?"

"No."

He wondered if she was thinking of the interrupted kiss, like he was. And if she, like him, wanted the moment back. He was aware of every movement she made, of the little adjustment she gave when she bent her knee too far and felt pain, of the way she cradled her left hand.

Black anger burned through him when he thought of the Hammonds' assault. In his mind's eye he could see the scene as he had then, tailing the pickup from a distance, seeing it turn around, seeing the men converge on an unsuspecting Jodie. Then being delayed in traffic…and having to watch as she was knocked to the ground.

No matter what Jodie said, he was going to have them picked up. He wanted another little talk with them. Maybe he could yet instill the fear of God.

He turned into the hospital parking lot and pulled the patrol car as close as he could to the front entrance.

"I didn't think you'd want to go in through the emergency room. A doctor might see you and think you're an accident victim."

She turned her lovely yellow-green eyes on him and his heart skipped a beat. "Tate," she said sincerely, "I didn't thank you for scaring those terrible men away, for ministering to my wounds, for—" her lips curved into a dry smile "—not giving me away to your mother."

He shrugged. "Would you like me to go inside with you?"

She motioned to Harriet and LeRoy's car and the two Parker Ranch pickups parked nearby. "No. Everyone's here now. It'd just draw attention."

She sighed lightly, then reached for the door handle. But before she could open it, he said, "Jodie?"

She looked back at him, and Tate couldn't help it. He leaned over and completed the kiss they'd begun earlier. Kissed her hard and with feeling.

"You take care," he said huskily when at last he pulled away. "Don't go gettin' yourself hurt any more. Stay away from where the Hammonds can find you."

Jodie blinked as if dazed. Then she smiled. "Something tells me it's a good thing your mother interrupted us when she did."

"Or?" he probed, compelled.

Her smile deepened. "Or...who knows?"

She wriggled away from him and out of the car, not without a degree of difficulty as she tried to protect her leg. Then she waved to him before disappearing through the entrance. As he watched, her limp lightened, until it was disciplined into nonexistence. She was determined that her family not learn of the incident.

ELISABETH JANE HUGHES was born two hours later. Blond like her father and weighing a little over six pounds. There was no difficulty with her birth, either for mother or child.

Afterward the entire family crowded into the room. "She's beautiful!" was the general consensus.

"She might have light hair, but look at that face!" Mae pronounced loftily. "That's a Parker if ever I saw one!"

Harriet rushed back into the room from having called LeRoy at the ranch to give him the good news. "LeRoy and the boys have already started to celebrate!"

"That's what we keep a couple of bottles of ol' Jack Daniels' around for," Rafe said, grinning.

Morgan stood at one side of his wife's bed, while Erin stood at the other. It was difficult to tell who was proudest. Both were beaming broadly. Shannon and Rafe were holding on to each other, while Mae thrust out her chest. Gib, as usual, was a little off to himself, but smiling hugely. And the paternal grandparents, Delores and Dub Hughes, could barely contain themselves. A new Parker, merged with their bloodline, had been born into the clan.

Jodie shared in the joy, hugging and being hugged. She, too, was very happy for Christine and Morgan. And for Erin. Hopefully the cloud of doubt that had continued to haunt the young girl's life would be completely dispelled by the birth of her sister.

Shortly afterward, the crowd moved back into the waiting room to give the new family a bit of privacy, and minutes after that they left for home.

Dusk had fallen by the time they arrived at the ranch. There was a small get-together at Mae's house to toast the new arrival.

The effort to keep her injuries secret had exhausted Jodie. By day's end it was almost too much. When she thought no one was looking, she discreetly massaged her aching hip.

"What's wrong with you?" Mae demanded, coming up behind her.

Jodie jumped. "Nothing," she lied.

"I've been watching you. Somethin's not right. Don't try to fool me, Missy. I've known you for too long."

"I...My hip. I stumbled. It was silly really. A stupid thing to do."

Mae pursed her mouth. "Somethin's not right about that, either," she said, "but it's been too long a day." Her dark eyes were shadowed, and she looked almost as tired as Jodie felt. Still, she had enough energy left to say, "You did a good job of caring for Christine. An excellent job. I'm proud of you."

To top it all off, praise from Mae! "Thanks," Jodie said huskily.

Her hip ached, her knee ached, her hand still stung from the burn. She had plenty of things to get misty-eyed about. So why did a few words of approval from her great-aunt hit her with such force? Because when Mae gave praise it really meant something? Because deep down she'd do just about anything to gain her aunt's respect?

Jodie hobbled along the driveway to her house and for the first time that day found true relief when she closed herself in her room.

TATE AVOIDED his mother when he arrived at the station the next morning. He knew she was burning with curiosity, but he wasn't in the mood to satisfy it.

As usual there was a stack of phone messages waiting, but the one that gained his immediate attention came from the sheriff in the next county noting he'd located an individual by the name of Joe-Bob Tucker.

Tate grabbed the phone, punched in the number and within seconds was connected with the sheriff, Frank White.

"What's this about a Joe-Bob Tucker?" he asked. "You think he's my man?"

Frank's gravelly voice growled, "Fits your description to a T. Fresh from a ranch in Montana, working at a small place on the far edge of the county. Brown hair, dark eyes, right age—about six-two and brawny."

"If it's not him, it's his twin," Tate said. "You had a chance to talk with him yet?"

"Thought you'd like to do the honors yourself."

"Got the number of the ranch?"

"I was just about to give it to you."

Tate jotted the number down, thanked his friend and dialed it. Minutes later he shot up from his chair.

"I'll be gone for two, maybe three hours," he told his mother and Rose Martinez as he headed out the door. "Over in Debolt County. If anybody needs me..." They knew the rest—contact him only in dire emergencies.

"Tate?" his mother called, stopping him.

He looked back.

"I'd like to talk with you later, all right?"

"Sure," he agreed. "Later." He could feel her worried gaze follow him outside.

It wasn't that he was still annoyed with her for interrupting any possible intimacy with Jodie. He was annoyed with everybody and everything! He hadn't gotten much sleep last night, but he hadn't really expected to. He'd stayed out as late as he could, spelling one of the deputies who needed a few hours off. Then he'd stopped by the jail, always good for an extra hour or two. But finally he'd had to go home, where he'd felt Jodie's presence as strongly as if she was still there. Just as he'd been afraid he would.

She *was* teasing him. He knew it. But why? Because she was bored? Because she actually did find him attractive? What did it all mean? Where was it going to end up? Where could it *possibly* end up?

Such questions had tortured him for the remainder

of the night. And when he'd dozed off toward morning, other more intimate images had jerked him awake more than once.

He wasn't in a much better frame of mind when he arrived at the small ranch in Debolt County, shook hands with the owner and was introduced to a large man, close to his own age, with big rough hands and a surprisingly soft voice, who carried with him a good helping of range dust.

"You ever been in Clayborne County, Colorado?" Tate asked.

"Only passin' through."

"How about at a ropin' contest nearly two weeks back?"

Joe-Bob Tucker tilted his head in consideration. "Yeah."

"You enter the contest?"

"I sure did. Didn't win, though."

"You do anything else?"

The cowboy smiled. "You mean legal or illegal?"

"Let's just say some circles might frown on it."

"I played cards."

"Who with?"

"Some friends of mine."

"Who exactly?"

"Couple of brothers I know from Colorado, a friend from Montana and another ol' boy I've known off and on for years."

"Names would be helpful."

"Will and Matthew Daniels, "Little Hat" McGraw and Rio Walsh."

Bingo! Tate thought, his solar plexus tightening. "When exactly did this card game take place?"

"Lemme see. The contest started on Saturday, with the finals on Sunday. There were card games Friday night and Saturday night."

"And you played cards with these people both nights?"

Joe-Bob laughed. "Well," he said, rubbing a thick finger along his chin, "Rio practically cleaned us out the first night, so we kinda hid from him the second. I don't even know if he was in town Saturday night. I didn't see him."

"This card game Friday night, how long did it last?"

"All night. Like they usually do."

"And Rio Walsh was there all night?"

"Only left to pee."

"What about the others?"

"Way Rio was winnin', you couldn't've dragged any of us away! We didn't think his luck could last! Man's luckier than a damned—"

Tate had heard enough. "All right, Mr. Tucker, that's all. Except, I'll need you to make a statement to this effect to Sheriff White, and I'll also need the phone numbers and addresses where your other buddies can be reached."

"Sure, yeah, I can do that. It's easy." He paused. "Is Rio in some kind of trouble?"

"He could've been."

"So, in a way, his luck finally did run out?"

"Yeah," Tate agreed, "for a little while it did."

JODIE'S FIRST THOUGHT when she awoke that morning was that time had almost run out. It was Wednesday, and Rio was going to leave at sunset if he didn't hear from her. She had to *do* something. But what?

"You fall off a horse?" her father asked curiously as he watched her limp about the kitchen while making breakfast. She'd been too preoccupied to hide her injuries from him.

"I wish," she sighed.

Gib energetically cut his fried egg into tiny bits, then stabbed at them with a corner of toast. Jodie didn't feel the least like eating. Her toast was more prop than food. She sipped her coffee mechanically.

Gib captured her tender left hand. "This doesn't look too good, either. Wanna tell me about it?"

"I can't, Dad, not right now. I wish I could, but..."

"Tell me what you want, when you want, if you want. I never was a believer in making people talk. That could be one of my great failings, though. Sometimes people *need* to talk and don't know how to start. So...just so you know I'm here."

"I know," she said tightly.

He went back to his egg. "I've made up my mind," he said after a moment. "About the exhibition. I'm gonna do it! I only hope people don't end up laughin' at me."

"They won't!"

His smile was like a little boy's. "Somethin' like this has been a dream of mine for years, but I never thought it'd actually happen."

"Can I come?" Jodie asked.

"You'll be my most important guest."

That bit of good news brightened the rest of the meal. Jodie even managed to eat her toast. But when her father left to take Mae and Delores back to town for a nursery visit, her sense of doom returned.

She hadn't told Tate about the deadline. Should she have? Was it now too late?

She stared at the telephone and debated whether to call. She thought of yesterday—of what had almost happened at his house and later did in the patrol car. Something was definitely brewing between them. But could she count on whatever it was to be strong enough to see her through the trying times ahead? She had to. Otherwise she didn't want to think about what would happen when Rio left and she'd be forced to admit the full truth.

She called the station and was greeted by an unfamiliar voice.

"May I speak to Tate, please?" she requested.

"I'm sorry, Sheriff Connelly isn't in. Would you like to leave a message?"

"He isn't in?" Jodie echoed, her voice rising.

"No. He's away on county business."

"For how long?" Jodie asked.

The other woman responded negatively to her pressure. "For as long as it takes. If you have a problem, ma'am, we can report it to a deputy in your area. Do you have a problem?"

Jodie hung up. Did she have a problem? She had a *huge* problem! She'd never thought she'd be unable to talk to Tate. Where was he? What was he doing? Should she demand to be put through to him?

Maybe she could talk to his mother, get her to— She groaned. No, not after yesterday.

She took several deep breaths, struggling for composure. Tate was sheriff of the whole county. He had a lot of responsibilities. It wasn't unreasonable that he'd be away from the station from time to time. She'd call again in a little while and this time leave a message. And if necessary do it again and again. If nothing else, he might call in for his messages and be told she desperately needed to talk to him. And then...

And then the real trouble could begin.

TATE RETURNED to the station and went straight to his office, shutting the door behind him. He had some important calls to make. The first was to the Daniels brothers, who worked on the same ranch outside Clayborne County. The second was to "Little Hat" McGraw, currently working on a ranch in New Mexico. He wanted to see if they'd confirm Joe-Bob Tucker's story. If they did—and he expected they would—it would blow the lid off Sheriff Preston's case against Rio Walsh.

He saw the flurry of messages from Jodie and his first instinct was to call her, to tell her what he'd learned, but he wanted to be sure. Just in case.

It took an hour to get confirmation, and this from only two of the three men. One brother was out riding fence and wouldn't be back until nightfall. His brother swore, though, to the truth of his own statement and vowed that his younger brother would say the same thing.

Tate was convinced.

He made one more call before dialing Jodie—to Sheriff Preston in Clayborne County. His news didn't go over very well. The sheriff didn't enjoy being shown up. But he did agree to talk with the brothers and get their statements, as well as contact "Little Hat" McGraw to hear what he had to say.

"Rufus sure as hell ain't gonna like it," Bill Preston said.

"Rufus Hammond and his boys are already skatin' on thin ice with me. They've come real close to havin' charges filed against 'em. If I had my way, they would have. Best thing they can do is head back home."

"He's still not gonna like it," the other sheriff warned. "He hates that Rio guy. Thinks he was after Crystal's inheritance. She wasn't Rufus's daughter by birth, but he loved her like she was."

Jodie answered his call on the first ring. "Tate!" she cried. "I'd just about given up!"

Apprehension flooded through him. "Has something happened?" He'd been so intent on verifying Rio's alibi he hadn't taken into account anything else. "Have the Hammonds—"

"No, no. Nothing like that! It's... Tate, I have to tell you something."

When she hesitated, he stepped in. "I've got some good news for you. It's why I called."

"What is it?" she asked quickly.

"Looks like your friend is off the hook. Got all kinds of backup witnesses who're willing to swear he was playin' cards with them on the night that girl was beaten. So good job, Jodie. You've helped keep an innocent man out of jail."

His words were met with silence.

"Jodie?" he said.

He could hear the overwhelming relief in her voice

when at last she choked out, "Oh, Tate, I just I can't tell you how happy I am. How relieved! I knew he couldn't have done it. But then—" Her words stopped. "Oh, God! What I wanted to say, Tate, I kept something back! Rio was only willing to wait around for so long. We agreed—I made him agree!—to wait three days before he started running again. Today is the third day! Wednesday, at sunset. And it's what now?" He knew she looked at her watch, just as he automatically glanced at his. "It's already two o'clock," she groaned.

"There was a time limit?" he asked flatly.

"I know I should have told you! But I was afraid you'd refuse to help...or try again to make me tell you where he was."

"And what would've happened if things hadn't worked out so conveniently?" he asked stiffly. "What if it had taken another day? Another week to find Joe-Bob? Were you ever gonna let me know?"

"I was trying to tell you earlier...before you interrupt—"

"Enough!" he broke in tightly as anger roiled through him. *Again* she'd taken sides against him. And all for the sake of the cowboy she'd once loved. Maybe *still* loved! He was fooling himself thinking that there could be anything between them. Jodie Parker had picked the man she wanted to be loyal to a long time ago, and it wasn't him! "This is still serious business, Jodie. The Hammonds are on the loose. They've been lying low since they accosted you, didn't spend the night in their motel room. No one's seen 'em. So that means they could be anywhere. And they don't know the truth like we do. As far as they're concerned, Rio's still the killer, and given half a chance—less than half a chance—they'll kill him. So, what I want you to do is stay put. I'll be there in forty-five minutes. Then we can go get him and place him in protective custody, if we have to, to keep him safe. At least until we can convince the Hammonds he's innocent.''

''No!'' she surprised him by saying. ''That's wasting too much time. Where he is, it'll take hours to get to him. And if he sees me with you, he won't come. He'll think I've turned him in. I have to go on my own.''

''No, Jodie.''

''Goodbye, Tate.''

''Jodie! Okay, okay! But if not me, then take someone else—Morgan, because of his training. The Hammonds have already tried to grab you once. They're crazed. There's no telling what they'll do.''

''I told you, I can't take anyone. Rio won't show himself if I do.''

''Let Morgan come partway, then. He can wait while you make the final push. Talk to Rio, let him know it's safe to come in, then Morgan can be sure you get back to the ranch without trouble. By that time I'll be there and I can talk to him, too.''

''Morgan's with Christine and the new baby. I'm hanging up now, Tate.''

''Jodie, *don't!*''

The line disconnected, and Tate fumbled through his index until he found the number for the ranch's main office.

All the while he cursed himself for his bad handling of the situation. It was a textbook example of why a lawman shouldn't let his emotions rule. He had to stay calm, cool and in complete control of his faculties. Not let anything rattle him.

A sentiment he had to repeat to himself yet again when he clumsily misdialed.

JODIE HURRIED down the path to the corrals, paying little heed to her sore knee and hip. As she passed the business office, she saw Rafe inside sitting at his desk. Then she heard the phone ring. Undoubtedly it was Tate, calling to warn him, trying to ensure she did as he directed.

Only, doing things the way he wanted would entail detailed explanations. As far as her family was concerned, she knew nothing about Rio's whereabouts, much less being neck-deep in helping him.

Let Tate handle that particular bit of dirty work for her if he wanted, she thought irritably as she hurried on. It might help defuse the erupting volcano she would face later, but most important, it would give her time now to get away.

As luck would have it, she found a horse already saddled and waiting. She mounted him, thumped her heels against his sides and took off at a gallop. She didn't plan to push the animal hard for long in the heat, just until they were out of sight. Rafe would have no idea where she was going—that she was riding out to the rough country of Big Spur division—and neither did Tate, so he couldn't tell him.

By the time she'd gone a couple of miles, she was grateful for the full water bag that hung on the saddle.

She hadn't thought to herself how badly she would need it.

Her hip was throbbing again, her knee protesting, but still she pressed on. Tate had done what she'd promised Rio he would. He'd learned the truth. And she couldn't let Rio leave thinking he was still being pursued. At one time she'd hated him enough to let that happen, but not now.

Her primary concern at the moment was that he'd jump the gun and leave early. That he wouldn't wait until sunset.

The last portion of the journey was the most difficult. The brush was thicker, the ground craggier. Jodie had to pick her way around and through large rock outcroppings and small ravines. Then up and up, into the foothills.

Finally she spotted the trapper's shack. If you didn't know it was there, you'd miss it. Tucked into the canyon, it was almost fully surrounded by grasses and overgrown bushes, its weathered boards bleached to the same color as the soil. She encouraged the tired horse to move forward, keeping an eye out for Rio.

She didn't see him, though, until she was upon him. He stepped out in front of her, causing the horse to start. Causing *her* to start.

He looked far rougher than when she'd last seen him. His clothes were filthy, his dark blond stubble had turned into a short beard, but it was his eyes that had changed the most. She knew for a fact that Rio was only twenty-nine, yet he had the look of a man twice that age.

He had suffered these past three days, and not

merely because of the harsh conditions. It had been proved he'd told her the truth about Joe-Bob. It only stood to reason he'd also been truthful about his love for Crystal. And Crystal was now lost to him, as was their child.

"Since you're here," he said gruffly, "I suppose that means you've got good news?"

Jodie nodded.

"Well, that's somethin'."

Jodie slid out of the saddle, keeping the horse's reins in her uninjured hand. The blisters had popped shortly after leaving ranch headquarters, but she'd done her best to ignore them.

"Tate found Joe-Bob," she announced simply. "He confirmed your story. So did the others. Just like you said."

Rio's body jerked when she said Tate's name. He hadn't wanted her to confide in him. Still, he repeated, *"Just like I said."*

"So you can come back with me. You don't have to hide out anymore. Everything's cleared with the authorities."

"Who told you all this?" he asked suspiciously.

"Tate."

"Tate, the sheriff."

Jodie gave an impatient sigh. She'd put herself through hell for this guy. Taken a lot of risks. "Yes, Tate, *the sheriff.* It took his connections to find Joe-Bob. I couldn't do it myself. I tried, but it didn't work. I told you that."

"How do we know we can trust him?" he demanded.

"There's no *we* to it. *I* trust him!"

"Sure you do—and a lot more."

His answer made Jodie so angry she kicked dirt on him. And she kept kicking it until he howled in protest and jumped away.

"That is about the most *ungrateful* thing I've ever heard anyone say!" she reproached him. "You come here, ask for my help. Me! The woman you duped! And now that Tate and I have saved your scrawny butt, you're being nasty about it? You make me wish I'd turned you in the first second I saw you! You make me wish I'd—"

Rio raised a hand from a safe distance. "Hey! Hey! It's okay. I apologize. I'm sorry. I—"

"You know what you can do with your apology!" she shot back.

He continued trying to placate her, "I truly am sorry, Jodie. I didn't mean nothin' by it. Not against you. I know you've helped me. Lots! It's— I'm just not used to a sheriff goin' out of his way to do somethin' good for someone like me. That's all."

"So," she said, not particularly mollified, "are you willing to come back? Because there's something else you should know before you go off on your own. The Hammonds are still looking for you. They don't know what Tate's found out, because no one can find them."

He instinctively looked around. "The Hammonds?"

She nodded. "Tate says he'll meet us at headquarters and the two of you can talk."

Rio thought for a moment, then nodded. "All right. Seems I still don't have much of a choice."

Jodie gazed at him intently, unaware of the new maturity that had strengthened her features. "Rio?" she said. "When this is all over, I want you to get the heck out of my life and *stay* out of it."

CHAPTER THIRTEEN

TATE ARRIVED at the Parker Ranch approximately
forty-five minutes after talking to Rafe.

He'd had to reveal a good deal of Jodie's situation
to get Rafe to understand the danger she was facing.
She shouldn't be going anywhere unaccompanied, on
or off the ranch, as long as the Hammonds were on the
loose. Especially not to meet Rio.

Rafe, though bowled over by all he'd been told, had
reacted immediately, telling a cowboy in the ranch office with him, "Cecil, I'm gonna need your help," then
he'd quickly hung up.

Tate didn't hold out much hope that they'd be successful in intercepting her. Between his fumbled dialing and the time it had taken him to fill Rafe in, she'd
probably made a break for it. She'd been bound and
determined to do it her way. And she'd known he
would immediately contact Rafe. She wouldn't have
wasted any time.

Rafe was waiting for him on Mae's front porch, and
Tate knew instantly by the set of Rafe's face that Jodie
had eluded them.

"We musta just missed her," Rafe said in disgust.
"Cecil's horse was all saddled and waitin' for him out
at the corral, and when we got there, he was gone. We

saddled up some other mounts, but by the time we started a search, we couldn't find hide nor hair of her. You sure she didn't give any hints about where she was goin'?''

"Not a one."

Rafe shook his dark head. "It could be too many places for us to go ridin' off half-cocked. Not enough men to cover it. I've given word for the boys to keep a close eye out, though."

"And I've told the deputies watching the roads around here the same thing."

Rafe shot him a hard look. "So what else can we do?"

Tate shrugged, tension eating away at his insides. They'd reached the worst point of any crisis—the sit-and-stew stage, where nothing was left to do but wait.

The housekeeper brought them something cold to drink, but neither man did more than look at it.

"Where's Mae?" Tate asked.

"In town, thank the Lord."

"Jodie thought what she was doing was right," Tate said in her defense. "And as it turned out, it was."

"But it could've been different."

"Sure could."

"Girl always was headstrong. Now she's gone and done this. Mae'll be fit to be tied!"

"She kept an innocent man from being charged with murder."

A flash of anger tightened Rafe's lips. "I just wish she was a little more careful in who she chooses to help." Then, looking curiously at Tate, he asked, "Don't you?"

Tate knew all about catching a suspect off guard—surprise him with an unexpected statement or question and watch the way he reacts. "Sure," he said easily, not letting his emotions show. "She can get into a lot of trouble if she isn't."

"Like she did this time," Rafe agreed.

"Yeah," Tate said, and let the moment fade. If Rafe had suspicions about his feelings for Jodie..well, he could just have them. Tate wasn't going to confirm or deny anything.

The next hour and a half passed with the speed of a glacier. Other Parkers joined them on the porch—LeRoy, Harriet, then Shannon. They came and went as their regular tasks allowed. Once or twice Rafe had to leave to take care of ranch business, and occasionally the children and a puppy ran over to see what they were doing. The more Tate was around them, the more he liked what he saw. They were *the* Parkers of the Parker Ranch, but they were also very nice people. Each had a hard time believing the depth of Jodie's involvement in protecting Rio. Or that because of it, his name had been cleared. Tate told no one about Jodie's run-in with the Hammonds. He felt he'd already said enough.

Word finally arrived from two sources. A cowboy rode into the compound and announced that a pickup truck had been spotted coming across the valley with two people inside, "driving like all get out" toward the compound. And one of them had bright red hair. *Jodie!*

The second source was Tate's police radio. One of his deputies had spotted the Hammonds cruising slowly along the highway that fronted Parker land. Tate told him to keep an eye on them until the other deputy patrolling the highway arrived, then they were to take them into custody and bring them to ranch headquarters. The second deputy responded that he'd heard and had already turned his patrol car around to assist.

Shannon gathered the children in Mae's house with promises of cookies and ice cream in the kitchen.

Everyone else stayed where they were, once again waiting.

AFTER RIO HAD FINISHED gathering his limited possessions from the trapper's shack, he and Jodie had made their way out of the canyon. At times Jodie had ridden the horse, at others—when the going was especially tough—she'd walked, all the while following Rio, who was leading the way to where he'd left his borrowed pickup three days before.

He'd done a good job of hiding it, slipping it into a ravine and covering it with a tarp and plenty of brush. As he'd dug it free, Jodie had seen to the horse. Using Rio's hat as a container, she'd offered the remainder of the water to the animal. He'd drunk thirstily. Then she'd removed the saddle and blanket and rubbed him down with a towel she'd found among Rio's things. Finally she'd patted his neck and removed the bridle. He'd seemed startled at first to be free, but soon remembered his unencumbered youth. When Jodie gave his rump a friendly slap and told him to run off and find his friends, he'd done just that, excited at the prospect of being on his own.

"Whose horse was that?" Rio asked, coming up beside her.

"I'm not sure," Jodie said.

"Hope he's not someone's favorite mount. He's gonna be harder'n hell to catch again."

They watched as the horse whinnied and kicked his rear legs, then took off in a ground-covering trot.

The closer they got to ranch headquarters, the more nervous Rio became. Jodie had insisted on driving for just that reason. She didn't want to have to fight him for the wheel if or when he flipped out.

"I don't know about this, Jodie," he said, his body twitching. "Rafe told me a long time ago not to come back. He's not gonna like seein' me again."

"He's not going to like *anything* about this, Rio."

"So maybe you should let me out right here. I can make my way to the highway and catch a ride from there, and—"

"You're forgetting the Hammonds."

"I'm not forgettin' anything! I just don't want Rafe or Mae gettin' their hands on me!"

"Tate said to bring you to the compound."

"Tate's not Rafe!"

The pens and corrals and cluster of outbuildings came into sight. To discourage him from doing anything foolish, Jodie increased the truck's speed. Dust billowed high into the air as they bounced along the cleared but uneven roadway.

Tate's patrol car was parked in front of Mae's house and people were on the porch. Close to three hours had passed since Jodie had talked to Tate. He'd had plenty of time to get there and plenty of time to fill everyone in.

Jodie suffered her own qualms as she pulled the truck to a stop, her gaze sweeping over all those who waited. Tate and LeRoy looked grim, Rafe's temper was obviously smoldering, and Harriet, holding the screen door open, appeared anxious and concerned. Mercifully Mae and her father had yet to return.

Rio had stopped talking after his earlier outburst, and when she glanced at him now, he looked frozen. All the more so when Rafe jerked into motion and strode down the steps, not stopping until he was outside the passenger door. Without a word he opened it, reached in and dragged Rio out.

Rio whimpered high in his throat, his arms hanging at his sides, completely unable to help himself.

Jodie jumped out of the truck. "No, Rafe!" she cried.

Tate rushed off the porch. Both had been caught off guard by Rafe's sudden action.

Rio hung limply in Rafe's grip, his shirtfront bunched near his throat. Rafe glared at him and said softly, "I thought I told you not to set foot back in Texas. Are you reckless, boy, or just plain stupid?"

"Easy, Rafe," Tate said, catching his arm.

Two more patrol cars drove up and stopped behind the truck. One by one the deputies stepped out.

"Where you want 'em?" the nearest deputy called to Tate.

"Bring 'em over here," Tate called back, "and keep 'em cuffed!"

Rafe's grip on Rio eased, to be replaced by Tate's

quick neck hold. "If you know what's good for you, you'll keep real still and real quiet for a piece," he warned. "Rafe, watch him," he instructed the other man.

Jodie's gaze slid away from Tate as he turned. She knew he was still angry with her. She wouldn't even chance a close look into Rafe's set face.

The Hammonds were extracted from the patrol cars—Rufus from the first, his sons from the second. They were already highly out of sorts, protesting their treatment to the deputies who accompanied them. Then they saw Rio. One bellowed, another cursed, and all three fought hard against their restraints.

Tate took charge of Rufus while his deputy hurried to help his counterpart contain the brothers. Both brothers ended up on the ground, their cheeks pressed into the grass.

Rufus Hammond behaved like an enraged bear. Tate let him fuss and fume and strain until he was temporarily spent. "Are you through?" he asked calmly.

It took Rufus a moment to become coherent. Finally he sputtered, "What the hell's goin' on here? Why are we bein' held like this when he's the one who—"

"I'll tell you if you shut up a minute. Are you gonna shut up? Or are you gonna keep talkin' and fightin' and makin' life all around difficult for everybody?"

Rufus drove forward again and Tate gave his bound arms a quick upward jerk. Rufus cried out in fury.

"I asked nice," Tate said mildly.

Rufus roared another protest, before his head slumped forward in grudging compliance.

Tate signaled his men to help the brothers up. Nasty

resentful looks were thrown around, but they, too, were more subdued.

"All right," Tate said. "Let's get this over with. Rio Walsh has an alibi for the night your daughter was beaten, Mr. Hammond. An alibi that's been checked and double-checked and it holds true. He didn't do it."

Rufus Hammond's head snapped up, his mouth curling into an ugly snarl.

Rio tried to hide behind Rafe, but Rafe wouldn't allow it. He grabbed the back of his collar and made him face his accuser.

"He was playing cards in a town near you," Tate went on, "where a ropin' contest was bein' held. Do you remember it?"

"That still don't mean he didn't do it!" the younger of the brothers cried.

"It does when everyone he played cards with says he was there all night," Tate shot back.

"They're his friends! He coulda *told* 'em what to say!" the younger brother countered.

"Only one was his friend."

"He coulda *paid* 'em!"

"With what? He's not rich, and most of the money he had that night he won from them. What man is gonna risk giving a false statement on a murder case, turning himself into an accessory, just to get his gambling money back? We're talkin' twenty years here in exchange for a few piddlin' dollars. And three of these men didn't know Rio Walsh from Adam! Uh-uh. I don't think so."

"It's the truth!" Rio burst out. "I never hurt her! I *loved* her!"

"You loved the money you thought was comin' her way!" Rufus Hammond roared. "You…" A string of hard-edged venom spewed from Rufus Hammond's lips. Rio twitched at each increasingly abusive epithet as if receiving a physical pounding.

Tate broke in shortly with, "That's enough!" Then when Rufus didn't stop, he repeated more authoritatively, "That's *enough!* I've been givin' you a lot of room, Mr. Hammond, because of your situation, but there are children inside who shouldn't be hearin' this, not to mention these women."

"Room, you say!" Rufus snarled. "If that's the case, then what am I doin' with these things on?" He turned sideways and rattled his handcuffs. "Me and my boys haven't done a thing! Either charge us with somethin' or let us out of 'em!"

Tate was not the least bit intimidated. He turned pointedly to Jodie and said, "Here's another chance to change your mind. You sure you don't want to press charges?"

Jodie could feel her family's attention turn on her, could almost hear their minds working. *There was something else she hadn't told them?* "No, let them go. As long as they don't try to hurt Rio."

"You heard the lady," Tate said flatly, turning back to Rufus. "As long as you don't try to hurt…Rio."

Rufus's eyes narrowed as he mulled over his answer.

Tate simplified things for him. "Because if you do," he continued, adding his own admonition, *"I'm* gonna charge you. And believe me, I use all my spare time thinkin' up things I can do to make people's lives miserable, people who irritate me, especially people who give me their word and then break it."

"All right! All right!" Rufus agreed belligerently. But when Tate made no move to free him, he changed his tone to something slightly more amenable. "All right."

"And the boys?" Tate asked, extracting the key.

"What I say goes for them, too. They know that."

Tate freed Rufus while his deputies did the same for the brothers. Each lawman remained on alert.

Tate said, "You can check with Sheriff Preston if you want. By now he's probably talked to everyone involved. He's some kind of relative of yours, isn't he?"

"Yeah," Rufus said, rubbing his wrists.

"Then you'll trust him when he gives you the same information I just did."

Rufus frowned and motioned to the still-cowering Rio. "If he didn't do it, who did?"

"That's somethin' I don't know," Tate said.

Rufus Hammond's tiny eyes moved from Parker to Parker, settling longest on Jodie. He looked at her for a long time. Finally he warned, "You better watch that girl if *he* stays around. My Crystal was a good girl. Never did a thing wrong in her life. Then *he* came to the ranch and got her pregnant. You're not denyin' that, are you?" he demanded of Rio. "That baby was yours?"

"Y-yes," Rio stammered. "And that's why *I* wanna know who did it, too! I *loved* her! We were gonna get married! That's the reason I was playin' cards. So we could get enough money together to...Then when I got back to the ranch and found out she'd been hurt, one of the boys told me you thought I did it. So I took off!''

"And never gave her another thought! Never mind what she might be goin' through."

"I thought about her all the time! I just couldn't do anythin'. But I didn't think she was hurt that bad. I—"

The younger round-faced brother lunged forward, evading the deputy's reach. "But she *was* hurt that bad, wasn't she, you little—" He jerked Rio off his feet.

"Phil!" His father intervened sharply.

"I just don't believe 'em, Dad! It's a trick to make us leave! Crystal never would've agreed to marry him! He musta raped her for her to get pregnant...and then she was afraid to tell us what happened! It had to be rape! She'd never—"

Rio clamped his fingers over those holding him and pried them loose. "She was afraid, all right!" he blurted as he jumped back, panting. "Of *you!*"

"Shut up!"

Rio began to circle him, tired at last of being made the goat. "She was! She told me she was! She also told me how you used to look at her, how you'd watch her every move—"

"I was just bein' a good brother!"

"*Step*brother!" Rio said. "And that ain't the way she said you looked at her, either. So if anybody raped anybody, it was you! Crystal came to me 'cause she wanted to, not 'cause she—"

Phil struck with the speed of a snake, knocking Rio to the ground. But when he reared back to deliver a hard kick to the ribs, Rafe grabbed him, while Rio scrabbled back to his feet.

"That's right!" Rio taunted, growing angry. "She said you even came into her room some nights sayin' you just thought you'd adjust the window shade, or you wanted to check on a noise you thought you heard, but she wasn't fooled." He tilted his head. "You know why she was in such a hurry to get married? 'Cause she wanted to get away from *you!*"

"What's this?" Rufus Hammond said, turning pale.

Rio stuck his hands in his back jeans pockets and rocked on his heels. "Yeah, you heard me. You didn't know about it, though, did you? But if she'd said anythin', would you've believed her? Your own son makin' a beeline for your daughter, or your 'good as' daughter?"

Color returned with a rush to Rufus's face. His expression turned mean, his mouth a thin line. "Is what he sayin' true?" he demanded of his younger son.

Jodie wanted to look away but couldn't. It all seemed too private to be played out on a public stage. But it was the Hammonds, or at least, one of them, who'd pressed the issue, insisting that Tate wasn't telling the truth. She examined the younger brother curiously. Up till now Phil had been the quieter of the two. Hanging back, not putting himself forward. Leaving the belligerence to his older sibling, Tom. But Phil was sweating now, his elbows caught in Rafe's strong arms. He wasn't going anywhere and he knew it.

"*Is it?*" Rufus roared.

The antagonism on Phil's face faded fast. He moved from aggression to contrition to misery all in the space of a few seconds. He was a big man, but everything about him seemed to get smaller. Then he started to cry. Great racking sobs shook his body. "I didn't mean it," he whined in a wet whisper. "I just wanted to talk to her and she wouldn't listen! She—"

Rufus stepped closer, his low voice ominous. "Are you sayin' what I think you're sayin'?"

Phil Hammond shrank even more. "Daddy, please—"

"You killed her?"

"I didn't mean to! I loved her."

Rufus smashed a fist into his son's face even as Rafe tried to twist him away. Phil Hammond screamed in pain. Then Tom broke from his stupor to join in the attack.

Tate pushed Jodie toward the porch, to keep her free from harm, then he waded into the fight, as did his deputies. Moments later it was over, with all three men under control.

Rio had jumped onto the porch with Jodie. When she realized he was right behind her holding on to her, she quickly shook him off. But not before Tate had seen them together.

Shannon came running from the back of Mae's house. "What is it? What's happening? I heard someone scream!"

Harriet answered her. "Everything's okay. Don't worry." Then, "Don't let the kids come out."

"I gave them a second helping of everything," Shannon said, breathing her relief that no one, particularly Rafe, was hurt. "That should keep them busy for a while.'' She looked around at the captured men. ''What's going on?''

''I'll tell you everything later,'' Harriet promised.

Jodie turned away, no longer listening. The full import of what had occurred was just beginning to hit her. Phil Hammond had confessed to killing his own stepsister? To beating her so viciously, so savagely, that she'd lost both the child she was carrying and her own life. And all because he ''loved'' her. Because...he was jealous.

She felt more than a little sick to her stomach.

He'd then been content to let Rio take the blame, which might have worked if she hadn't agreed to help or if Tate had turned a deaf ear to her plea.

The melee in the front yard started to sort itself out. Phil Hammond was taken into custody, the handcuffs back in place, while the remaining Hammonds worked to collect themselves.

''Take him in, put him in a cell, get the doc to look at his cuts and I'll be there shortly,'' Tate told one of his deputies. To the other he said offhandedly, ''Hang around a bit.''

As mean and disagreeable as Rufus Hammond was, it was difficult to look at him and not think of his shattered life.

Tate inquired evenly, ''You want to get your son a local lawyer?''

''Who?'' Rufus inquired flatly.

''The lawyer in Del Norte's pretty good. Her name's—''

''I meant, get *who* a lawyer. I only have one son and he's right here. He don't need a lawyer.''

Tom Hammond stared hard at the ground.

Tate nodded. "Sure. Okay. I guess I can see that."

The deputy started to take Phil away. "Daddy?" he called plaintively. "I didn't mean to hurt her none. Everything just…"

Rufus turned his back and made sure Tom did likewise.

Nothing was said as the deputy put his prisoner into the patrol car and drove off.

Moments later Rufus Hammond cleared his throat. "I, ah, owe everyone here an apology," he said stiffly. "If there's any hurt feelin's, I'm sorry. The way things turned out…" He swallowed, then shook his head, unable to go on.

Tate motioned to his deputy. "Why don't you take these people back to their truck," he said quietly. "Then maybe help 'em find their way to the main highway. We're sorry about your losses, Mr. Hammond. And if you change your mind and want to see—"

"We're goin' straight back to Colorado," Rufus interrupted him. "We got a girl to bury."

They ducked into the back seat of the patrol car and the second deputy drove away.

"Whew!" Rafe breathed after a moment in which no one seemed able to move. "That's pretty well one of the worst things I've ever had to witness."

LeRoy nodded, while Harriet buried her face in his shirt.

Rio swaggered off the porch. "I was pretty sure it was him all along," he bragged. "I didn't want to say nothin', but—"

Tate looked at him as if he were a worm. "You still here?" he asked.

Rio held out his hand. "I wanna thank you," he said grandly. "Jodie told me you found Joe-Bob."

Tate seemed of two minds whether or not to accept. He finally did, but the handshake was brief.

Jodie hurried down from the porch. She'd seen the way Rafe was glaring at Rio and knew it wouldn't be long before he'd toss him off the ranch. And even though she'd just as soon not draw attention to herself, knowing what would follow, she felt she had to intervene. "Rio, you know where the bunkhouse is if you want a shower. And I'm sure you could talk one of the boys out of a change of clothes."

Rio looked down at himself. "Yeah, I could sure use one."

"Yeah, you stink!" Rafe agreed. But everyone knew he was referring to more than Rio's ripe body odor.

Tate shifted position, drawing Jodie's attention. She knew he was angry—because of the way she'd gone against his directive, because she hadn't told him about the time limit, because he seemed to think that she and Rio were closer to each other than they really were. She wanted to speak privately to him, to explain. But there was no chance of that at the moment. She could feel her family's pent-up questions bursting to be asked. There was no way she and Tate could go off alone together. And no way, from the look of him, that Tate would even agree.

"I'd better get back to town," he said. "I have to make a call or two and see to the county's newest guest."

"What'll happen to him?" Harriet asked.

"Sheriff Preston'll probably send somebody to get him, or he might even come himself. Either way, it won't be our worry for long."

"Poor girl," Harriet whispered, still leaning against LeRoy. "She must have had a terrible life."

A horn tooted repeatedly as the black Cadillac tore down the road, then turned into the compound driveway. Mae and Gib were returning.

"Tell Miss Parker I'll talk to her another time," Tate said, climbing into his patrol car.

"Will do," Rafe said, then added, "Hey, Tate, thanks. We appreciate everything you did."

"Yes," Jodie said softly.

"Sure do!" Rio added.

Tate's brown eyes went from Jodie to Rio and back again. Then with a tight little nod, he drove off.

Almost at the same instant the black Cadillac rocked to a halt. And after only a little trouble getting out, Mae stood by the front fender, ready to stare everyone down. Even with wisps of white hair trailing from the normally impeccable knot on top her head and her increasing reliance on a cane, she still cut a formidable figure. Her dark eyes whipped round them. "Well, what's happened?" she snapped. "We met two county patrol cars comin' from this way, then we see another one parked out front, and it leaves before we can get here. Was it Tate? What did he—"

Her barrage of questions instantly broke off when she spotted Rio and did a double take. Her gaze had touched on him before, but his presence was so unexpected it hadn't registered.

The moment might have been comical in other circumstances. Mae's eyes widened as she realized just who Rio was. She gasped, then in a voice that could cause shivers to run up and down any listener's spine, she demanded, *"What in heaven's name is that worthless sack of misery who calls himself a cowboy doin' here in my front yard?"*

CHAPTER FOURTEEN

"THAT'S THE MOST foolhardy thing I've ever known anyone to do!" Mae railed from the comfort of the overstuffed sofa in her living room after the family moved indoors. Rio had slunk off to the bunkhouse immediately after Mae learned of his exoneration to scrub the days of dirt and grime from himself. "How could you, Jodie?" Mae continued. "How *could* you? I don't think I'll *ever* understand!"

"What gets me, Jodie," Rafe said, joining in, "is that you were doin' it all along! When did Rio first contact you? You didn't know he was here when Tate came to tell us about him, did you? You sure acted surprised."

"And what was it Tate said about you pressing charges against the Hammonds?" LeRoy asked. "Why would you want to do somethin' like that? Unless..."

Jodie had completely forgotten her ailments. The pain in her knee and hip was fading, and the blisters on her hand were barely noticeable.

Shannon had come in from the kitchen to sit with Harriet on the second sofa. Both women looked at her with dismay and compassion. Neither had condemned her.

Her father, who'd been just as shocked as everyone else, stood just a little outside the group.

Jodie cleared her throat, her first chance to speak. "I didn't do it to spite anyone or to go against what you said. I helped him because I believed him. I told you I did."

"Yes!" Mae fired back. "But you didn't tell us everything, did you?"

"I only learned about it after the barbecue. That's when he found me and asked—"

"He asked you to hide him?" Rafe interrupted.

"He asked for my help." She gazed at each of them, silently appealing for their understanding. "He's changed. He's not the same person you used to know. He was only twenty-two then. He—"

"He was old enough to know better!" Mae snapped.

"I never said he was perfect," Jodie retorted. "Or is. Just that he's different."

"What you did was against the law, Missy," Mae came back. "It's a wonder Tate didn't arrest you, too!"

A light tap sounded on the door, and when Shannon answered it, Rio stepped hesitantly inside. As if to add credence to Jodie's words, he looked different than he had a short half hour before. Clean, with fresh clothes, his hair combed, his beard shaved and his mustache trimmed, he might have been a neighbor's son come to pay a call. But he wasn't given that kind of reception.

Rafe jerked to his feet. Mae strained forward on the sofa.

"You're pressin' your luck comin' into this house, aren't you?" Rafe drawled darkly.

Rio swallowed, then motioned to Jodie. "I just wondered... I'd like to talk to Jodie for a minute. I wanna thank—"

"You can do it from where you are," Rafe growled. "Then you can get goin'. You have about five minutes to cart your mangy hide off this ranch."

Rio ducked his chin nervously and worked his old black Stetson in his hands. He glanced at Jodie.

Jodie jumped up, angry that what should be her decision was being taken away from her, but she kept her voice studiously calm as she countered, "I'll talk to you, Rio. And we'll talk for as long as we want. This is either my home or it isn't." Her gaze moved around the room. "Everyone's also forgetting that Rio is an innocent man. He didn't hurt that Hammond girl, so he shouldn't be treated like a criminal."

She waited for someone to contradict her. No one did.

She followed Rio out onto the front porch, feeling everyone's eyes on her as she did. Once outside she drew a deep breath. Contesting the conventional Parker wisdom, especially when they presented a united front, was never easy. As a youngster she'd fought against the authority of her elders—mostly Mae—and sometimes even succeeded, but she'd always felt herself in the wrong. As if she was a spoiled child, misbehaving. Now she didn't. She had a right to feel the way she did and to do whatever it was she wanted to do. They were just going to have to learn to trust her judgment. Mae especially.

Rio whistled low under his breath. "Wow! That took guts!"

"Let's go out in the courtyard," Jodie suggested.

Several lawn chairs were in place under the trees, but Jodie ignored them. She wanted to talk to Rio, but she didn't want the talk to be extended.

"Jodie," he said, still holding on to his hat, "I truly do want to thank you for all you did. You saved my life."

"Tate did that really."

"He wouldn't have helped if you hadn't asked him."

Jodie shrugged.

He stuffed his hat on his head, grabbed her hand and held it against his chest. "From the bottom of my heart I want you to know I'm a changed man. I used to think only of myself, nobody else. If there was a cute little gal around, that was all I lived for. But not any more. You changed me. Crystal changed me. Crystal most of all, I guess." His face brightened. "I wish you two could've met! You'd've liked each other. She was..." The brightness faded and a bleak look took its place. "I'd like to go to her funeral, if Rufus Hammond'll let me. If not, I'll wait around until after they leave, then go pay my respects." He lapsed into silence, obviously thinking about what lay ahead.

"You're going back to Colorado?" Jodie asked, removing her hand from his grasp.

"I have to take my friend's truck back."

"Then what?"

"Look for work. Not with the Hammonds of course."

"In Colorado?"

Rio shrugged. "For sure not Texas! Rafe'd track me down if I did that."

"I can get him to change his mind."

"They'll think you're sweet on me again," he teased.

"Rio, seven years is a long time. Too long to hold a grudge. I was just as much at fault for what happened between us as you were. I used you almost as much as you used me. The only difference was, I made plans for the future."

"If I'd married anybody back then, it would've been you!"

Jodie smiled. "Sure it would."

"Naw! I mean it!" His smile widened, the old Rio making another comeback.

Jodie cocked her head. "Just how many times have you used that lucky coin since you used it with me?"

He dug in his pocket and brought out his key chain. The silver coin dangled from its loop. "Tell you what," he said, pulling it off. "I'm gonna give it to you—for old time's sake." He handed it to her. "Take it," he urged. "Then, if you ever get into any kind of trouble—hopefully not the kind of trouble I was in— you just send it to me and I'll come runnin'!" He smiled until she took it. "I wonder," he said quietly and with as much sincerity as he was capable of "do you think we could be friends? I'd like it if we were. Friends, now, nothin' else. Not unless you—"

Jodie slipped the coin into her jeans pocket. "How about we just take this one step at a time? But it can never go beyond friendship, because I...I think I'm in love with someone else. So..."

"Tate Connelly," Rio said. Then, at her surprised expression he explained, "I saw the way you looked at him."

Jodie gave a half nod, but didn't answer.

They parted a moment later. Friends, but not friends. Odd confidants from a fractured past. Jodie had wanted to shake hands, but Rio wasn't satisfied until he leaned close to kiss the side of her mouth.

"You always were a good kisser," he said.

"Drop me a line. Let me know what you're up to," she called after him.

He tooted the truck's horn and waved as he pulled out of the driveway.

Jodie watched him go. Who would have thought their relationship would end this way? She doubted she'd ever hear from him again. And that would be fine with her.

She walked slowly back into the house, bracing for what waited. She would meet the inquiry head-on, with her chin up, her back straight and the light of confidence in her eyes.

"I'm sure Tate told you everything there was to tell," she said once she'd rejoined them. "But if you insist, I'll go over it again. What would you like to know?"

In the pause that followed Gib moved close and put his arm around her shoulders. He looked at the others. "Don't you all think she's been through enough? Do we really have to ask more questions? We know what happened. She helped save Rio's sorry ass and now he's gone. He is, isn't he?" he asked Jodie.

She gazed into her father's dark eyes and saw the

warmth of unconditional love. In that moment she couldn't have loved him more. She nodded. "Yes."

He smiled. She'd noticed a few days back that he didn't chew as much gum as he used to. Maybe as he'd gained confidence in his painting, he didn't feel so emotionally exposed in his everyday life, and he'd been able to conquer the nervous habit. She rested her cheek against his shoulder.

"There is one thing," Mae said stiffly. She seemed the only one still wanting a hearing. "What LeRoy said earlier—about pressing charges against the Hammonds. Is that why you were limping last night? You pretended nothing was wrong, but somethin' was. Did they hurt you?"

Rafe, who'd settled back in his chair content to follow Gib's lead, grew tense. "You were hurt?" he asked.

Jodie wasn't about to tell them everything. The Parker men could easily take it into their heads to catch up to the Hammonds and vent their displeasure. "It wasn't all that much," she said. "They wanted to talk to me, I didn't want to talk, and I ended up slipping. I hurt my leg a bit, that's all."

"They knocked you down?" Mae demanded, looking fierce.

"I fell."

Mae's frown showed she didn't believe her.

"Where were you when this happened?" Rafe asked.

"Outside the hospital, getting coffee. The hospital cafeteria was closed, so I went to a café down the street." Her explanation petered out.

Mae's fierce look deepened. "You left the hospital—*alone*—when you knew—"

"I'd forgotten!" Jodie defended. "Driving Christine, I forgot everything!"

"It *was* a hair-raising experience," Harriet contributed, trying to help.

Mae waited for Jodie to say something more. But Jodie couldn't. She'd used up all the energy her body had stored for the day. Too much tension, too much worry, too much emotion. She had nothing left to argue with.

Gib, sensitive to her needs, said firmly, "I'm takin' her home, Aunt Mae. Any more questions are gonna have to wait till tomorrow."

Mae gave a dismissing motion with her cane, but Gib had already started for the door. This time he hadn't waited for her permission.

Her father carried her the last steps to their house, then, after she'd quickly changed for bed, returned to her room to tuck her in. "How many years has it been since I've done this?" he questioned softly, sitting on the edge of the bed.

"A long time," Jodie murmured.

He adjusted the cover under her chin and ruffled her bright hair. "Do I have to tell you to sleep tight?"

She shook her head. "I can barely keep my eyes open."

It made her feel all warm inside to have her father's undivided attention. She'd missed these infrequent moments from her childhood. She'd missed them even then, when she didn't have them.

He got up to switch off the lamp and was ready to leave when Jodie said, "Daddy...I love you."

"I know you do."

"And?" It was important to her to hear the words. She needed to hear them from him.

Her father hesitated, not because he was unsure or because it wasn't true, but because saying it was difficult for him. "Yes, little girl," he said at last, "I love you, too."

Then he slipped out the door and closed it behind him.

Tears sprang to Jodie's eyes and one rolled onto her pillow. She smiled, sniffed, then fell instantly asleep.

IT GALLED TATE to leave Jodie and Rio together. He knew the Parkers were going to make hanging around the ranch a problem for him—they disliked him intensely—but it was Jodie's feelings that counted.

He remembered how he'd felt when, after pulling the Hammonds off each other, he'd glanced up to see Jodie and Rio standing together, looking for all the world like the cover on one of those romance novels—two lovers, bravely facing the world, the hero's hands tightly clasping the heroine's shoulders, drawing her back against him. He'd wanted to pull them apart, too!

All the way into town Tate thought about what he'd like to do to Rio Walsh. Cocky little... It was a good thing no women or children were privy to what was in his mind, because then he'd have to censor himself just as he had Rufus Hammond.

What if Rio was to get work as a hired hand on one

of the surrounding ranches? What if he and Jodie took up where they left off? They certainly looked friendly enough. Where did that leave *him?*

He was in a foul mood when he walked into the station. He didn't say anything to anyone and barely heard what was said to him.

From the way he felt you'd think he was in love with her.

"Oh, hell!" he growled, shutting the office door. It was fortunate his mother was off duty. She'd probably have read him like a crystal ball.

Was he in love with Jodie? Tate raked a hand over his close-cropped hair. He'd never been in love before. Not like this, if that was what *this* was. So how was he supposed to know? He liked her, wanted to be around her, wanted to get to know her better, wanted to…

To help keep his thoughts off Jodie, he dialed the sheriff's office in Colorado and found that Sheriff Preston had kept late hours that evening, as well.

"Got some good news and some bad news," Tate said levelly, aware of the bombshell he was about to drop in the other man's lap. "I found out who killed that girl of yours up there, and it's somethin' you're not goin' to like to hear. Seems Phil Hammond had some strong feelings for her and didn't take too well to the idea that she was expectin' Rio Walsh's baby. He confessed what he'd done in front of his dad and his brother and most near everyone who lives on the Parker Ranch. I have Phil in custody in my jail. His dad and brother are on the way home—they don't want to have anythin' to do with him. Won't even see to gettin' him a lawyer. So, how do you want to handle it from now on? When do you want to come get him?''

There was a stunned silence. Tate had to repeat some points, but finally Bill Preston put together what he wanted to do. His plans satisfied Tate and Tate soon hung up.

In a few minutes he needed to check on his newest prisoner. After that, he was going home.

Then he remembered his mother—and his promise that they would talk.

Might as well get it over with, he thought tiredly, and gave her a quick call to let her know he was on his way.

"I JUST STOPPED BY to see what you needed, Mom, then I've got to go. It's been a long day." Tate knew darn well what his mother wanted: to talk about Jodie. It wasn't what *he* wanted, but he didn't see how he could avoid it unless he avoided her.

"I heard what happened out at the Parker Ranch," she began.

"Yeah, it was somethin'."

"So Rio Walsh is a free man?"

"I don't have anything to hold him on."

"But you wish you did?" his mother guessed.

Tate rubbed the back of his neck. "Is this all comin' to something, Mom? Because if it's not…"

Emma patted the chair across from her. "Sit down, Tate," she requested softly.

"I want to get home, Mom."

She smiled. "Just for a few minutes. You can spare me a few minutes, can't you?"

Tate sat, feeling totally ill at ease.

"I heard something about that fall of Jodie's," she stated. "I heard three men tried to kidnap her and you put a stop to it. Is that true?"

"Who told you?"

"Is it true?"

Tate frowned. "Yes, but it's not something I want put around."

"Why not?"

"Because Jodie doesn't want her family to find out about it. She doesn't want to cause any more hard feelings. So I'm goin' to ask that you not tell anyone, Mom, and that you tell whoever told you not to say anything, either."

"A number of people saw it happen. I don't think you can keep it a secret."

Tate grimaced.

His mother watched him carefully. "Just how much has she come to mean to you, Tate? The other day, at your house, I sensed—"

"She doesn't mean anything to me," he denied.

Emma arched a brow and reminded him, "This is your mother you're talking to."

Tate frowned, then shook his head, admitting, "I don't know. Everything would be a whole lot easier if I did, but I don't."

"I've also heard something else," Emma said. "I've heard you've been offered a position on some kind of special state task force and you're not sure if you're going to take it."

"Has Jack been talking to you?" Tate demanded.

"It's not because of me, is it? You aren't unsure

about taking it because of my medical situation, are you? Because I'm fine now. I've learned to manage this disease. I love having you nearby, but I'll be fine if you decided to move away tomorrow. The only reason I had trouble before was that I didn't know I had it. Tate, it was bad enough when you gave up your job in Dallas to move back here, but I'd really be upset if I thought…''

"It's partly that," he admitted, "but a lot of other things, too."

She went quiet for a moment, while he regretted having spoken.

"I don't want you to consider me for a minute," she said finally. "You make up your mind purely for your own wants and desires. Just remember—I wouldn't be alone. I have loads of friends. *And* an active social life. You didn't know that I've been taking square-dancing lessons, did you? Or that Mark Lovell has been taking me around."

Mark Lovell. Chief Lovell! Tate was surprised.

Emma grinned. "It's nothing serious and never will be. But we're both without partners and thought we could have some fun together. He's my square-dancing buddy."

Tate smiled. "When did *this* start?"

"A little over a month ago."

"I never knew a thing."

"You've been too busy. Tate, is it the sheriff's job that's holding you back?"

"Well, it does look a little funny to be thinkin' about leaving so soon. I only took office a year and a half ago. How long was Jack sheriff? Thirty years?''

"But you're not Jack."

Tate frowned. "No. And I'm not my dad, either."

Emma looked at him closely. "What does your father have to do with this?"

"I've been trying to figure out what he'd do if he were in my situation. And I don't think he'd leave. He probably wouldn't even consider it."

His mother placed a hand over his and said softly, "You said it yourself—you aren't your father." She went to get a photograph from the piano and handed it to Tate. It was one he'd seen numerous times. Dan Connelly, dressed in what passed as a county uniform twenty years before—white Western shirt with a five-pointed Texas star pinned over the left pocket. The exact same badge Tate wore now. Dan's handsome face was smiling with open friendliness.

"Tate," Emma said, "your daddy was a special man and a good lawman. And he loved the work he did here. Do you truly think he'd want you to follow in his footsteps if you weren't happy doing it?"

"I'm happy!"

"Are you? What about all that special training you've had? How much do you use it?"

"I use it," Tate defended.

"Do you enjoy looking after the jail?"

Tate grunted. "No person in his right mind would enjoy that."

"What about the long hours?"

"I don't mind hard work. You know I don't."

"Do you have any time left for a private life? What if, say, you wanted to take a little time to trail after Jodie Parker—" Tate made a sound she ignored

"—could you do it? A picnic, something simple. Could you invite her out and not be interrupted? And remember, I know the hours you put in."

That was the trouble. He couldn't lie. He couldn't even fudge the truth. If his mother didn't know first-hand, from having taken and delivered the calls herself, she could easily find out. "Are you telling me I should take the job?" he demanded.

Emma set the photograph back in its proper place. "No. I'd never presume to do that. It has to be your decision. I'm just trying to get you to see you don't owe anything to anyone. Your dad gave his life for this county. You don't have to do the same."

Tate drew a quick breath.

His mother turned to face him. "I have a feeling Jack's getting a little antsy out on his place. I saw him the other day. He seems…restless. You should talk to him."

IT WAS AFTER TEN O'CLOCK before Tate unlocked his own front door and let himself into the house he did little more than camp out in.

Was it because nothing about his job—both as deputy and as sheriff—had seemed permanent to him? Was that why he'd hesitated to put down solid roots?

But maybe all he needed to put down roots was the right woman in his life. Jack had had Maureen. His father had had his mother. He could have…Jodie.

But could he? Here, in Del Norte? In this house? As his wife?

He laughed with very little humor and sat down for

a minute in the recliner. Only, when his eyes fell shut, it was morning before they opened again.

JODIE SAT UP, breathing hard. Something was chasing her, about to get her. She had to— Suddenly she realized where she was—in bed, in her father's house, on the ranch, safe and sound. The terrible menace existed only in a dream.

She fell back against the warm sheets, panting. She was hot. Was that what had disturbed her sleep? Then memory came flooding back. Rio, Phil Hammond, *Tate*... It was a wonder she'd slept at all!

She checked the time—2:00 a.m. Was she the only person awake on the ranch?

She longed to call Tate. Just to hear his voice. But would he talk to her, as angry as he was? Especially at two in the morning?

She'd told Rio she was in love with Tate. Why? As a way to keep Rio at arm's length? Or because Rio was leaving and she never expected to hear from him again—and she'd wanted to test out saying the words?

Rio was oddly easy to talk to about such things. Maybe because he viewed society's rules as restrictions placed on *other* people.

Jodie had been governed by rules all her life. Mae believed firmly in right and wrong and saw little in between. Rio existed in the shades of gray. He'd spent his whole life there.

She switched on the bedside lamp and flipped open the lid of a lacquered box, her favored cache for her most prized possessions since childhood. She withdrew Rio's lucky coin and, turning it this way and that, let the bas-relief carvings catch the light. Was she wrong to have accepted it?

No. It was a part of her life, just as Rio was. She could no more deny either of them their place than Phil Hammond could change the fact that he had destroyed the person he loved and in so doing cut himself off permanently from his family.

She could almost feel sorry for Phil Hammond. Almost. Until she thought of the young woman he'd killed.

Rio had said she and Crystal would have been friends. Might they have been?

Jodie switched off the lamp after returning the coin to the box, then lay back to stare up at the darkened ceiling. For a time she kept her mind purposefully blank, until an earlier thought could no longer be denied.

She'd told Rio she was in love with Tate.

So…was she?

CHAPTER FIFTEEN

"LOOK! A POSTCARD from Darlene and Thomas!" Harriet exclaimed as she brought the mail to Mae's house. "From Alaska. She says it's absolutely beautiful there. And they're having loads of fun."

"Thomas, on a sea cruise," Mae said, shaking her head.

Harriet laughed, still reading from the card. "Darlene says Thomas won the captain's costume contest—he dressed up like a gangster. Can you believe it?"

Mae was speechless. All she could do was continue to shake her head.

Harriet looked at Jodie and Shannon and winked. The morning so far had not been easy. Everyone else had decided to put the incident behind them, particularly when they found out that Jodie didn't care that Rio had gone back to Colorado. But it still rankled Mae. She'd said less than ten words to Jodie since first seeing her, having gone out of her way not to say more.

It had been Shannon's idea that they pay a call on Mae to try to smooth the way to reconciliation. The attempt didn't seem to be working. That was why it was so surprising when, in the early afternoon, Mae called Jodie over to request that *she* drive her to Little

Springs to visit Christine and the new baby. She'd received word only a short time before that Morgan had brought them home.

"Daddy's available," Jodie said, unsure if Mae was aware of it.

"Of course he is, but I'm askin' *you*. Are you going to turn me down?"

"No."

"Then be back here in an hour with the Cadillac."

Jodie nodded. Her great-aunt hadn't cracked a smile. Instead, she'd worn her fierce matriarchal look and carried herself with distant dignity.

An hour later Jodie waited outside Mae's house, the Cadillac's engine running. Her father had told her often enough that Mae didn't like to be kept waiting.

Had only two days gone by since she'd rushed Christine into town in this car? It seemed longer.

Mae emerged from the house and what Jodie saw made her eyes widen. Her great-aunt had taken a great deal of care with her appearance, wearing a soft pink linen dress, short white gloves, black dress shoes and a narrow-brimmed straw hat with a matching pink band. She came directly to the car and slid into the back seat, pointedly maintaining her distance.

"Aunt Mae," Jodie said, "I really wish you'd—"

"I'd rather not talk about it," Mae said shortly.

"But we can't go on like this!"

"Shouldn't you have thought about that before you did what you did?" She tapped the floorboard with the tip of her cane, signaling her impatience to be off.

"I *did* think about it," Jodie said, putting the car into drive.

"I said I don't want to talk."

Her great-aunt's intransigence was becoming irritating. "Aren't you the person who told me to pick a direction and stick to it? Well, I did. I decided to help Rio—and I was right!"

"Only a child needs to be right all the time."

Jodie gritted her teeth. She had a mind to stop the car and refuse to go on until her father agreed to switch places. Obviously Mae had asked her to drive so she could take potshots at her. Talk about a person who always needed to be right!

"Anyway," Mae continued, her jaw jutting, "this isn't the appropriate setting. This is little Elisabeth's official welcome to the ranch and I'd like it to be special."

So she was playing the role of Queen on an official visit! That really made Jodie want to stop the car and get out, but instead, she turned toward Little Springs and kept her mouth tightly shut.

Everyone at Little Springs was delighted to see them. Delores and Dub greeted them at the car, and Morgan came out on his porch to invite them inside.

Christine was on the sofa, smiling softly as Erin, seated next to her, cuddled the baby in her arms. After accepting the newcomers' hugs, Christine murmured warmly, "Isn't this the most beautiful sight? I wish I'd had a little sister to love or a big one to look up to."

"I always wished that myself," Mae said gruffly. "I had to make do with two older brothers. When I was born, they thought I should've been another boy."

Mae waggled a finger inside the baby's tiny fingers. And Elisabeth instantly latched on. Mae's face brightened with a huge smile. "Look at that! This little girl's already showin' some spunk."

Mae settled in a nearby chair, and after the usual niceties were exchanged and Delores had served coffee, she dug in her purse for a box covered in green velvet. It looked old, an antique, and when she handed it to Christine and Christine opened it, she said, "That belonged to me when I was a child. I was told it was my mother's. I thought maybe little Elisabeth might like to have it now, to welcome her into the family."

The diminutive gold bracelet gleamed. "Oh, Mae, that's so sweet," Christine said.

Mae withdrew another small green box. "And this is for you, Erin," she said, again handing the box to Christine, who opened it for her daughter. It was a narrow gold ring that matched the bracelet. "They're a set," Mae said. "One for you, one for your new sister. I thought maybe you could wear it on your little finger."

Erin said, "Thank you," very politely, and maneuvered her hand so that Christine could put the ring in place. It fit perfectly.

"One day you can pass it on to your daughter, just like Elisabeth can pass her bracelet on to hers. That's what's so special about being part of a family like ours. The past generations are never far away. All you have to do to feel close to them is look outside or, in your case, look at your ring and your bracelet."

Erin nodded solemnly and again offered her thanks.

Jodie watched the gift-giving with a mix of feelings. It touched her, as it did everyone else, that Mae was being so thoughtful. But it also gave her the answer she'd been searching for—the real reason Mae had wanted her along. It was another push to get her to see the importance of family.

Christine and Erin had been on their own for years before arriving at the Parker Ranch. Now they were no longer alone. They were Parkers. An accepted part of the family.

Jodie wondered if Mae's message had been received with as much enthusiasm by Christine as it had by her daughter. She glanced at her and caught her gazing at Morgan. All the love Christine felt for her husband was there in her eyes, increased by the addition of their child.

Would *she* ever look at a man with that same degree of feeling? At Tate...if they were to have a baby together?

A shiver of presentiment passed over her. She and Tate? A child?

Jodie took a quick sip of coffee and tried to pretend she hadn't just thought that, hadn't just felt it. But she wasn't at all successful. Each time she looked at Christine and Morgan, she thought of Tate.

A short time later Mae went to the other house with Florence. Dub and Morgan disappeared, and Erin hurried to answer the telephone, which it turned out, was a friend calling her. So Jodie and Christine were left alone with the baby, who was sleeping soundly in a portable bassinet a few feet away. Voices didn't seem to bother her yet.

"Did I ever thank you for getting us to the hospital so quickly?" Christine asked.

"I'm only glad we made it!" Jodie returned.

"Me, too. I was worried there for a while." She glanced at the bassinet. "But she's worth every ounce of trouble it took." Her gaze swung back to Jodie. "I heard what happened at the ranch yesterday. The whole town knows. Jodie—you took such a gamble!"

Jodie frowned. It stood to reason that word would spread. What had happened wasn't the sort of thing that could be kept secret. And who'd want it to? Practically the whole county had been alerted to watch out for Rio. It was only to be expected that the whole county would be interested in the result.

She shrugged. "It came out right in the end."

"I know, but—"

"Mae's still mad at me. Do you see how she's ignoring me?"

"I did notice a certain coolness. But that's just the way Mae is sometimes. She—"

"She's made it part of her family-loyalty campaign. She can't understand why I don't fall into step. I wonder if that's the way it is in other families. I doubt it. But then, I don't know. Being a Parker is so much like being a part of this huge beast that devours everything in its path."

Jodie began to pace, making no pretense that she was doing anything else.

"Does this have something to do with the way you were feeling the other day?" Christine asked. "I thought it was Tate, but—"

"It *is* Tate! And it's Aunt Mae! And it's...oh, I don't know, everything! Ever since I've gotten back it's been one thing after another.'

The baby made a fretful sound and Jodie guiltily lowered her voice. "I'm sorry," she whispered.

Christine patted little Elisabeth's back and smiled as she resumed her seat. "No harm done."

"I wish I could say that," Jodie murmured miserably.

Christine said, "Come on. Sit down. Let's talk."

Jodie hesitated. She felt too much on edge to relax. But Christine was the person she most wanted to talk to, besides her father, and this was her opportunity. "Are you sure you're up to this?" she asked, uneasily taking a seat.

"I'm so happy I'm up to anything," Christine assured her. "And I'd like to see you happy, too. From the first time we met I knew we had a lot in common. Me not knowing my father, you not knowing your mother. It's not something other people understand unless they've experienced it. How it leaves you feeling somehow...incomplete."

Jodie was silent a moment, then said, "Do you remember when you first came here? How you had to stand up for what you thought was your and Erin's rightful share of the ranch, and how, later, it made all the difference in the world to Aunt Mae because you truly were a Parker?"

Christine nodded. "Yes."

"And how you didn't want the share then but finally accepted it because of Erin?"

Christine nodded again.

Jodie rubbed her arms. "Well, that's the way I feel sometimes. I wish I could give my share back. That I wasn't a Parker."

"And what would you do then?" Christine asked.

Jodie shrugged. "I have a degree. I could get a job."

"And be all on your own?"

"Yes."

Christine watched her levelly. "And what does that have to do with Tate Connelly?"

"He thinks I'm a spoiled brat. At least, he used to think that. Now, I'm not sure. But I do know one thing—like a lot of other people, he thinks we use our name and influence to get what we want around here. That we have too much power."

"He said that?"

"He as good as."

Christine murmured, "I used to think that, too. But I've learned a few things along the way, Jodie. The Parkers have power and prestige because of who they are, more than how much money and land they have. Think about Rafe for a second. Do you believe he needs the Parker Ranch behind him to have people listen? No. People listen because they sense he knows what he's talking about and because he's willing to back it up. So's Mae. Morgan's the same, and he's not a Parker. No one from the ranch throws their weight around." She paused. "There's something subtle that happens, though, and I bet that's what you're talking about more than anything else. The Parkers may not ask for preferential treatment, but they don't *have* to ask. It's simply given to them. There's this natural hauteur you all have—yes, you, too! It's part of your personality, and people respond with deference. I saw it then, I see it now." She laughed. "I've even caught myself acting haughty on occasion before I make myself stop.''

Jodie remembered the incident at Tate's house—how she realized that she couldn't let herself cry because she was a Parker and how aghast she'd been at her behavior. She nodded in recognition. ''What can we do about it?'' she asked.

''Just be aware of it, I guess. Try not to take advantage.''

''But I do that all the time. I do!''

''Jodie—'' Christine smiled ''—you're as forceful in your own way as Rafe and Mae are in theirs. You're a Parker. It comes with the territory. It's part of who you are.''

''But—''

''Stop fighting it. Stop trying not to be something that oozes out of your every pore. It's nothing to be ashamed of. And if Tate loves you, he'll love you for who you are. Not for what you're not. Does that make sense to you?''

Jodie nodded, but still wasn't convinced.

''Just remember,'' Christine continued, ''I was on my own for most of my life before I came here. And, Jodie, it's hard having no one to fall back on. No one to help you when you need it. No one to give you even a simple pat of encouragement. I may still have disagreements with some of what it means to be a Parker, but I wouldn't trade the support I have here for anything. Morgan, Delores and Dub, Rafe and Shannon, Harriet and LeRoy, your father, Darlene and Thomas, even Mae. We're a family, warts and all. And most times you ignore the warts.''

While driving Mae back to ranch headquarters, Jodie thought about what Christine had said. She seemed to have adjusted well to what at one time had been anathema to her. Christine had had such a huge chip on her shoulder when she arrived at the ranch, defying Rafe and Mae and rejecting Morgan. Her views certainly had changed.

Now Jodie was going through changes of her own. And it wasn't easy. Sometimes it hurt. Sometimes it was difficult to tell which way to turn, which way to look, what to say or do.

She glanced at Mae in the rearview mirror, willing her to say something. But not a word had passed her lips since leaving Little Springs.

"Pull off the road up here," Mae directed a few minutes later, making Jodie jump. The order was so unexpected.

"What for?" Jodie asked.

"Because I said to," Mae replied coolly. "Right here."

Jodie braked and cut the engine. Then she watched her great-aunt step outside.

"Come with me," Mae ordered again, and Jodie scrambled to follow.

Her aunt had some difficulty with the uneven ground and, afraid she was going to fall, Jodie took her arm.

Mae stiffened at first, but didn't draw away.

"Where are we going?" Jodie asked. "What's..."

And then she knew. The Parker cemetery. Located on a small rise that gave a nice view of the wide valley, it was only a moderate walk from the compound if you cut across an open field. Jodie hadn't been up here in years, not since she was a child.

A wrought-iron bench was set among a natural grouping of trees, encouraging a visitor to linger. Across the way, near the edge of the slope, was a fenced off area containing numerous tombstones.

Her great-aunt was puffing by the time they arrived at the bench and she sat down for a moment to rest. Dust covered her black dress shoes and the lower part of the black cane.

"You remember this place now?" Mae asked, throwing her a look.

"Yes."

"You and I used to come up here and pull weeds every weekend—until you decided you didn't like it. I always wondered if you thought a ghost was going to come out of the ground to get you. You didn't need to be afraid of any of the ghosts from here, though. None of 'em would hurt you."

Jodie did remember feeling spooked by the place, but mostly she hadn't liked pulling weeds. She'd rather have been riding or searching for the lost gold Parker legend said was buried somewhere on the ranch and generations of Parker children had spent their spare time trying to find. "I remember," she said quietly.

Mae took a deep breath and said, "Come on."

They found their way inside the low fence. "Look here and here," Mae said, pointing. "Look at the names and dates."

Jodie couldn't help but see them. Gibson Parker, Virgil Parker—the two brothers who founded the Parker dynasty. Deena, Sue, Watt, Byron—some of the names dating back into the previous century. Theodore, Mae's brother, the soldier who'd died near the end of the First World War. Jeff and Sara, Jodie's grandparents, who'd passed on long before she was born. Ward, Rafe's father. Name after name, all Parkers by birth or marriage. It was like a history book spread open on the ground. As was the custom of the time, some markers explained the cause of death: died of fever, died in childbirth. A number said "beloved mother" or "beloved father." Jodie sighed.

"This is what I'm talkin' about, Missy," Mae said fiercely. "*This* is your connection, and if you can't see it, if you can't feel it, then I don't know how to make you! Parker land, Parker blood! I'm going to be with them soon—I can sense it comin' on. And I don't want to go without knowing that you're set right in the world. Set right in your mind. In here!" She tapped Jodie's forehead with a gloved finger.

"Are you ill?" Jodie asked, startled.

"I'm eighty-eight! I'm tired. I'm wearin' out."

"You didn't answer me. Are you ill?"

"No."

"Then how do you know?"

"I told you. I can tell."

Jodie turned away, a hand covering her mouth. Emotion swelled in her breast, threatening to overwhelm her. She'd been right all along! She could see more clearly than those who'd been living with her day by day for the past year that her great-aunt had gone downhill physically. She could see the differences, the changes. And not just Mae's use of the cane she'd taken to recently.

Mae's hard stance softened when she saw Jodie's reaction. She put a hand on her shoulder and squeezed gently. "It's gratifying to know you care. Sometimes I've wondered. Now don't get all blubbery on me. I'm not expectin' to drop off tomorrow. Anyway, what if I did? I've had a long life and it's mostly been a good one."

Then she dug at a newly sprouted weed with the tip of her cane. "My only worry is what I'll say to these people when I meet 'em at the Pearly Gate and they ask me how I did managing the present-day Parkers. I'm afraid they won't think I did a good enough job. That I made too many mistakes."

"With me, you mean," Jodie stated flatly, beginning to see this stop for what it really was. If Mae couldn't get her to change her ways by fury and couldn't convince her by persuasion, why not try a little guilt? The terrible thing was, the guilt was working.

"I've come up here almost every day for the past nine or ten years, did you know that?" Mae went on. "I talk to them, tell 'em my problems."

"And what do they say back?"

"Nothing. They've earned their rest and won't say a thing." She smiled wryly. "So don't expect any answers from me after I'm gone. I'll have earned my rest, too!" Mae stopped to dig in her purse. "Here," she said gruffly, and handed Jodie a green velvet box like those she'd produced earlier.

"What's this?"

"Open it."

Jodie did, and inside she found a locket that perfectly matched the child's ring and bracelet.

"I've been holding on to that for years," Mae murmured. "It's yours—part of the set. You can use it now or save it for a future baby. Just don't throw it away."

Jodie's throat closed again. She could barely speak. "I'll never throw it away, Aunt Mae," she whispered.

Mae led the way back to the car, spurning any offer of assistance. But instead of installing herself in the rear seat, she slid into the passenger front and nodded her desire to complete the journey, instead of using the more imperious cane tap.

RESTLESSNESS KEPT a firm hold on Jodie as she tried to get through the remainder of the day. She didn't know what to do with herself. After all the tension surrounding the Rio episode, as Harriet now termed it, an ordinary day, void of worry, seemed somehow unnatural. And every time she let her mind drift, it moved automatically to Tate. Should she call him or wait for him to call her? Had she made too much of a few brief episodes? And how, exactly, did she feel about him?

Her father came to her rescue. "If you're not doin' anythin', why don't you come help me pick out which paintings to send to the exhibition?"

Jodie jumped at the opportunity. She followed her father to the old storage shed he'd converted into a studio. Canvases were set on edge in jumbled rows, leaning against old ladders and house-paint cans. Several easels held partially finished works. Tubes of paint, from new to tortured, were scattered about on makeshift shelves, and numerous sketches, ideas for new works, were tacked onto the rough wooden walls, while various-size brushes bathed in turpentine.

This was her father's inner sanctum. His refuge.

He replaced the partially finished paintings with canvases that were complete. Then set up some others about the space. "I've narrowed it down to these," he said. "What do you think? I can only send six."

Jodie studied the paintings. She liked all eight. Three were of horses and riders at work on a roundup, two were of cowboys doing the ill-favored job of mending fence, one was a scene of cattle gathering at a stock tank in the shadow of an old windmill, one was of a pair of well-worn boots, and another was of a cowboy preparing a young horse to be ridden for the first time.

She shrugged and admitted, "They're all good."

"I can't send more than six," he repeated.

Jodie pursed her lips and hardened her judgment. Finally she said, "These two of the roundup, this one of the fence, the boots—definitely, the boots—the windmill and the horse. That's Rafe, isn't it, with the horse? The last one?"

Her father grinned. "Look on the back," he said, and showed her the *x* he'd put on the two paintings she'd left out. "We have similar tastes," he said. Then he answered her question. "Yeah, that's Rafe. I usually try to disguise the faces, but I liked the way this one set up. I've shown it to him and he doesn't mind."

"I'm surprised Shannon doesn't want it."

"She does. I'm not to sell it."

Jodie fingered through some drawings in a folder as her father gathered their choices and put them aside. She was surprised to see an image of herself. "This is me!" she exclaimed. "Dad! It's me! When did you do it? My hair's long, so it was before I went to Italy, wasn't it?'' She smiled at him happily, then noticed he wasn't smiling. She looked at the drawing again and began to notice the subtle differences. A thinner nose, a rounder chin, eyes that tilted just a little more than hers did. The same smile, though in a fuller mouth.

She stared at her father, stunned. "Daddy? Is this…?" She'd never seen a picture of her mother. Mae had burned them all.

Gib snatched the drawing from her hands. He started to tear it up, but she stopped him. "No, Daddy, don't. Please!''

He stopped.

She pulled it free of his grip and tried to smooth any creases. "It's her?" she asked softly, looking up.

"Mae's gonna kill me for holdin' on to that."

"This is my *mother?*" Jodie breathed.

He nodded wordlessly.

Jodie studied the drawing again. "No wonder I don't look like the Parkers. I was curious, but— She never seemed real enough for me to imagine. She was always this mysterious woman—out there somewhere, trying to get money, not caring that she left you and me." Jodie shook her head, still stunned.

Her father cleared a collection of newspapers off an old nail keg and sat down. "You want a seat?" He motioned to a second keg.

Jodie shook her head. If she moved, her legs might buckle and she would fall. "What…what was she like?" she asked. Never mind that it was a subject they'd always avoided. Never mind that Mae would be displeased. Jodie had gone through her whole life not knowing. She wasn't going to waste another second.

Her father swallowed, ill at ease. "She was beautiful. Like you are."

"And?" she prompted when he dried up. "Did you meet her at a bar like Mae said?"

"Just like Mae said."

"And you got married right away?"

He nodded.

"Then you brought her back here and she and Mae..."

"Mae had a hissy fit. She didn't like her the moment she set eyes on her. And the feeling was mutual. I never saw two people take such an instant dislike for each other."

"Did you love her?"

He was silent for so long Jodie thought she was going to have to prompt him again. "I loved her," he said at last. And Jodie knew he meant it.

She cleared her throat. "Do you still?"

"No."

"Why not?"

"Because she left you. I was hurt, but I could understand. You couldn't."

"Aunt Mae told me she gave her money. How much?"

"Enough so she'd agree to a legal separation. I'm sure she got herself set up pretty good."

"With her rodeo cowboy."

Gib nodded.

"So she was a bitch, just like Aunt Mae said."

"Did she tell you that?" he demanded, his tone suddenly angry.

"All but the word. I got the idea, though."

"My God."

"You didn't know?"

He shook his head.

"Why didn't *you* tell me, Dad? Why didn't *you* ever talk to me about her? Didn't you think I'd wonder?"

Gib got up, grabbed a brush, smeared it in some paint and began to work on one of the unfinished paintings. "I never knew what to say. Mae...Mae told me she'd handle it. But I never—"

"Didn't you realize I might think that if Aunt Mae disapproved of my mother, she'd disapprove of me, too? That no matter what I did, it would never be enough? Ruby was my mother! If she was a terrible person, I was a terrible person!"

Jodie didn't know where that had come from—it had just burst out. As if it had been waiting for years.

Her father looked at her in anguish. "No!" He went to set the brush down, but he fumbled and it fell. "Jodie, no." He came to her, but she didn't want to be cuddled. She avoided his touch.

"Is she alive or dead?" she asked tightly. "Or do you know?"

"She died when you were eight. In a car wreck. Somehow someone connected us and sent word."

"I should've been told," Jodie said.

"Yes," her father answered, his chin down.

Jodie was silent, trying to take in all she'd heard, most of which was confirmation. Still...she looked at her father, angry at first, then with growing compassion. The whole affair must have been tremendously hard on him. To love someone, to have it fall apart, to have money mean more than you and your child.

She touched her father's cheek. He looked up, his

gaze tortured. And without further argument, they moved into each other's arms.

"I didn't mean for it to happen this way," Gib said huskily. "I kept wantin' to talk to you about it ever since you grew up, but every time I tried, the words just wouldn't come." He pulled back and cupped her face. "You may look like your momma, but you aren't *like* her! Not one tiny little bit! Your momma had a hard edge, probably from bein' raised hard scrabble. She didn't think about anything but what was good for her. Clothes, jewelry—she wanted the best and couldn't get enough of it. I wish I could tell you that havin' you made a difference, but it didn't. I think she loved you—she used to rock you and sing to you all the time right after you were born—but when it came down to it, she took off with that cowboy. I didn't know about it until Mae told me the next morning."

"She was a silly woman to leave you," Jodie said thickly.

Gib gave a half smile as he let her go. "I don't seem to have the right touch with women. Not even my own little girl."

"Why don't you let me be the judge of that?"

Jodie left her father in his converted studio. She'd asked for and been given the drawing of her mother. She took it to her room, smoothed the edges, then tacked it on the wall near her cheval mirror. One day soon she'd get it framed. Not because she admired what she knew of the woman who was her mother, but because it *was* her mother. A face to put with the name. A connection, of sorts, to her past, as Mae was so determined she make.

JODIE LAY ACROSS her bed and tried to sleep, but she couldn't get the day out of her mind. Christine's advice, Mae's portent, her father's assertions. She wasn't going to have any rest until she thought it all through. She went outside, then, restive, started to walk. Ending up, as if drawn, at the Parker cemetery.

A rosy twilight lent the valley a rugged fairy-tale quality. Cattle clustered here and there, barbed-wire fences separated sections. The compound was like a green oasis, with its large trees and civilized comforts.

Jodie's gaze settled on the final resting place of the people who, through generations, had created the ranch with their blood, sweat and tears. They'd fought for it, died for it, then passed it on to their heirs for care. The Parkers. Her people.

She bent down, gathered a handful of dirt and slowly let it trickle through her fingers. Good West Texas dirt—dry, but rich in nutrients, so that when water came in the seasonal rains, life sprang into being and the growing cycle began again.

Jodie gathered another handful of dirt, then another and another, until she finally did what Mae had talked to her of doing. She rubbed it into her skin. At first experimentally, feeling slightly silly. Then with more intensity of purpose.

She wanted to make the Parker connection!

She wanted to feel what Mae and the others did!

She was tired of trying to stand alone!

And as she rubbed it on her neck and throat, then down across the rise of her breasts, she began to laugh. Because as her heart opened on a swell of feeling, the years of determined detachment broke away and a newborn peace with who she was settled into place.

CHAPTER SIXTEEN

TATE LEARNED through the grapevine that Rio Walsh had packed up and left for Colorado. At first he experienced a jolt of primal pleasure. A rival, vanquished! Then he thought about how Rafe's boot and Mae's shotgun had no doubt been a part of the equation, and most of his pleasure disappeared. The question remained: how did Jodie feel?

He thought about going out to talk to her, to see for himself. But the duty of office kept getting in the way—an attempted robbery at a convenience store outside town, a reported livestock theft, some teenagers who drank too much the night before and were causing no end of trouble this morning in jail, and the parents who objected to their children's incarcerations.

In between, Tate made his decision. He was going to do it! He would accept the position on Drew Winslow's task force. It was work that interested him, would advance his career along the lines he'd originally intended and would—he laughed darkly—get him away from that infernal jail!

Only two things had yet to be worked out: his replacement as sheriff and whether or not Jodie Parker was going to play a part in his life. The first needed to be seen to right away, but the second...well, he had at least six weeks before he had to report for duty with Drew Winslow. He could afford to take it slow. Not press her. Not press himself. They could let things evolve naturally. *If* they were going to evolve. *If* she hadn't already recommitted herself to Rio Walsh.

Just thinking his name made Tate's skin crawl. What she saw in him, now or in the past, was beyond his understanding. Rio was good-looking in a brash kind of way, but he'd already proved himself unreliable. And not nearly enough of a man to stand up for himself, even in the most recent crisis.

Tate set his hat in place and left the office. He didn't care if space aliens staged a Hollywood-type landing on Del Norte's main street, he was going to talk to Jack. Then he was going to see Jodie.

"YOU'VE DECIDED, haven't you?" Jack said almost as soon as he set eyes on Tate, his famous intuition still operating.

"Yep."

"And?"

"You're the first to know. I'm gonna do it. I'm accepting Drew Winslow's offer. Which leaves me with a big problem."

"Another one?"

"Who's gonna take my place." Tate leaned on the fence near the stock pen where Jack was working and listed his requirements. "It has to be someone who can hit the ground runnin'. It'd also be best if he knows the procedures, knows the personnel—that kinda thing."

Jack nodded sagely.

"And be someone the men can respect."

Jack nodded again.

"Someone like *you*." Tate put emphasis on the last word.

Jack kept working, cleaning dirt from a shovel. "I'm retired."

"You can *un*retire."

Jack shook his head. "Why would I wanna do somethin' like that?"

"Because you're bored stiff livin' all the way out here. Away from all the excitement. Away from all your friends in town."

"Did your momma tell you that?" he demanded, straightening.

Tate smiled. "Her exact word was 'antsy.' Or, if you prefer, 'restless.' But she didn't have to tell me. I saw for myself the last time I was out here. It just took me a while to put together."

"Son, I quit because I thought it was time for new blood."

"Are you tellin' me you *aren't* bored? Look at this place! There's not a blade of grass growin' where it shouldn't, there's not a wood surface that's not been painted. You prob'ly run around after the cows with a shovel and a plastic bag!"

Jack glanced at the shovel he was cleaning, then back at Tate. The light of amusement brightened his dark eyes. "One of us is sure shovelin' something all right."

"Tell the truth, Jack," Tate said seriously, "are you happy out here?"

The old sheriff finished cleaning the shovel, then meticulously hung it from a nail on the side of an out-building. Finally he turned to Tate. "I dreamed about havin' a place of my own for thirty, maybe forty years. Maureen did, too. We'd stay up till the wee hours plannin' how we were gonna do things. She made me promise that first thing I'd build her a wishin' well, like one she'd saw in a book when she was a little girl. An' I did." The wishing well was off to one side of the house, complete with hand crank and wooden bucket. A profusion of pink flowers overflowed the sides of the bucket. "I even planted the petunias she wanted," he added, then sighed. "But it's not the same. She's not here."

Tate thought of Maureen. Her warm wonderful smile, the way she loved to work crossword puzzles, the way she shooed everyone out of the room when it was time for her favorite TV soap opera.

"So what's your answer?" Tate asked. "Will you come back to bein' the sheriff? Or do you want me to tell the county supervisors they're gonna have to look for another man to fill out my term?"

Jack cast a long look around. "I think what happened," he said slowly, "is that I came out here too soon. Maybe in four or five years I'll be ready. Right now?" He glanced at Tate. "You know anybody who might like to lease the place?"

Tate grinned. "You sure you don't want to think this through some more?"

Jack shook his head emphatically. "You hit the nail almost straight on the head—this mornin' I came a little too close to findin' me a plastic bag!"

Tate hooted and Jack slapped him on the shoulder, then the two men started back for the house.

"When do you have to report for duty?" Jack asked.

"Not for six weeks. But like I said, you're the first to know. I haven't even told Drew Winslow yet. He may have changed his mind and not want me anymore."

"Little chance of that. Not when he handpicked you. I'd tell you what all he had to say about you, but I wouldn't want to swell your head."

Tate suffered Jack's teasing with fond regard.

"So," Jack said as they neared the patrol car, "that means you haven't told your momma yet, either, right?"

"Nope."

"How's she gonna take it?"

Tate cocked his head. "Did you know she was goin' around with Mark Lovell?"

Jack's grin widened. "Sure. Didn't you?"

Tate shook his head as he settled into the driver's seat. "No. But then, there seems to be lots of things I'm just learning about."

"That always happens when you're fallin' in love. Your head's in a cloud and all you smell is roses."

"Now I know you're goin' nuts." Tate started the car.

Jack bent down to see him better. "When you gonna ask her to marry you? Better get busy!"

"Bye, Jack," Tate said dryly, and escaped.

TATE REHEARSED in his mind what he was going to say. *I know this might not be any of my business, Jodie, but...where does it stand between you and Rio Walsh? Is there something going on? Or is it over? And if it's over, are you willing to see what it is that's been happening between us?* Simple, direct, yet still slow-paced enough not to cause alarm.

Only, he didn't get to use it. He received one of the few calls guaranteed to take him back immediately to Del Norte—one of his deputies had been injured while trying to referee a domestic dispute.

Tate arrived at the hospital to find both Jimmy and Evie Evers being treated in the emergency room, as well as Deputy Bob Stewart. The injuries ranged from scrapes and bumps on various parts of the three anatomies to the deep gash in the deputy's upper arm.

Jimmy Evers immediately started to whine excuses. He knew he was in trouble, since he was out on bail from the previous altercation with Evie and would have the bail revoked if he proved to be the instigator. Evie, of course, blamed the deputy for everything.

Tate went to stand beside Bob Stewart while the doctor sewed up the wound. "What happened?" he asked briskly.

"They were havin' an argument, a neighbor called it in, I arrived—thought I had everything under control—then when I started to take Mr. Evers to the car, Mrs. Evers grabbed a kitchen knife and came at me. I let go of him, tried to take the knife away from her, he grabbed me, she started to scream at him, and the next thing I know, I'm cut."

"Which one did it?" Tate asked, his eyes narrowing on what he could see of the pair in the next cubicle, where another deputy stood guard.

Bob looked embarrassed. "I don't know. She had it last time I looked, but things kinda got confused."

Tate nodded. He told the deputy to stop at the station to make his report, then go home if he needed to.

"I'm fine," Bob said. "It's not as bad as it looks."

Tate stopped off to speak to the Everses. "Looks like you've gone and done it this time. This is serious business, assaulting a police officer. You can both end up doin' time."

"I didn't do anythin'!" Jimmy wailed, and ever the gentlemen, blamed his wife. "She did it! She had the knife! I never—"

"You took it away from me! I was cuttin' onions, that's why I had it in my hand. I—"

Tate hushed them both. "I don't want to hear any more right now. Deputy? Bring 'em on over when they get done here."

"Yes, sir," the deputy said.

Tate turned a deaf ear to their continuing pleas as he walked away. By now, if his plans had been left undisturbed, he'd have been talking to Jodie.

Stymied anticipation formed a knot in the pit of his stomach.

It could be hours before he'd get another opportunity, or with his luck, even days!

THERE WAS SOMETHING different about Jodie that everyone, herself included, noticed. And it wasn't merely a release from the stress of the week before. The change that started when she stood up for her right to deal with Rio after his exoneration had only continued.

Several times she caught Mae watching her, trying to gauge what had happened but remaining puzzled. Finally Mae could stand it no longer. "All right! What is it?" she demanded. "What've you done? What are you smilin' about?"

"Is it a sin to smile?" Jodie asked.

Mae frowned. "It's not the smile. It's what's behind it I'm worried about!"

Jodie left the side table, where she'd been filling a vase with some of Harriet's beautiful summer flowers, to sit beside her great-aunt on one of the twin sofas. Mae's house had cleared out as the morning wore on. Harriet and her younger children had gone to take Gwen and Wesley to the fair being held at the county park outside Del Norte, and Shannon had gone home to work some more on Jack Denton's family history.

"There's absolutely nothing to worry about," Jodie said sweetly.

Mae snorted. "Now I really *am* worried."

"There's not! It's…" Now that the time had come, Jodie found it hard to put into words without sounding trite. "I took your advice. I thought about what you said, about what everyone said, and…I think you're right."

Mae narrowed her eyes. "About what?"

"About being a Parker. About *me* being a Parker." She paused. "Aunt Mae, I think I'm beginning to see that I am who I am, and there's nothing I can do about it. There's nothing *you* can do about it, either. I'm my mother's daughter as much as my father's." She tilted her head. "Why didn't you tell me I look like her?"

Mae sputtered, "Who told you that? How do you know?"

"If we're going to get through this, we have to do it by laying all the cards on the table. No holding back. I look like her. I saw a drawing Daddy did. It's hanging in my room now. He gave it to me when I asked for it."

Mae sat forward. "A drawing?"

Jodie smiled wryly. "It escaped the ritual burning."

Mae blinked and repeated, "Ritual?"

"Yes, when you burned every photograph of her. I heard about that years ago."

For once Mae seemed unnerved.

Jodie asked, "I know you hated her, but did you hate her that much?"

Mae quickly conquered her disquiet, and her eyes flashed. "Yes, I hated her! For what she did to Gib— he's always been something of a disappointment when compared to the other Parker men, but he's good to the bone. Wouldn't hurt a fly. He didn't deserve what she did to him. And for what she did to you. You were such a tiny little thing. You needed her!"

"You disliked her on sight, Dad said."

"I knew what she was."

"Her *name* was Ruby."

"I know that!" Mae snapped.

"How much money did you give her?"

Mae pushed to her feet, wobbling a bit before she gained control of the cane.

Jodie suffered her own moment of disquiet, but knew they had to get through this. For both their sakes. "And when did you offer it to her? Right away or just before she left?''

"Why should that matter?" Mae demanded, turning around.

"I'm just curious if you influenced the breakup of the marriage.''

"Me? No! It didn't stand a chance from the beginning. Didn't your daddy tell you that, too? She only married him for the money. All I did was supply it.''

"If you hated her, did you hate me?''

Mae, genuinely confused, asked, "Why would I do that?''

"Because I'm Ruby's daughter.''

When the fog of confusion parted, Mae looked at Jodie as if she'd uttered something sacrilegious. "I didn't hate you! I never hated you! How can you...?'' She groped her way to the nearest chair and Jodie rushed to kneel at her side.

"I thought you did, don't you see? The way you sounded when you told me about her! I was too young to understand. I thought I'd done something wrong, too! That you'd found yourself saddled with me and were making the best of a bad situation.''

"Oh, Jodie." Mae's aged hand reached for her head and, trembling, smoothed the copper red hair. "No! If only I'd listened to Rafe. He didn't think I should tell you the way I did or when I did. He thought I was bein' too harsh, and now..." She took a breath. "I'm about to tell you something your daddy doesn't know about. Not even to this day. She threatened to take you with her, and I couldn't let her do that. All she wanted was more money, so I gave it to her. I couldn't let her take a Parker away from the Parker Ranch! She didn't know the first thing about raising a child. And that boyfriend of hers—he made the Hammonds look good! That's the kind of people she came from. The kind of men she ran around with. I had her investigated."

Jodie sat back on her heels. "You gave her more money—for me?"

"Not *for* you. To keep her from takin' you away."

"Was that all it was? My Parker blood?"

Mae twitched, then admitted, "By the time she was threatening to take you with her, you'd already stolen my heart. I'd never been around babies much—I was always too busy for that kind of thing. But you—" she smiled with unfeigned richness of memory "—you were different. It was almost as if you were *my* baby, too. I couldn't let her take you away and never see you again. I couldn't let her take you from your dad, either."

Jodie was silent for a long moment. Then she wrapped her arms around her great-aunt's normally unyielding neck and kissed her on the cheek.

She hadn't expected such a confession. For Mae to have loved her so much!

"I love you, too, Aunt Mae," she said quietly. "And I want to thank you. I can't imagine growing up anywhere else or not being with these people. Not being with you. Not being with my dad."

Mae watched her intently, studying her face, studying what she really meant behind the words. Then a huge worry seemed to lift from her shoulders, and she smiled warmly at her great-niece.

JODIE GREW DISSATISFIED with waiting for Tate to contact her. She knew he'd been angry the last time he'd seen her, but she hadn't expected it to last. Over the past couple of days she'd been getting things in her life in order. She wanted to get this settled, too.

That was why, when Harriet returned from delivering her older children to the fair and mentioned, seemingly in passing, she'd seen Tate there, Jodie promptly decided to go to the fair herself.

She paid special attention to the way she looked, remembering that the last few times they'd seen each other, she'd not exactly been at her best. She'd either been going out for a ride, picking herself up off the ground or disheveled from collecting Rio from his hiding place. Because of the continuing heat she decided on a soft cotton dress, but it was a very flattering cotton dress that made the most of her figure and her coloring. Then she added her favorite perfume—sensual, delicate, yet incredibly potent. And a subtle application of makeup. Around her neck, she wore the locket Mae had given her, threaded on a long gold chain.

She checked the full effect in the mirror and gave a short nod, before going out and settling in the Cadillac, which Mae had given her permission to borrow.

All the way into town she tried to decide her approach. March straight up to him and kiss him full on the mouth was her first instinct, but sensible thought prevailed and she decided just to talk to him—maybe thank him again for helping her and helping Rio. Let him know casually that she and Rio weren't together, as he seemed to think. Then take it from there.

Butterfly wings fluttered in her stomach as she entered the county park and found a place to leave the car. The fair had drawn a big crowd. Numerous cars and pickups lined the narrow roadway leading to the entry gate.

Someone had gone to a lot of trouble to make the event festive. Clusters of balloons and miles of crepe-paper ribbon had been strung from place to place. There were booths selling snack food and drinks, booths where you could win a homemade cake and enter contests for best pickles, best pie, as well as numerous game booths and a dunking stall. Areas had been roped off for children's competitions—three-legged races, sack hops, egg-and-spoon races. Adults got into the act, too, with similar competitions.

Jodie tried her hand at a game or two—attempting to snare the neck of a soda bottle with a series of plastic rings and tossing a beanbag through the mouth of a swinging clown face—but all the while she kept an eye out for Tate.

And all the while she was aware of people looking at her. This was really her first trip into town since her return from Europe, if you didn't count the birth of little Elisabeth. She understood they were curious to see her again. She also knew they'd heard about the recent trouble involving Rio, which brought up her past trouble with him.

People were friendly to her, though. Some even to the point of welcoming her back.

If this had been an ordinary day, Jodie would have enjoyed it. With her newfound ability to be at ease with herself, she didn't question the motives of others quite so readily. If a person smiled, then said something in private to their companion, she didn't wonder if they were saying something negative about the Parkers. But this wasn't an ordinary day. She was on a mission, and only when she located Tate would it truly begin.

And then at last she saw him. He was dressed in civilian clothes—slim-fitting black jeans, a dark T-shirt and a light blue shirt he wore unbuttoned and loose. He was carrying a large box for his mother, who walked beside him.

Jodie turned away, her heart thumping wildly. This was going to be far more difficult than she'd thought. Even from a distance she was sensitive to his appeal. How was she ever going to pretend she wasn't?

His mother saw her and stopped. "Jodie?"

Jodie turned around slowly. She forced herself to smile at Emma Connelly, then her gaze was drawn inexorably to Tate. The box was filled to overbrimming with paper products—plates, cups, napkins. It was more bulky than heavy, and Tate shifted it easily so his view of her was unobstructed.

Jodie's forced smile stayed in place. "Ah yes... hello!" she returned brightly.

"You're the last person I expected to see here today," Emma said starkly.

"Yes, well, I heard about it and—"

"You're welcome, of course," Emma amended, obviously having realized how impolite she'd sounded. "Everyone's welcome."

"It...it looks like the fair's going well," Jodie said, glancing around.

"It is," Emma agreed. "We were starting to run out

of supplies. Lots of people came hungry. The barbecue's disappearin' faster than we can cook it!''

"Hello, Jodie," Tate said, his voice soft, melodious.

Jodie's insides were jumping. Her primary instinct was flight. What did she think she was going to accomplish by this? How had she thought she'd ever be able to talk privately with Tate in such a circus-like atmosphere? She should never have come. Should never have—

"Don't let me stop you, then," she said quickly, starting to duck away. "I...we...I'll see you another time, Tate."

"You wanted to talk to me?"

"Only to thank you again. It's not important. I can—"

"I want to talk to you, too."

The surrounding noise and bustle seemed to disappear as she looked across at him. Time stood still. Then a little boy, running away from another little boy, misjudged distance and bumped into her as he tried to dart past. Reality rushed back with a resounding *whump*— conversations, laughter, cries of triumph and disaster at the races.

Emma caught hold of Jodie's arm and asked with concern, "He didn't hurt you, did he? You look so...odd."

Jodie shook her head. She hadn't felt a thing.

Emma, still frowning, directed Tate to pass her the box. "You see to Jodie," she said. "I can handle this. I just have to take it over there." She indicated a pavilion a short distance away where numerous people were eating at long picnic tables.

Tate hesitated. "It would only take a minute for me to carry it over."

"I won't hear of it. It's not that heavy."

Tate made sure his mother had adequate control before she started off with the box, then his frown cleared when another woman came rushing out of the pavilion to assist her. He turned to Jodie. "Come on over here," he said, pulling her away from the booths and into the shade of a gnarled old tree.

Plenty of people were still about, but in his company Jodie felt protected. And excited. And nervous.

His hand, encasing hers, was warm and strong and vital. She wasn't sure she'd continue breathing if he didn't let go soon. Yet when he did, she wanted the contact back.

She'd always thought him attractive. Now she understood why. It was Tate himself—his compelling features, leanly muscled body and the steady confidence he maintained in himself and in his abilities. It all added up to an innate virility he was barely conscious of. Which made him even more appealing.

He was the complete opposite of Rio, who wore his attraction for women on his sleeve and used it—and them—to his advantage.

"Jodie?" he said.

Jodie's attention jerked back to the present and she blinked up at him.

His mouth slanted into a smile. "I didn't mean to startle you."

"You didn't," she lied, and knew he didn't believe her.

"What did you want to talk to me about?" he asked

after a slightly awkward moment. "You've already thanked me."

Jodie could see exactly how this strained conversation was going to play out. She'd say her bit, he'd say his, and then they'd part—no worse off, but certainly no better, either. She couldn't let that happen. Just as she had with Mae and her father, she had to break through to the truth. And the only way to do that was to take a chance.

"Rio's gone," she blurted. "Back to Colorado. And I hope I never see him again."

Tate remained stubbornly still. "I heard he'd left," he said.

"So why didn't you come out to the ranch? Why?" She took a deep breath. "Tate I think I love you. That may not be something you want to hear, and I'm sorry if that's so, but I just had to say it, because—"

Tate, stepping closer, placed his fingers over her mouth, effectively hushing her flow of words. "If you say that, you'd better mean it!" he murmured huskily.

Jodie looked up at him, lost in embarrassment from her unilateral declaration, then—as his body moved against hers—in amazement at his reaction. She broke her mouth away enough to retort, "Of course I mean it! Why in the world would you think that I—"

Once again she wasn't allowed to finish. But this time, instead of hushing her words with his fingertips, he stopped them with his lips.

At first Jodie struggled, intellect not yet having caught up with reality. Then, as physical bliss dawned, reason finally understood.

CHAPTER SEVENTEEN

ONLY WHEN TATE and Jodie became aware of the whistles and teasing comments aimed at them by passersby did they break apart. Jodie felt her color heighten, Tate laughed and returned the teasing comments, then they left as quickly as they could.

Both were breathing hard as they reached the exit, yet they were still able to laugh at the absurdity of what had just occurred. And both were very much aware of what it meant. A declaration of sorts had been delivered by both of them. In public, in front of a small-town population. The news would travel fast.

The prospect of gossip couldn't dampen the brightness of the moment, though. Jodie didn't care and neither, it seemed, did Tate.

"Where can we go?" she asked, meaning to talk, but not discounting other possibilities, either.

"My place," Tate said.

He directed her to an old Ford sedan and she hopped in happily. As they rolled past Mae's Cadillac, Jodie had a moment of disquiet, but that vanished when she realized she could collect the car later.

The drive into town seemed to take forever. She had scooted close to him, her hand on his thigh, where he'd placed it, then covered it with his own.

Jodie had never felt so excited. No man had ever brought her to this sense of anticipation. When they parked in the driveway of his house, she was in just as much of a hurry to get inside as he was.

The door had barely shut when he pressed her back against it, his mouth devouring hers between heated explorations of her neck and breasts.

She moaned his name, her fingers threading though his short hair, pulling him closer, using her body to heighten his need.

He uttered something unintelligible, then lifted her into his arms and carried her into the bedroom, kissing her all the way.

Next she was on the bed and he was stretched out beside her. Her floaty summer dress presented little problem. One tug on the zip and it was free. His clothes were a little harder, though. The overshirt, the T-shirt, the gun he had clipped to the side of his belt

Jodie's hand jerked away at the discovery. Tate removed the weapon, placing it safely on the bedside table.

"Being sheriff is a full-time job," he murmured in explanation.

"Mmm," Jodie responded, no longer caring, her fingers busy with what she'd started previously.

Their bodies free of the last encumbrance, each was able to revel in the physical beauty of the other. Tate—long and lean with sculpted muscles. Wide shoulders and deep chest narrowing to slender hips and the strong legs of a natural athlete. Jodie—willowy, yet with rounded breasts and a soft layering of flesh that kept her from being bony.

His hands caressed her, gliding easily along her spine and over her hip. "My, God, you're beautiful," he breathed. "I used to dream, but—"

Jodie rained kisses over his shoulders and chest. "Shh," she whispered. "Later."

Finally they could put the moment off no longer.

Their bodies joined and Jodie lost touch with everything but sensation, which kept growing ever stronger. She couldn't get enough of him or give him enough of herself. Making love with him was the most wonderful, most profound thing she'd ever done. She cried out in ecstasy and felt him tremble, even as he tried to extend her pleasure.

Once collapsed, their bodies remained entwined. Minutes passed before Jodie could move again, then with her breathing still heightened, she smoothed a hand over his hair and down his neck.

She hadn't thought about being together in this way when she'd fallen in love with him the first time—in the spring of her twelfth year. Adult love was something mysterious then. She'd wanted him to notice her, to *like* her, to maybe hold her hand. She wouldn't have known what to do if he'd actually done that.

Her fingers wandered over him, exploring the way he was made. His ribs, the sprinkling of dark hair on his chest, and down over his flat stomach to the indent of his bellybutton.

"You'll give me ideas again if you don't stop right there," he warned.

She hadn't been aware that he was watching her, but when she looked up, his head was propped on his hand.

He gave a sexy grin. "But go ahead if you want. I don't mind."

Jodie tingled from head to foot, her body alive to every nuance of his. It was tempting, very tempting. But she controlled the urge. For now.

"You're quite a lady, Jodie Parker," he said huskily.

She smiled. "I could say the same about you, only change it to gentleman."

He dropped back onto the pillow and pulled her with him, so he could continue to hold her. Her cheek rested against his chest. Minutes passed as he stroked the silky smoothness of her hair.

Finally he asked, "Did you mean what you said earlier?"

"Yes."

"You love me," he repeated.

"Yes."

"Since when?"

"Since seventh grade."

He raised his head to look at her. "You're kidding me."

"No," she said, grinning. "You were my first love. I remember trying to get you to notice me and all I succeeded in doing was to get you angry. You threatened to toss me off the school bus several times when you were the driver. Do you remember?"

"You were a brat!"

"See?" She cocked her head and reminded him, "You haven't told me how you feel yet."

"We're here together, aren't we?"

"Is that your way of telling me you love me? That you'd never do this unless you were in love?"

"I wouldn't do it with you."

Jodie climbed partway onto his body and looked him straight in the eye. "I'd like to hear the words, if you don't mind. Humor me."

He dragged her the rest of the way up, until she was resting on him fully, then he cupped her face and said, "I didn't think it was possible to love a woman the way I love you. Even if you are one of the high-and-mighty Parkers."

"Since when?" she echoed his earlier demand.

He frowned. "Now that's a little harder for me than it was for you. It's been a long time, I think. Only I didn't know it. It kinda came to a head when you got back to the ranch this time."

"You were still horrible to me."

"When?" he challenged.

"You tried to give me a ticket!"

"You were drivin' like holy hell!"

Jodie shifted position a little and received an instantaneous response.

"Jodie," he warned.

She wiggled again and grinned. "What if I was 'drivin' like holy hell' to get back to you? Would you give me a ticket then? Or would you—"

Her question was cut short by the best kind of answer. At least from their point of view.

TO LESSEN the distractions they both thought it prudent to get out of bed and get dressed before they talked.

Jodie met him in the living room.

It felt a little strange at first. For them to have been so intimate, then to come together for serious conversation. But Tate took it upon himself to put her at ease, crossing the room to kiss her sweetly before leading her to the only chair.

Jodie watched as he brought in a kitchen chair for himself. And when he leaned forward to collect her hand, her heart warmed toward him even more. He was a thoughtful considerate lover, as well as a demanding one. And she knew that, as the future unfolded, their lovemaking would only get better.

"I realize you'd probably rather not think about this right now, and I wouldn't, either. But, Jodie," he said, his voice softening on her name, "we *have* to think about it. If we lived in a big city, no one would care. If we were both on our own, with no families to consider, no one would care. But that's not the way it is for either of us. You have your family and I have my mother."

"Does she dislike me?" Jodie asked quickly. "I always have the feeling that I've done something I shouldn't. Something she doesn't approve of. I know that's a problem I have sometimes, and I'm trying to work on it, but with your mother, it's really there!"

Tate studied her hand before looking up. "When I tell her I love you, she'll like you. She's already guessed, anyway."

Jodie gazed at him. "She's already guessed?"

Tate nodded, smiling slightly.

"And she didn't tell you not to?"

"No. She knows better. And she doesn't dislike you. She just doesn't know you."

"It's because I'm a Parker. But I can't help that. I am what I am, Tate! What is it she has against us?"

Tate ran a hand through his hair. "It's not that exactly, either. It's more...Jodie, when my dad was killed, my mother and I had to work our tails off to maintain a decent life. She's resentful of people who have it easy, I guess. People who don't have to work hard for what they have."

"The Parkers do work hard! I used to be ashamed of that!" She shook her head. "I probably was the spoiled little brat you thought me to be. I was ashamed because all my friends' families got to play with their expensive toys. They showed horses or went to gallery openings or were members of country clubs in their respective towns. They only came to their ranches on weekends or in the summer. And we were stuck here all the time." She paused. "Rafe works as hard as any cowhand, probably harder. Aunt Mae did, too, until she got too old. LeRoy keeps all the ranch machinery running, and Thomas does all the ranch carpentry. My dad...well, my dad is at Aunt Mae's beck and call at all hours, and that, believe me, is a tough job. Everyone does something. Shannon does the histories, Harriet writes children's books—"

"What about you? Are you going to find somethin' to do or do you have...other plans?"

Jodie frowned. "What do you mean?"

"Are you going to stay on the ranch? Or go off back to Europe somewhere?"

Jodie tried to pull her hand free. How could he ask that when she thought...Oh, God, she hadn't made another mistake of planning ahead too far, had she? Rio had disappointed her; surely Tate wouldn't, too!

"I'm only askin'," Tate continued, "because I'm

not gonna be here myself.'' He stood up, drawing her gaze with him.

Jodie's heart skipped some beats. What was he trying to tell her?

"I've accepted a position with my old supervisor from Dallas. He's heading up a task force that will have state-wide enforcement power, and he's asked me to be a part of it. I wasn't sure at first, but it's somethin' I really want to do.''

"Where...where will you be? Dallas?'' Jodie asked quietly, her throat tight with dread.

"There or Austin. I'm not sure.''

"When?''

"I talked with Drew Winslow last night—he's my old supervisor. I have six weeks. I've already handed in my notice to the county.''

Tate was leaving? Again? Jodie remembered the last time he'd left West Texas, first to go to school, then to the police force in Dallas. "Will it be dangerous?'' she breathed. She'd worried about him before, on an unconscious level she was only now recognizing. But after today, she'd be petrified!

"Not any more than here, maybe less.'' He squatted down in front of her and reclaimed her lifeless hand. "Jodie, I don't have time for a personal life on this job. Like I said, I'm on call twenty-four hours a day—I'm surprised I haven't gotten a call since I've been with you! One could come at any second and I'd have to leave. With the task force, I'd have regular time off. At least, the time off I'd have I could pretty well count on. I couldn't ask you to be a part of the mess here, ask you to leave your family. Not when I was rarely home. But as part of the task force—''

Jodie's gaze lifted.

''—as part of the task force, I could. Now I don't wanna rush you. This thing between you and me has come up pretty sudden. I don't want you to feel obligated in any—''

Jodie placed her fingers over his mouth.

He continued talking. ''Just because we…you know, in there…'' He indicated the bedroom.

As he'd done earlier at the fair, she substituted her lips, kissing him long and hard so he knew she meant it. ''Just say the word and I'll be there,'' she said, smiling.

''What about your family?'' Tate asked. ''How will they feel about me? I'm the outsider, a town person.''

''My family doesn't care about that. It's what's inside that counts. The makeup of a person. And you, Tate, would pass any test. They already like you and respect you. Aunt Mae thinks you're 'such a nice boy.' And Harriet thinks you're a hunk. And Rafe said you're as good a sheriff as the county's ever had.''

Tate smiled. ''Then I'm in, but it's a little different when I'm wantin' to marry one of the clan.''

Jodie grew still. ''Marry?'' she repeated.

Tate frowned. ''What did you think I was talkin' about all this time? Us shackin' up together?''

''Well, I—''

''If it makes a difference, if you don't want to do it…well, that's okay, too. I'll take you any way I can get you, Jodie. Any way at all.''

The telephone rang and Tate went to answer it. When he came back he said simply, "I'm needed."

Jodie started to stand up.

"Wait there. I have to change," he said. "I won't be a minute. Then I'll run you back to your car."

"It's not out of your way?" she asked.

"Where I'm headin' is just down the road."

He disappeared into his bedroom and seconds later Jodie followed him.

He'd already changed into his uniform pants and was just donning his tan shirt when she entered the room.

He turned at her footstep, a little smile on his lips. "Are you plannin' on makin' me late?" he asked.

Jodie slipped her arms around his naked torso. It was so wonderful to be free to touch him, to claim him for her own. "Aren't you forgetting something?" she asked sweetly.

"What?" he asked, his arms coming around her, as well.

"The answer. It's *yes,*" she said.

It took him a second to make the connection, then his smile grew brilliant. "You mean it?" he asked.

"I've never meant anything more in my life."

"When? Where?" He glanced in frustration at his half-donned shirt. "Dammit, Jodie, I have to go! I can't—"

She smiled. "I understand. I only wanted you to know." She stood on tiptoe to kiss his forehead, then stepped back. But Tate wasn't satisfied with that.

"C'mere," he growled, and spent the next few precious moments cementing their betrothal with a proper kiss.

After that he let her go and she laughingly helped him finish dressing. His tie was a little askew, his badge not perfectly centered. But he didn't seem to mind.

Then they hurried out the front door—although not as fast as they'd hurried in.

CHAPTER EIGHTEEN

JODIE HAD WANTED a big wedding ever since Shannon and Rafe had gotten married. *The bigger the better,* she remembered herself saying. But not now. All she wanted now was to marry Tate quietly and for them to get started building a life together.

Mae had been shocked at the news of their engagement. "But, Jodie, you just got back!" she'd exclaimed. "Are you sure you aren't just jumping into this, too? I know you've changed recently, but doesn't that mean it's much too soon for you to be making another big change? And Tate Connelly! I like him, he's a fine young man, but I had no idea..."

"If you truly love each other, you can wait," Harriet had advised. "You want to be sure, Jodie, for both your sakes."

"Give it some time," Shannon had agreed. "Rafe and I waited over six months, and I don't regret it, even though at the time it was hard."

Even Christine counseled, "You want to be sure."

But Jodie *was* sure. And she grew surer by the day. She wasn't jumping into this in order to jump away from something else. For the first time in years she knew exactly what she wanted. And because of that she had an inner serenity that, in the end, even Mae couldn't ignore.

Jodie gazed at herself in the full-length cheval mirror. She was in a short dress of white satin, frilled at the neck and cuffs with lace. She wore matching shoes and a bridal wreath of tiny white silk flowers. Her hair, a little longer now and freshly styled, was like a bright flame in contrast. She wondered what Tate would think.

She gazed at herself for another long moment, then slowly undressed. Tomorrow she would become Mrs. Tate Connelly. She'd be giving up the Parker name. The prospect wasn't as welcome as it once would have been. In fact, she did it now with a certain sadness. She'd come late to an appreciation of her heritage, but despite her tardiness it was something she would always treasure. *Jodie Connelly. Jodie and Tate Connelly.* She loved the sound of it, even as she loved Tate.

It was beyond her understanding how she could ever have thought she loved anyone else. Or that she'd spent a year away in Europe, searching. Searching for what? Exactly what she'd found with Tate. All she'd had to do was come home.

A light tapping sounded on her door as she secured the last button on her pajamas. The dress had been carefully hung on her closet door.

Her father came in, glanced at her, then at the dress. "You been practicing?" he asked, grinning.

"I love putting it on."

Gib moved aimlessly about the room, looking at this and that she'd yet to pack. Almost everything was off her walls, and almost everything else had been put in boxes to be sent on to her new home. He ended up at the dress again. "You, ah, don't regret havin' a small wedding, do you? I mean, I remember the last big one. Rafe and Shannon's." He shook his head good-humoredly. "Now that was somethin'! Everyone was here—all the relatives. All the neighbors. The governor even came, didn't he? Or he sent a gift."

"I think he sent a gift."

"That's Mae's long reach. Wonder what it's like for everybody in the state capital now that she's slowed down. A lot fewer notes that it burns their fingers to read. A lot fewer irate visits." He glanced at her. "I suppose you've noticed she uses the phone more often now. Used to hate it, but she's finally come around. Saved me a few trips, I can tell you."

Jodie sensed why her father was there. And it wasn't to reminisce about Mae or even Rafe and Shannon's wedding. She crossed over to him and hugged him tightly. "I'm going to miss you, Daddy," she said quietly, emotionally.

Jodie and her father had grown much closer in the past two months. She saw him as more of a whole person now, from the perspective of her own adulthood. He wasn't the ineffective bumbler that she, to her shame, had once considered him. They'd taken tiny steps toward understanding before, but not gone far enough. Not to where they were now.

Gib patted her back as he returned her hug. Then he wiped his eyes. "That goes double for me, little girl."

She smiled up at him. "Austin isn't all that far away."

"I know."

"We'll come for a visit every month. I promise."

"Tate'll take good care of you," Gib said, more to assure himself than to assure her. Jodie didn't need convincing.

"He will. Like I'll take good care of him." Her eyes fell on the drawing of her mother, which she'd framed and hung on the wall beside the long mirror. She went to get it and brought it to her father. "Why don't you keep this?" she said quietly. "It's been with you all these years. And...and I don't need it anymore."

Gib studied it. "She was so beautiful—just like you."

Jodie wanted to pull him from the past. She grinned and asked, "Are you ready to walk me down the aisle tomorrow?"

Gib answered in true Texas fashion, "Sure. You bet."

"At least it's a short aisle—only to the front of Aunt Mae's living room."

Her father laughed. "You shoulda seen Mae today. You'd've thought the Queen herself was comin'! She was runnin' poor ol' Axel ragged, gettin' this and that, makin' sure all the rented chairs were properly placed. All I can tell you is those flowers better arrive on time tomorrow mornin' or there's gonna be a florist in Del Norte who'll regret the day he was born."

"I'm sure everything will be fine."

"Harriet and Shannon are tryin' to make her settle down, but she's like a stubborn horse that's taken the bit in its mouth. She's gonna do it her way or else!"

"She's having fun. You know Aunt Mae."

Her father tilted his head. "You notice how she's

taken a new lease on life? Got more energy. Gotten feistier again. For a while there I started to wonder. Then— It happened about the time you got engaged to Tate. You know, for a woman who never had one herself, she sure seems to like weddings.''

''Maybe that's why she likes them so much,'' Jodie said softly.

Gib nodded. ''You might be right.''

Once her father left, Jodie moved about the room, seeing to a few last-minute details, then climbed into bed.

She and Tate had agreed not to be with each other tonight. To keep to tradition. She would see him tomorrow for the first time in Mae's living room, where together, gathered in front of their families and a few friends, they would exchange their vows.

She wondered what he was doing now. If he was thinking of her.

A COUPLE OF HIS OFF-DUTY deputies threw Tate a small bachelor party at the Watering Hole. Jack was there, as was Mark Lovell. They laughed together and told off-color jokes and drank a beer or two, then broke up.

Tate dropped Jack off at his new place—which was Tate's old place—and Tate continued on to his mother's. She'd requested he spend the night with her and he'd agreed.

Emma was still up when he let himself inside. She was playing solitaire at the kitchen table in her lightweight robe and fuzzy slippers, just as she used to do when he was a teenager.

He went over to kiss her cheek, just as he also used to do. "Waitin' up?" he asked.

She patted his hand on her shoulder. "My very last time," she said.

He hooked a foot around the leg of a chair and settled into place beside her. "Who's winnin'?" he teased.

"The deck is," she retorted, and pushed the cards away. Then she looked at him for a long moment. "I guess you know what you're doin' for sure, hmm?"

Tate met her gaze steadily. "I love her, Mom."

"And she says she loves you."

"She does love me."

Emma considered for another long moment, then said, "I wasn't very happy when I heard about this, you know that. A Parker…marrying into our family! Who'd've believed it? But you're good enough for 'em, Tate. You're more than good enough!"

"They couldn't be nicer to me, Mom. Even ol' Mae. She even seems happy now that she's gotten used to the idea."

"Because you're from town?" Emma demanded, sensing a slight.

"Because she wasn't sure Jodie was ready to settle down. Now she is. Jodie's convinced her."

His mother shifted in her chair. "She's been nice to me, too, I have to admit."

Tate smiled fondly. "With reason, I'd say, but then, I'm prejudiced. I think you're the world's finest mom!"

"Flattery will get you out of all kinds of trouble— but you already know that."

"It never used to get me out of trouble when I was a boy."

"It took you growin' up to know how to use it." A brief silence ensued, then his mother said, "I'd like to give you a special present. I know you and Jodie aren't going to need a lot, because Jodie has her own money and you'll be getting good pay on your new job. But, I thought—if Jodie would like it, too—I'd give you the quilt my great-grandmother handed down to me. She won all kinds of prizes for it and it's so very pretty. She made it as her wedding present for your great-grandfather." She waved off Tate's protest. "I don't have any use for it anymore. I'd rather give it to you. That is, unless you think Jodie wouldn't like it."

"I'm sure she'd like it! You know the locket she wears? It was Mae's when she was a child. The Parkers set a lot of store on family traditions."

"I didn't think Jodie did. I thought she used most of her energy trying *not* to be a Parker."

"That was before. Not now."

"Well, now she's gonna be a Connelly," Emma said firmly.

Tate smiled. "Yes, she is."

"It'll be hard thinkin' of you with a wife," Emma admitted. "I still remember you as that tiny little thing your daddy and I were afraid to hold after you were born. We thought we'd break you." She paused. "Your daddy would be so proud of you, Tate. You know that."

"I hope so."

"I *know* so. Come here. Give your ol' mom a hug,

then get yourself off to bed. Tomorrow's gonna be a big day for everyone."

Tate did as his mother requested and added a warm kiss. His mother had always done her best by him. Raised him to the best of her ability. He would be forever grateful.

Minutes later he was stretched out on the bed in the spare room, his hands clasped behind his head as he stared at the darkened ceiling. Tomorrow he was going to marry Jodie.

Then five glorious days in Hawaii—somewhere neither of them had ever been before—and two days to set up their apartment in Austin before he had to report for duty with Drew Winslow.

It was as if some kind of lucky star had hovered over him sprinkling magic into his life.

Jodie...his wife.

When he drifted off to sleep, Tate was smiling.

"JODIE! YOU LOOK..." Shannon stood back, admiring the bride-to-be. Harriet hovered nearby, while Christine continued to fluff and smooth and fuss with the dress.

"Perfect," Christine finished for her.

They were in an upstairs bedroom at Mae's house. For the past ten minutes they'd heard family and friends assembling.

"Is Daddy ready?" Jodie asked in a mild panic, having remained calm until that moment.

Harriet peeked into the hall. "He's here. At the top of the stairs. And he looks so handsome I almost didn't recognize him."

"And you're sure Tate's here," Jodie said, needing additional reassurance.

"I saw him myself. And talk about *handsome!* Wow!" Harriet wagged her fingers as if they burned. "He came with his mother and Chief Lovell."

Jodie shifted from foot to foot. She was ready for the ceremony to begin.

Thankfully the flowers had arrived on time, the cake was on the dining-room table, the champagne had been iced, the minister welcomed. All that remained was for the organist to start playing. At that exact moment organ music floated upstairs.

Gwen tapped on the door and opened it. Nearly twelve, she was mature enough to really appreciate this wedding. Her gray eyes, so like her mother's, were shining with excitement. "Aunt Mae said to tell you everything's ready downstairs."

Jodie's heart gave a strong beat, then a number of quick smaller ones. Her fingers felt like ice in comparison to Shannon's as she accepted the bouquet.

She laughed giddily. *It was happening! It was truly happening!*

She accepted kisses and smiles of good wishes from all around, then as she stepped into the hall, she reached for her father's arm.

Gib did look handsome in his tuxedo. And very proud.

The others hurried downstairs to take their seats.

"All the luck in the world, sweetheart," her father murmured as they started forward.

Jodie could hear her flowers shaking, a low rustle just below the sound of the music.

The entryway looked like a spring garden, as did the living room. Mae had spared no expense. Most of the furniture had been removed and white wooden chairs set in place. A cluster of white blossoms and greenery marked the side of each aisle chair.

Everyone watched as Jodie and Gib proceeded down the narrow walkway. Smiling faces, a few with tears of happiness. Jodie looked from one to the other—the people who meant so much to her life. She saw Tate's mother, tearing up. And Jack Denton, urbane in a suit.

Then she saw Tate. Waiting for her beside the minister.

Tate, in his tux. Strong and handsome and vital. Looking at her as if she was the most wondrous vision.

Jodie increased her pace, ready to get *on* with it! The ceremony and their life!

HARLEQUIN SUPERROMANCE®

Hope Springs

Hope Springs Eternal...

Faith O'Dare loves living in the tiny town of Hope Springs, where all good things happen. But now things are happening just a little too fast. It seems as if half the women in town are pregnant—and only one of them is married.

Faith believes her out-of-town boyfriend will *want* to marry her, though—until she finds out he's already found wedded bliss with someone else. His law partner, Sean, wants to make amends for his wayward friend, but what can he do...apart from help decorate her nursery, raise her child and marry her himself?

March 1998—**BABY BOOM** (#780)
by Peg Sutherland

Look for further tales from Hope Springs
in the coming year.

FATHER: UNKNOWN (#784)
by Tara Taylor Quinn

Her name is Anna. And she's pregnant.

That's all she knows, all the doctors can tell her. Anna's been in a subway accident, and when she regains consciousness, she has no memory of who she is or where she came from. She has no idea who the father of her baby might be.

Jason Whitaker sees her on the TV news...and recognizes her. She's Anna Hayden. The woman he still loves. The woman who rejected him *three* months before—and is now pregnant.

Two months pregnant.

Detective Jackie Kaminsky is back—and this
time *First Impressions* aren't adding up…

Second Thoughts

Jackie Kaminsky had seen enough break and enters to know
that intruders usually took something. This one left a calling
card and a threat to return. The next visit was from a killer.
Jackie had a list of suspects, but as they became victims, too,
she found herself thinking twice about *everything* she
thought she knew—professionally and personally.…

**"Detective Jackie Kaminsky leads a cast
of finely drawn characters."**
—*Publishers Weekly*

MARGOT DALTON

Available in March 1998 wherever books are sold.

MIRA BOOKS

**The Brightest Stars
in Fiction.™**

Welcome to *Love Inspired*™

A brand-new series of contemporary inspirational love stories.

Join men and women as they learn valuable lessons about facing the challenges of today's world and about life, love and faith.

Look for the following March 1998 Love Inspired™ titles:

CHILD OF HER HEART
by Irene Brand

A FATHER'S LOVE
by Cheryl Wolverton

WITH BABY IN MIND
by Arlene James

Available in retail outlets in February 1998.

LIFT YOUR SPIRITS AND GLADDEN YOUR HEART
with *Love Inspired!*™

Steeple
Hill™

Don't miss these Harlequin favorites by some of our top-selling authors!

HT#25733	THE GETAWAY BRIDE	$3.50 u.s.	☐
	by Gina Wilkins	$3.99 can.	☐
HP#11849	A KISS TO REMEMBER	$3.50 u.s.	☐
	by Miranda Lee	$3.99 can.	☐
HR#03431	BRINGING UP BABIES	$3.25 u.s.	☐
	by Emma Goldrick	$3.75 can.	☐
HS#70723	SIDE EFFECTS	$3.99 u.s.	☐
	by Bobby Hutchinson	$4.50 can.	☐
HI#22377	CISCO'S WOMAN	$3.75 u.s.	☐
	by Aimée Thurlo	$4.25 can.	☐
HAR#16666	ELISE & THE HOTSHOT LAWYER	$3.75 u.s.	☐
	by Emily Dalton	$4.25 can.	☐
HH#28949	RAVEN'S VOW	$4.99 u.s.	☐
	by Gayle Wilson	$5.99 can.	☐

(limited quantities available on certain titles)

AMOUNT	$	_____
POSTAGE & HANDLING	$	_____
($1.00 for one book, 50¢ for each additional)		
APPLICABLE TAXES*	$	_____
TOTAL PAYABLE	$	_____

(check or money order—please do not send cash)

To order, complete this form and send it, along with a check or money order for the total above, payable to Harlequin Books, to: **In the U.S.:** 3010 Walden Avenue, P.O. Box 9047, Buffalo, NY 14269-9047; **In Canada:** P.O. Box 613, Fort Erie, Ontario, L2A 5X3.

Name: _____

Address: _____ City: _____

State/Prov.: _____ Zip/Postal Code: _____

Account Number (if applicable): _____

*New York residents remit applicable sales taxes.
Canadian residents remit applicable GST and provincial taxes.

Look us up on-line at: http://www.romance.net

075-CSAS

HBLJM98